Lucky Strike

Pat Wilson
and
Kris Wood

RendezVous Crime

Cover design: Trudy Agyeman and Vasiliki Lenis

LE CONSEIL DES ARTS | THE CANADA COUNCIL
DU CANADA | FOR THE ARTS
DEPUIS 1957 | SINCE 1957

We acknowledge the support of the Canada Council for the Arts for our publishing program.

RendezVous Crime
an imprint of
Napoleon & Company
Toronto, Ontario, Canada

Printed in Canada

11 10 09 08 07   5 4 3 2 1

Library and Archives Canada Cataloguing in Publication

Wilson, Patricia, date-
        Lucky strike : a Maritime mystery / Pat Wilson, Kris Wood.

ISBN 978-1-894917-51-3

        I. Wood, Kris   II. Title.
PS8645.I57L82 2007   C813'.6   C2007-900509-8

To our families
and to our friends
on the Eastern Shore

One

I stood just inside the terminal doors, watching the people leaving the arrivals area. No one looked suspicious, but then, how would I know? I was new at this game.

I turned up my coat collar and pulled down the brim of my hat. For the tenth time, I checked my pocket to make sure the instructions were still there. I'd tried to memorize them, but I'd been so distracted by the thought that any one of the hundred other passengers on the plane might be there for the sole purpose of ending my life, that the various numbers and directions on the slip of paper slid through my brain like an assassin's blade between the ribs.

I watched most of the people on my flight disappear, picked up by waiting friends and relatives, or heading for taxis and parked cars. I decided that it was safe for me to leave.

Juggling the cat carrier, my new laptop and my bulky suitcase, I stumbled over to the car rental desk. "We try harder", it promised me.

"Name, sir?" a bored young woman asked me.

"Trenchant. Charles Trenchant." I tried to sound casual. Would she believe me?

"Oh, yes. We have you down for a three-month long-term rental. Driver's license and credit card, please."

I fumbled in the new wallet they'd given me in Ottawa along with my tickets. After some struggle with the unfamiliar snaps, I found both items and I pushed them across the desk with shaking fingers.

She gave them a cursory glance. "If you would just sign here, initial here and here and here."

I licked my lips. For a horrible moment, I realized I'd forgotten my new name. I glanced at the top of the rental contract. Charles Trenchant. That was it! I did as she bade me, hoping that the signature matched that on the credit card and driver's license which I'd signed some days before.

"Here you are. Ford Focus. Grey as per your request. Third car in the second row. Out the double doors, turn left at the sign." She handed me some keys.

I picked up the keys and put them in my pocket along with the rental contract.

Outside, the fog was thick, so thick that it was like rain. The airport lights were dim yellow orbs in the murk. I doubted that any more planes would be landing tonight. I took a deep breath and stepped off the curb.

Two headlights dazzled me as a large, dark car sped towards me. I threw myself backwards, landing on top of the cat carrier. The cat hissed in alarm. My heart pounded in my chest and my breath came in ragged gasps. Was this to be my life from now on, always on guard, always watching for dark shadows, always afraid? Was this just the first of many attempts on my life?

I debated going back into the safety of the terminal, but the car had disappeared into the night. In any event, I needed to get going. It was already late, and I had a long way to go to my final destination.

I found the car, stowed my bag in the trunk, put the cat carrier on the back seat, and laid my laptop on the front seat beside me. I checked the map given to me by the rental agent, flicking the light on just long enough to read the instructions, but not long enough to make me an easy target if they were out there in the parking lot.

I headed off into the dark night, the fog swirling about my headlights, a fine mist coating the windshield with a greasy film. Within minutes, I was out of the airport area, and turning onto the main highway into the city. Always, I kept my eyes on the rear view mirror. However, the traffic was light, and at my cautious speed, it flowed past me in a continuous stream.

It had been some time since I had driven a car. Once my initial nervousness wore off, I began to relax a little. The fog continued to hamper my visibility, thickening as I neared the coast. I peered at the signs looming up over the roadway, trying to remember the instructions.

Soon I found myself on Highway 107, heading eastwards. After twenty kilometres of reasonable highway, the road deteriorated into a narrow, pot-holed two-lane nightmare that wound up and around the various headlands along the shore. After a while, I saw few houses, no stores, no gas stations, just thick forest on one side and the ocean on the other. The traffic had thinned to an occasional pick-up truck. At several points where the fog lifted, I caught a glimpse of waves below me on the passenger's side of the car, and on my side, an unbroken hill of endless trees. I was aware that if I were to go off the road here, no one would ever find me.

It was at this point that the interior of the car lit up with the glare of headlights behind me. The vehicle was inches from my bumper, its high beams blinding me. I sped up. So did it.

I slowed down. Ignoring the fog, the blind corner and the double lines, a large black SUV swept past me, its headlights cutting a swath in the darkness. It pulled back in front of me and slowed down as if to stop. I knew that if they succeeded

3

in stopping me, I wouldn't stand a chance. I wondered if I had the skill to swing my car around the SUV and make a break for freedom. Just as I was calculating distances, the SUV turned off onto a dark sideroad. I watched in disbelief as its taillights disappeared into the fog.

Were they playing cat and mouse with me, I wondered? Was this just a ploy to put me off my guard? How long before the next attempt?

I pulled off onto the side of the highway and tried to gather my wits about me. My hands were shaking and wet on the wheel. The sweat ran down the back of my neck in a cold trickle. It seemed as if I'd been trapped in this car for hours, bumping along this endless dark road to nowhere. I wasn't cut out for this kind of thing. Maybe James Bond could handle it with equanimity, but I was made of less heroic stuff.

Taking a deep breath, I pulled back onto the highway. The kilometres continued to click by under my wheels. Heads, harbours and coves swept past. An hour later, I drove through the small coastal village called Cormorant Harbour, the final leg of my journey.

It was only ten o'clock at night, but the streets were deserted. The stores were closed, and only a few streetlights looming out of the fog indicated it was any sort of a centre of civilization. I parked under one of the lights and consulted my notes. Just one more kilometre, and I should see the sign for Lupin Loop. Then, first house on the right.

The cat meowed, a demanding cry for food, for water, or perhaps a litter box. I didn't know. "You'll have to wait," I told it. "Not long now."

Minutes later, I pulled into an overgrown driveway, deeply rutted and thick with weeds that brushed the bottom of the car. I had arrived.

TWO

Five days after my long journey from the airport, I began to believe that I would be safe in this place. I felt the anguish and upheaval of the past six months fade like the memory of a nightmare as I realized that the trial, the threats and the fear were now behind me.

They said it would be a small cottage beside the ocean in a rural fishing community on the remote Eastern Shore of Nova Scotia, fully furnished and ready to move in. I looked around me. Indeed, the cottage *was* small, the ocean *was* at the back door, and the community of Cormorant Harbour *was* only a short walk away. I could not dispute the facts.

However, beyond the facts lay a modest little house stuffed with depressing furniture, sitting on an acre of scrubby spruce trees and alder bushes which served to hide the accumulated debris of years of habitation by people with no garbage service.

Standing on a patch of rough lawn at the side of the house, I felt well hidden from anyone's curious eyes. Behind me, the wide Atlantic spread to the horizon, its expanse broken by several small, uninhabited islands. In front of me, only the shack across the road bore evidence of any other human activity in the area.

For the first time in twenty-five years, I was without the constraints of a job. At first, I'd enjoyed the sense of unstructured time, much like being on a holiday. But now I felt the first stirrings of a need to "do" something. I decided to ignore the overgrown yard which desperately cried for attention. It was time for me to step into my new vocation—writer.

Again, I'd fallen in with this suggestion, but with a great deal more alacrity than I had accepted their other ideas. I'd always harboured a deep secret desire to be a writer. Although life had taken me to the towers of commerce, where any creative spark was soon extinguished by dull routine, I realized that this was my opportunity to re-light the fires of my ambition.

A search of the decrepit woodshed behind the house turned up some sagging lawn chairs, which I set up on the beach-rock patio beside the kitchen doorstep. With a sense of anticipation, I carefully opened my new laptop. The cat leapt onto the other chair. She was a nondescript breed, black with just a touch of white under the chin, a large neutered older female which I suspected had been obtained from some animal shelter. She fixed me with an unwavering yellow stare.

I hadn't planned on an animal. In fact, my former fiancée, Chloris, had always accused me of being indifferent to the point of dislike of her two Siamese cats. With some reluctance, I had agreed that I might benefit from the companionship and stress-relieving qualities of a pet. So far, Twinkles (the cat refused to answer to anything else) and I had yet to form the master-pet bond.

I tore my eyes away from the cat, ceding the staring match to her. Fingers poised over the keyboard, I searched for the perfect opening phrase that would capture the reader's imagination while leading into the heart of the best-selling novel I knew lay within me.

"RICKY!" The voice reverberated around the bay, shrill enough to shatter glass at forty feet. "Ricky! You get your ass in here right now! I'm not telling you again."

The cat leapt up in alarm and dashed into the bushes. My laptop fell to the ground with a thud. All the old terrors flooded my brain; my heart started to pound with a sickening force. I felt bile rise in my throat, and for a moment, the world swayed around me. I wondered if I could be having a heart attack. My rational mind realized that this voice had nothing to do with me or my past, but my tenuous sense of security shattered in an instant. Could they have found me already?

"RICKY! Get in here. I didn't make this hot dog for nothing!" The voice, if anything, increased in volume. It came from the shack on the other side of the road, a rundown clapboard box with a junk-filled yard and an air of abandonment. Having seen no sign of life in the past few days, I had presumed it was vacant.

A small boy, about eight years old, clutching a fishing rod, scrambled up from my rocky beach, raced across my lawn, careened onto my patio, paused two feet from my chair and responded in an ear-splitting screech, "Chill out, Ma! I'm coming!" I had a brief impression—ragged shorts, oversized shirt and roughly-cut hair. He looked ready to go on stage as a street-urchin extra for a production of *Oliver.* Oblivious to my presence, he rocketed across the road and disappeared down the overgrown driveway, dodging around several dead cars, a rusting furnace, a pile of bedsprings and an ancient water heater.

I sat stunned. This was a development I had not foreseen. Neighbours. And a child! One who felt entitled to fish from *my* wharf. A horrible thought crossed my mind. Maybe there was more than one child. Even a dog. What could be worse? I closed my eyes, trying to regain my composure.

"Howdy, neighbour."

A man stood in front of me, a large man. I had no idea where he'd come from. For all I knew, he was one of them. I half-rose from my chair, ready to flee, but his bulk blocked my escape.

"Care for a chug?" A huge hand wiped the neck of a brown bottle then proffered it to me. I fell back into my chair, speechless.

"I'm Kevin Jollimore. Folks call me 'Kev'. Welcome to the neighbourhood. That's Arleen over there, hollering for Ricky. He's my boy. Woulda come over to say hello sooner, but took the wife over to her Ma's for a few days. Old lady wasn't too well, but didn't look no less mean than usual to me." He paused to take a healthy swallow from the bottle. "Didn't get back until today and saw you was moved in."

He pulled up the other lawn chair, lowering his thick body into it. My heart was still pounding, and I could feel the cold sweat drying on my forehead. I tried to reconcile Kevin's intrusion into what I had thought to be my solitary sanctuary. He was not a reassuring sight. His filthy plaid shirt gaped open over an equally grubby, stained undershirt. Dirt-encrusted work pants hung under a bulging gut. I strove to hide a grimace of distaste when I saw the roll of pasty flesh between his undershirt and the straining waistband of his pants. Run-down boots with the tongues flapping over his bare ankles completed his ensemble.

"Are yous just visitin' like, or are yous plannin' to stay awhile? Arleen was wonderin', see, 'cause she likes to use your clothes line when she's done a big wash."

I had a brief, nightmarish vision of Kevin's underwear

flapping over my front lawn.

With an effort, I pulled myself together. "I'm here for awhile," I stammered. The words stuck in my throat so that I had to clear it several times. My brain spun, trying to marshal my thoughts in order to make some sort of coherent reply. I must appear normal, I reminded myself, but I felt anything but normal before this behemoth. "At least, I think so." I realized I had little to say in the matter. I was here until *they* decided to move me out. "I'm Charles Trenchant," I said, feeling a brief frisson as I used my new name. Just saying it again gave me a growing sense of control in the situation.

Giving up my real name had been more difficult than I had imagined, but even I realized that I could no longer be Eric Spratt, a name linked forever with the trial of Marcello Bacciaglia and his various hangers-on in the Toronto Mafia.

"Glad to meetcha, Charlie." Kevin pumped my hand in enthusiastic greeting. His eyes lit on my fallen laptop. He picked it up, handling it with exaggerated care. "Computers, eh? You one of them techie people? You heard about that hacker kid in Montreal, pretty much shut down most of the country? Wisht I could do that. Think you could teach me?"

"Ummm, er..." I paused, gathering my wits about me. I raised my hand to adjust my glasses, only to remember that I no longer wore glasses, but the new contact lenses they had substituted. It was crunch time. I lined up the facts they had given me for my new persona. With a sense of desperation, I trotted them out. "I'm not a techie, *per se…*"

Kevin's brow wrinkled. The foreign phrase stumped him. I guessed he wasn't bilingual. He was barely unilingual. "I'm actually a writer," I told him.

A writer. I straightened my shoulders as I reminded

myself of my new freedom from the grind of office hours, free from the daily familiarity of the commute, free from the drudgery of dry statistics, endless spreadsheets and soulless numbers. I felt much like a butterfly, newly emerged from its chrysalis of darkness into the sunlit future. I savoured the phrase, "chrysalis of darkness", and tucked it away for future use in my novel.

"Oh." Kevin dismissed the subject. He eyed me up and down. "You don't look like you'd be much of a handyman," he ventured.

Not like a handyman? What did Kevin expect? I knew that I didn't have the muscular frame of a labourer, but many smaller men, Napoleon leapt to mind, were capable of changing the world. I stroked my developing Van Dyke beard, something else that I had initially resisted. Now, I appreciated the air of distinction it gave me and thanked whatever gods there were for its lovely silky silver appearance, unlike the orange brush so many men sported. The beard said "writer", not "handyman". I could see why Kevin's hasty assessment placed me in the non-handyman category.

"You're right," I told him.

"Great! 'Cause if you was wanting any odd jobs done, stuff fixed, lawn mowed, whatever, why you just have to give me a shout, and I'll be over here like a shot. It's what I do, eh? Odd jobs. 'No job too big, no job too small, Kev's your man, he does them all.'" This last he rhymed off in a sing-song voice. "Everyone knows me around here. Kev Jollimore. Not much I can't fix or do." He took another long swallow and settled back in the chair, looking at me with an appraising glint in his eye. "I hear you writers pull in a good buck, eh? Like those broads on Oprah. Sell millions they do. They gotta make at least ten bucks a pop. That's gotta add up after a million books." He shifted his weight in the chair. I heard it creak under the strain.

I saw his eyes look around and take in my little home with an appraising glint.

"I can give you a good deal. Strictly cash, eh? Your pocket to mine. Fix this up for you. Little bit of paint. New siding. Wouldn't take much. Say forty per cent up front, and the rest when I'm done. We can work it out."

"Wonderful, Mr. Jollimore. I shall certainly keep that in mind." If his shack across the road was any testament to his handyman skills, I doubted I'd be calling on him any time soon.

I stood up, hoping he'd take the hint and go, but having got his business over with, Kevin settled in for a neighbourly chat. "So, got a wife? Little buggers?"

"What?" I asked as I placed my laptop on the top step of the back porch.

"Family? You got any?"

"I'm afraid I'm quite alone in the world. I tend to be a bit of a recluse." He looked puzzled. "I like to be by myself." In desperation, I folded up my lawn chair. "We writers are often solitary types."

Kevin took another long pull of his bottle. "No family, eh? Lucky you. Family's a bitch! Costs an arm and leg, specially with the little bugger. Raisin' a kid soaks up the dough. And the wife's always wantin' something new, too. Although it's nice to have a warm body next to you in bed on a cold winter's night." His lascivious wink invited me to share the joke. I shuddered at the thought of Kevin with anyone in a bed of any kind in any weather.

"KEVIN! Where the hell are you? Food's on the table!" The Voice crashed over us like a sonic boom.

"I'm coming, woman," he bellowed back. "Don't get your tits in a wringer." Kevin pushed himself up with a grunt, farted loudly, muttered, "Oops, better out than in," and scratched his belly. His bulk blocked the last rays of the setting sun. "Women!" he said with a shrug as he spat into the wild rose bushes under the kitchen window.

The cat chose this moment to reappear. It eyed Kevin's boots, keeping well out of range as it made its way towards the back door. It sat on the top step, poised to slip inside the minute I opened the door.

"That your cat? My old aunt Mildred usta have one like that. Bad luck, they say, a black cat. Don't let Arleen see it. She's that superstitious she'd shoot it."

"It's not all black. It has a touch of white under the chin," I told him, wondering why I felt I had to leap to the defense of the cat.

"Mebbe so, but it sure looks like a black cat from twenty yards away." Kevin shambled off across the road, swigging from his bottle as he went. "See you later, neighbour," he hollered as he turned into his driveway.

"Did you ask him about the clothesline?" The invisible Arleen might as well have been on the patio beside me as her words reverberated on the air.

"Yeah. The line's there, you might as well use it. Don't look like he will." The resounding slam of a door ended their discussion.

I stood in a daze for a moment, unable to move or think. This was the longest period in which I'd needed to maintain my new persona of Charles Trenchant. It had proved harder than anticipated. I felt as if I'd undergone a baptism of fire. Before I met and conversed with people with IQs substantially higher than Kevin's, I'd have to learn to think on my feet and improvise, until Charles Trenchant became as much a part of me as Eric Spratt had once been.

Thinking of Kevin reminded me of Arleen, The Voice. Oh, God! For all I knew, today could be her laundry day! The muse would have to wait; that clothesline needed to come down now!

I sought out the ladder I'd noticed in the back of the woodshed. Removing the clothesline proved to be difficult. Kevin had been right about my lack of practical skills. The line sagged between the house and a large spruce tree. The hook on the house came down with no trouble, but the hook in the spruce tree had become overgrown. In the midst of sawing off the short prickly, branches around it while hanging onto the ladder for dear life, not having much of a head for heights, I heard the crunch of tires in the driveway.

For five days, no one had come near me. Now, in the space of an hour, the world was beating a path to my door.

I took a deep breath. No doubt it was just the Welcome Wagon making a call, I told myself, determined not to give way to my continuing panicky fears of being discovered.

"Good day, sir. Are you putting it up or taking it down, not that you have to do either, of course, especially with the wonderful clothes dryers they have these days, not that Dottie would ever use such a thing, but some people do, not everyone of course, depending on whether they have enough power for it, the clothes dryer that is, not the wash line, although it is handy if the power goes off, not that it does very often, although last winter, it seemed every second day it was off…"

"For heavens sake, Donald. Don't get started." A second voice cut in, this one a woman's.

I realized in a moment that the man and woman at the

13

bottom of the ladder peering up at me bore little resemblance to the nemesis I feared. Not two goons, but a rotund middle-aged couple with welcoming smiles. Although a little voice whispered in the back of my brain, what better way to lull me into a false sense of security?

"Just taking this old clothesline down," I squeaked, trying to force my voice to sound normal and relaxed. I gave a mighty heave on the pulley, and, without warning, the whole contraption gave way, landing on my hapless visitors.

"I'm so sorry! Are you all right?" I scrambled down the ladder.

"Oh shoot! Oh my soul!" My male visitor struggled to remove several yards of clothesline wire from around his head and shoulders. "Oh my stars!" he exclaimed as he pirouetted around several times, which only served to tangle him further. "At least *I'm* all right, not a scratch, not that I know of. And you're all right, aren't you, Dottie? No harm done." I found myself facing a large man with a boyish face over his well-padded, middle-aged body. A shining white clerical collar and black suit proclaimed his calling, but his resemblance to Tweedledum made it difficult for me to view him in a spiritual context. The woman with him looked like his Tweedledee counterpart, albeit several inches taller and with a great deal more hair on her head.

"I'm the Reverend Donald Peasgood," he announced, stepping out of the last coils of clothesline wire. He shook my hand as he enthusiastically bounced up and down on the balls of his feet, which were shod in huge white running shoes closed with velcro tabs. "And this is my dear sister, Dorothy. We have come to welcome you to the Parish of Cormorant Harbour, and to bring you a copy of our parish letter, that is if you'd like one, not everybody takes them, at

14

least not everybody we visit, although I suspect that everyone at the church gets a copy, that is, when Dottie's able to run them off before the service, otherwise, I just pop them into mailboxes, although I'm not sure Canada Post would approve, the post mistress being a Catholic, and not a good Anglican, which isn't to say she isn't good, just Catholic, and I have known some bad Anglicans, not at St. Grimbald's of course, or any of the other churches in our parish, at least, not at the present…" He proffered a small mimeographed leaflet. "You wouldn't be an Anglican yourself, would you?" He peered at me through thick-lensed glasses in hopeful anticipation. "Not that it's any business of mine, although one might say that it *is* my business…" he tapped his collar. "Please don't think I mean to pry, it's just that we so seldom have new faces around here, well, not that's there's anything wrong with the old ones, not all old in years, although many of them are getting up there, and indeed, I see fewer and fewer young people in the pews each Sunday…"

"Donald!"

Father Peasgood stopped in mid-spate as if someone had pulled the switch. Dorothy Peasgood took my hand in a firm grip. I found myself looking up at her. In fact, since I had stopped wearing the two-inch lifts in my shoes, another suggestion I had been loathe to take, I found myself looking up at most people.

Her massive frame stood almost six feet tall. She had abundant grey hair pulled back into a messy chignon and wore a smear of lipstick as her sole cosmetic. Her brightly patterned summer dress had the unfortunate effect of making her look like an overstuffed upholstered chair. At odds with her matronly ensemble, she sported a large, garish, guitar-shaped brooch pinned on her left shoulder.

15

I felt her gimlet eyes appraise me in a glance, much as she might look over a particularly choice cut of beef at the butcher shop. This look I had seen before in the eyes of other ladies of a certain age who hoped that Prince Charming lurked just the around the next corner. "Call me Dorothy," she urged, "Mr....?"

"Trenchant. Charles Trenchant." I let my tongue roll a little on the 'r's. Every time I said it, the name felt more comfortable, more *me*.

"And Mrs. Trenchant? Is she home today?" Her voice rose on a hopeful note.

I had a bad moment in which I couldn't remember whether I was married or not.

"N..n..not married," I stammered.

"Ohhh." She smiled archly. "And are you just visiting, or are you planning to make your home here at Cormorant Harbour with us?"

"I've retired here." I raised a hand to push up my glasses, then again realized I no longer wore them. I converted the gesture into a sweep through my hair, now much longer than it had ever been. At least I hadn't had to shave it off or dye it some strange colour. The longer length suited me, I thought, and reinforced my new artistic image.

"Ex-civil servant, and I was fortunate enough to be one of the few who got a 'golden handshake' in the last round of cutbacks. This has enabled me to fulfill a life-long ambition to devote my time to my writing." The words tumbled out, sounding as if I'd learned them by rote, which of course, I had. However, neither Peasgood seemed to notice.

"Oh, how exciting! An author in our midst." Dorothy's girlish enthusiasm clashed with the predatory gleam in her small blue eyes. "You must give a little talk to the A.C.W.—

that's our church ladies' group. They'll be so interested. And perhaps, you might consider leading a writers' group, and we're always looking for someone knowledgeable to serve on the Library Board, and a qualified person to judge the high school poetry competitions. Oh, I just know you're going to love it here."

All through this exchange, Father Donald reminded me of a restless racehorse at the gate, waiting for his chance to plunge back into the conversation.

"Oh my stars, yes, we're quite a happy little family here, well, not all family, of course, although most of the people are related to one another in some way, although not to Dottie and me, of course, our being 'come-from-aways' like yourself, though not so far away, having just come from the North Shore, although some here think that's another world, and much to our surprise, we discovered that many have not ventured off this shore in their lifetimes." He paused and drew breath.

Dorothy took back the conversational ball. "And you're from?" She probed, making little effort to hide her curiosity.

I decided she was wasted here in this hinterland. She belonged in the Crown Prosecutor's office in some large Canadian city. "Tor…er…Ottawa," I said, almost forgetting my lines. "Yes, Ottawa."

Ottawa, I reminded myself. Yes. That was the story. Not Toronto, where I had lived. It was Ottawa, and now here, Cormorant Head, a remote community on Nova Scotia's Eastern Shore.

"Ottawa! Our Nation's Capital!" Father Donald announced. My slip went unnoticed.

"And your church affiliation is….?" Dorothy overrode him, continuing in her quest for information.

"I'm Anglican," I told her. This much they had left me of my former self. "In fact," I said, fingering my new beard, "I was a lay reader in my old parish." Too late! The words had slipped out on their own volition. I regretted little about leaving my old life except that I would no longer be part of the mystical ritual and spiritual pageantry of St. Thomas's. Standing at the lectern reading Morning Prayer, or processing down the aisle in full panoply, I had deemed my small role almost as important as that of the priest.

I could have bitten my tongue off. How could I have let such a thing slip? In a moment of despair, I realized that I had no stomach for this cloak-and-dagger existence. Slips like this would lead to my ultimate downfall, if not demise, should I make them in front of the wrong people. Certainly, the Peasgoods looked innocent enough, but I'd been warned not to trust anyone. I needed to remember that my enemies would never rest until they found me.

Father Donald beamed, almost apoplectic with enthusiasm. My heart sank as he bounced up and down. I realized that I couldn't retract my statement now. "How wonderful! An answer to prayer! Our lay reader passed away just six months ago, so sad, poor fellow, although a blessing in some ways, not that his dying was a blessing, especially not to me, but with his difficulties, you know, his failing health, and always, so determined to keep up his duties at St. Grimbald's, despite his increasing deafness, although at eighty-seven years, one must expect this, although I've know some people who've retained remarkable use of their faculties well into their nineties…" At this point, he stopped and looked bewildered. "Well! It's good to have you. We must get together for a long chat," he finished.

"Perhaps you will join us for lunch at the rectory after

church on Sunday?" suggested Dorothy, seizing the opportunity to consolidate our acquaintance.

"Oh, yes!" said Father Donald, picking up on the need to strike while the iron was hot. "That would be wonderful. It would give you a chance to see how our little church functions, and then, we could prepare a letter for the Bishop, not that the Bishop minds, he's glad to have anyone on board, well not anyone, he wouldn't want murderers or criminals or atheists, although I doubt an atheist..."

"Donald!"

Father Donald's musings on the suitability of atheists as lay readers in the Anglican Church ceased. Dorothy turned to me with a smile. "The service times are in our newsletter. We will see you on Sunday."

Any thoughts I had of excusing myself faded before Dorothy's implacable tone. I would be more likely to refuse a royal summons from the Queen of England than say "no" to Dorothy Peasgood.

I realized I had trapped myself by my own carelessness— the same kind of carelessness that had propelled me into this place and this situation. I still found it hard to believe that I, an honest, law-abiding citizen, a man of modest means, a simple accountant, had held the key to the biggest drug bust in Canadian history. Little did I know that when I had carelessly picked up the wrong briefcase one damp, October morning on the Markham to Union Station GO train, I would end up here. If I could have foreseen the danger that lay ahead of me, of the threats to my life, of the unending sense of insecurity, of the anxiety, the fear, the turmoil that my public-spirited act would lead to, I would have tossed the cursed thing into the nearest garbage bin.

And now, here I was, trapped in a situation far beyond

my experience or imagination, struggling to become someone else. Was it any wonder that I made a slip-up now and then?

I had no choice but to send a note to my contact in the Witness Protection Department. They would have to create a fictitious lay readership to replace the genuine credentials that I could no longer use without revealing that my new persona was a complete fabrication. Surely adding a few spurious details from some church in Ottawa wouldn't be a problem for people who had been able to wipe the entire fifty years of my previous existence from the face of the earth.

Three

The following Sunday, I felt a guilty pang as I sat down in a vacant pew near the front of St. Grimbald's church. Although I had planned to sit at the back, where I would remain unnoticed, it seemed that everyone else had the same idea. I found myself walking down the single centre aisle under the unwavering gaze of dozens of pairs of curious eyes. I knew that this action broke the prime commandment of my new life: don't get noticed. I hoped that none of the parishioners of Cormorant Harbour were connected to the Mob.

After a service that bore only a passing resemblance to what I had previously experienced at St. Thomas' (or for that matter, at any Anglican church anywhere in Canada), I duly presented myself at the Rectory door for lunch. Before I could ring the bell, Dorothy Peasgood welcomed me in.

"Do come in, Charles." She swung the door open wide. "Lunch is just ready, and we're waiting for Donald. Fortunately, this isn't a coffee morning, or we'd be waiting all day, since Donald is rather fond of home baking. If I'm not there to keep an eye on him, he'll stay until the last crumb."

I stepped into a dark hallway painted a bilious shade of bottle green. This didn't surprise me, since most rectories seem to be decorated in the least appealing hues on the colour palette. However, this rectory hallway had one additional feature not often seen in ecclesiastical dwellings—a large framed poster of Elvis Presley in concert at Las Vegas.

I gestured to the print and said, "Elvis? Father Donald didn't strike me as a rock 'n roll fan."

Dorothy's ruddy complexion deepened to an alarming shade of puce. "He's not," she said tartly, fingering the guitar brooch that she'd worn on our first meeting, now pinned to the lapel of her maroon and mustard striped blouse. "I am." Something in her tone deterred me from pursuing the subject further. I suspected I had, quite by accident, touched on the hidden depth of a girlish heart.

I followed her into an equally dark dining room filled with a massive table and sideboard, both gleaming with numerous pieces of highly polished silver. It looked like the dining room of a large country manor house, complete with maroon velvet curtains and Turkey carpet—except for the row of Elvis commemorative plates arranged on the mantle of the brick fireplace.

The tableware told me that lunch was going to be more than just soup and sandwiches, a welcome change for me. My culinary skills only encompassed simple meals. I tended to eat lightly and avoid rich desserts, since smaller men tend to run to pot-bellies when they overindulge. However, an occasional splurge on someone else's cooking wouldn't hurt, I decided. Before I could inquire about the menu, Father Donald arrived, no less exuberant than he had been two hours before at the start of the service.

"Oh, shoot! You're waiting for me! Dorothy told me not to dawdle, but once Mrs. Granger gets going, there's no escaping from her, not that she's not interesting, well, perhaps not interesting, but at least she has something to say, although she says it many times, well, not that often, but often enough you wish she'd come to the point, although I doubt there is a point, really, not that you have to have a point in all cases, but sometimes…"

"Donald!"

His words ceased. I wondered if I'd be able to master that same controlling tone. If my fate was to be a lay reader at St. Grimbald's, I would have to learn how to deal with Father Donald's ramblings. Here, another wave of guilt washed over me as I remembered how displeased my agent had been when I'd informed her of this new development. "Are you crazy?" she'd shouted at me in justifiable anger. I told her I thought it would create more attention if I tried to withdraw at this juncture. I'd been swept into the raging river of Peasgood enthusiasm, helpless to fight the current. I suspected that many people who'd come up against the Peasgoods felt the same way.

"Please, sit down." Dorothy gestured to me. "Donald, say grace, and make it short."

The delicious food kept coming in copious quantities, smothered in gravy, lavished with butter or doused in cream. I began to see the source of the Peasgoods' girths. Although Dorothy kept a tight rein on Father Donald's intake, she made sure that my plate remained full. I began to feel quite ill as my stomach, used to much lighter fare, bulged uncomfortably against my waistband. Dorothy and Father Donald seemed unaffected by the richness of the meal. When I bogged down in the middle of my dessert, a concoction of chocolate cake, syrup and whipped cream, Father Donald slipped the remainder onto his own plate, much to Dorothy's disgust.

As he spooned up the last crumbs, the ear-splitting wail

of an emergency siren filled the room, followed by the shrill beeps of a pager. I jumped up, knocking over my chair, and looked around wildly. Had the police come to protect me? Had I been lulled into a false sense of security by the Peasgoods' aura of amiable guilelessness? Dim memories of movie clips of gangster shoot-outs in Italian restaurants rushed through my brain, and I dove for cover under the table.

"Oh my stars! Oh my soul!" Father Donald hunted without success through his jacket pockets. "The beeper! It's a fire! Oh, dear!" If anything, the beeping grew more penetrating as he leapt up and began searching around the room. "Ah, here it is!" He snatched the beeper off the mantlepiece and silenced it. However, the siren continued, an ululating ear-splitting wail that hampered any further conversation.

Dorothy alone remained unaffected, continuing to eat her dessert as if nothing had happened. I crawled out from under the table, righted my chair and sat down, unable to grasp the situation, but thankful that none of the commotion seemed to be directed at me.

"Oh shoot! The keys! Where did I put the keys? Dottie, where did I decide to put them so I wouldn't lose them? Oh my soul! I know it was somewhere easy to remember!" He dashed from room to room. I could hear drawers and cupboards being opened and shut.

Without a word, Dorothy got up, walked through to the kitchen and returned with a large bunch of keys. Father Donald raced back into the dining room showing all the signs of a complete mental meltdown. "Oh my stars! The keys! The keys!"

"Here they are, Donald." Dorothy held up the key ring. "Right where I always keep keys. On the key rack in the kitchen."

Father Donald grabbed the keys and galloped out the door. I heard it slam. Even though the siren continued to wail, the room felt almost peaceful after his exodus. Relief washed over me. If I hadn't leapt to the wrong conclusions about the situation, it would have been laughable.

"Coffee?' shouted Dorothy. "I hope you like decaf," she bellowed, filling my cup. "We find that regular coffee is rather too much for Donald's nerves. Cream?" She continued to speak over the continuing wail of the siren. I was surprised how quickly I was becoming accustomed to the hideous noise. "Sugar?"

I declined both and took a sip. To my horror, I detected instant decaffeinated coffee. I made a mental note to avoid coffee at the rectory in the future.

"Is there really a fire?" I asked her, trying to shout above the continuing din.

"Oh, yes. The firehall is right next door to the rectory, so it seemed a good idea to have Donald drive the engine, since he's usually right here. It's a volunteer brigade, so our proximity was the deciding factor in Donald's appointment. He, of course, is quite thrilled. When he was a little boy, he always wanted to be a fireman." She took another sip. "Fortunately, we have few fires in Cormorant Harbour and area, so this kind of commotion doesn't happen very often. I'm sorry it disturbed our little luncheon…" At this point, the siren ceased. My ears rang, and Dorothy's voice seemed loud in the new silence. "…and I know Donald wanted to talk to you about joining us as lay reader, but there'll be plenty of time in the future for you two to talk business." She leaned forward, fixing me with a penetrating stare. "This will give us an opportunity to get to know each other so much better."

I quailed at the thought of enduring another one of her interrogations. If anyone could rattle me into making a mistake, it would be Dorothy Peasgood. In desperation, I turned the subject back to the fire. "How does Father Donald know where the fire is?" I had a mental image of Father Donald at the wheel of a bright red pumper truck, driving off in a mad search for smoke.

"Oh, when you call in, the civic address is noted. It's no problem, unless of course, Donald has to start off by himself. One or two of the others try to make sure that they're on board before he leaves the hall." She offered me another cup of the abominable coffee, but I declined, leaving her to finish the rest herself. "Most of the fires are false alarms. Otherwise, in the winter it's chimney fires, and in the summer, grass fires. Seldom is it a serious blaze, I'm happy to say. People have been educated to take more precautions against fire today. In the past, however, there were many more fires due to careless accidents. Then of course, some of the locals were always trying for a 'lucky strike'."

"A 'lucky strike'?" I queried the unfamiliar term.

Dorothy's face twisted in disgust. "I regret to say that some people had a reputation for setting fire to their own homes in order to collect the insurance. It's not so common now, but people will still try. If someone started to remove valuables from their home and then had a blaze a week later, you could be sure it was a 'lucky strike'."

"But why a 'lucky strike'?"

Dorothy sniffed. "It's a joke—in poor taste, if you ask me. There is a brand of American matches called 'Lucky Strikes'. The name stuck, I suppose. It seems applicable when someone ends up with a nice new house in place of the hovel they burned down."

"Surely a 'lucky strike' would be investigated?" I pressed.

"Indeed it is. That is why we seldom have these convenient fires any more. Only a very stupid person would try to get away with it today." Dorothy stood up. "Shall we go into the living room? Donald shouldn't be long."

I followed her into a room filled with the kind of antiques that would set a Toronto dealer's heart beating faster. On an elegant piecrust table beside the door sat a large photograph of Elvis Presley in an ornate silver frame. I read the inscription with unabashed curiosity. "To Dorothy, my faithful fan and president of the Canadian Maritime Fan Club, love, Elvis, 1964." The pieces fell into place. I could see now that Dorothy's infatuation with Elvis had roots deep in her past.

I sat down upon an antique horsehair sofa with great care. The surface proved slippery beyond belief. My continual struggle not to slide down in a heap onto the Axminster carpet helped me stay awake, since my intake of food at lunch had put me in danger of quietly dozing off at any moment.

"Well, now, Charles. Do tell me all about yourself." The only thing missing in the room was a bright light shining into my eyes. I now knew how the most hardened criminals felt when confronted with the top interrogator on the force. My sleepiness vanished under the threat of inquisition, and I began to marshal the facts in my mind.

Before I could muster a reply, the door bell cut off my words. It sounded like the opening notes of the Elvis Presley classic, "Are You Lonesome Tonight?" Surely not, I told myself. Then it rang again. "Dah dah daaah da da dah". It was. Dorothy excused herself with a sigh.

I could hear a murmur of voices from the front hall. I

pulled myself together, as usual anticipating the worst. I reminded myself that people often called at a rectory. I told myself that I'd have to get used to dealing with life's everyday little incidents without blowing them out of proportion. At this rate, if I didn't make these mental adjustments soon, I'd have a nervous breakdown.

Dorothy reappeared with a tiny lady in tow, a delicate woman who looked like everyone's idea of a sweet grandmother. Dorothy, however, glowered at her as she offered her a seat. I put this down to the fact that our little tête-à-tête had been interrupted.

"This is Charles Trenchant," she said to her guest. "He's just moved to Cormorant Harbour. I've discovered he's a writer, and I'm trying to persuade him to lead our little literary group. Donald and I hope he's going to be the new parish lay reader." I could feel the noose tightening. "Charles, this is Mildred Barkhouse, the president of St. Grimbald's A.C.W. and of the Firefighter's Auxiliary." A certain tension in Dorothy's tone gave me the impression that these two were not bosom buddies.

Mildred shook my hand with a dainty air, then perched on the edge of a straight-backed chair with an intricately worked tapestry seat.

"And what brings you to our little corner of the world, Mr. Trenchant?" Despite her sweet and silvery voice, I heard the steel beneath her words and recognized the touch of another top interrogator. My cover story was getting a lot of air time.

"I'm retired," I told her. "Ex-civil servant out of Ottawa." This time, the words flowed easily. Perhaps it only required practice to be an accomplished liar.

"My," she said. "How brave of you to come so far from

civilization." She tittered at her own small joke. "Whatever possessed you to choose Cormorant Harbour?" she pressed. "We're hardly a centre of culture and refinement, I'm afraid, and I can't imagine a man such as yourself finding our little bit of the world inviting." This last she said with an upward inflection. The question had been asked, and I knew I had to rise to the occasion. Mildred Barkhouse hardly posed a threat to me, but I needed to keep my wits about me at all times. I couldn't afford to make any more mistakes. My careless admission of a small part of my past to the Peasgoods had brought me to this pass.

I took a deep breath as I launched into the history I had been coached in. "Well, Mrs. Barkhouse, it is a most interesting little story. One of my colleagues in the Planning Department returned from a touring holiday of Nova Scotia raving about the beauties of the Eastern Shore. I'd always dreamed of a little cottage by the sea where I could pursue my writing. Ten minutes on the web, and I'd found myself a real estate agent, and just weeks later, I was the proud owner of Innisfree." I sat back and blew out my breath in relief. As far as I knew, I'd got it right. Next time would be easier.

"Innisfree?" Dorothy's brow wrinkled in puzzlement. "But aren't you living in the old Barnes place on Lupin Loop?"

"Well, yes, it is the old Barnes place." I knew they were picturing the rundown clapboard house surrounded by unkempt lawns on an unpaved side road, but to me, it represented freedom. "I call it 'Innisfree'. Yeats, you know." I quoted the first verse for them, raising my voice slightly to convey the beauty of the lines. 'I will arise and go now, and go to Innisfree…'" I liked the resonance of my voice echoing in the high-ceilinged room, so I continued, "'And a small cabin build there, of clay and wattles made; Nine bean rows will I have there, a hive for the honey bee, And live alone in the bee-loud glade."

The two women looked at me blank-faced.

After a brief moment of silence, Mrs. Barkhouse said, "The Barnes place on Lupin Loop? Why, you must be my nephew Kevin's new neighbour!"

My head reeled. I couldn't for the life of me reconcile this delicate little ladylike creature sitting in front of me, her pale pink suit immaculate, her hat a froth of feminine frills, her gloves and purse neatly placed on her lap, with the lout who had accosted me about the clothesline.

"Kevin?" I sputtered. "Kevin Jollimore?"

"Why, yes. Have you met him?"

I nodded.

"A dear boy. My favourite sister Mona's only son. Such a pity he married that Arleen creature. The Hubleys from Lower Cormorant were always a rough bunch. But what could he do? She caught him good and proper."

I noticed that her air of refinement slipped several notches as her indignation grew.

"Knocked her up, she claimed, as if we all didn't know there were half a dozen others sniffing around her at the same time. But dear Kevin was always a sucker for a pretty face. Married her just in time. Cat'licks don't care when the ceremony is as, long as it's before the baby comes. As it was, she practically dropped it at the altar steps. Wore white, too."

I felt uneasy and glanced at Dorothy to see her reaction to the change in Mildred Barkhouse's demeanor. From the look on her face, Dorothy knew how thin a veneer covered Mildred's spurious gentility.

"Yes, well… um..." I floundered for a suitable reply until Dorothy rescued the conversation by changing the subject.

"Is the Auxiliary still determined to have a Casino Night?" she asked Mildred, bluntly.

"Yes, that's why I popped in. I looked for you after church, but you'd disappeared. Now I know why." She smiled at me, her ladylike façade firmly back in place. "I wanted to let you know that we had a quick executive meeting last night, and it was unanimous—Casino Night is a go."

I watched a dark cloud settle over Dorothy's face. Her mouth turned down into a grim line. "Casino Night," she sneered. "I hardly think we should be encouraging the local people to gamble. Surely they have enough with bingo every other night and the buses running them to the real Casino. Not to mention the video lottery terminals at the Treaty Store in Upper Cormorant. I've said it before, and I'll say it again. It's not a suitable fundraiser for a responsible organization like the Volunteer Fire Department. Donald will be most disappointed with your decision."

"Oh, no. I spoke to Father Donald after church, and he's agreed to sell tickets at the door for us." Mildred smiled in sweet triumph. "In fact, the A.C.W. are going to cater the lunch." If she had torn one of the black velvet Elvis cushions on the sofa to shreds, she couldn't have gotten a stronger reaction from Dorothy than these words wrought.

Dorothy stood up, her large frame quivering with indignation. Her voice trembled with fury as she faced Mildred. "Donald! Agreed! Tickets!" She drew a rasping breath. "And the Anglican Church Women's group involved!"

I shrank back on the sofa, wishing myself anywhere but here. In fact, given a choice, I'd almost have preferred to be back in the courtroom facing the mob. It reminded me of a battle of the titans. Although only Dorothy physically fit the "titan" bill, Mildred Barkhouse's saccharine-sweet demeanor covered a determination to control, every bit as daunting as Dorothy's size.

Having delivered her payload, Mildred began to put on her gloves. She stood up, adjusted her hat and smiled at me. "It's been so pleasant to meet you, Mr. Trenchant. I do hope you'll enjoy living in our little community. I'm looking forward to seeing you again soon. Of course, if you become our lay reader, our paths will cross often." She turned to Dorothy, as if her angry words had never been uttered. "Well, I'll be off now, Dorothy, my dear. I can see myself out. Do give Father Donald my regards." She swept out of the room on a waft of flowery perfume.

Dorothy fell back into her chair. To my dismay, tears glinted in her eyes. From the look on her face, I realized they were tears of pure rage. "I could kill that woman," Dorothy said through clenched teeth, more to herself than me. "And Donald," she hissed, "how could he be such a fool? The Bishop will be furious. The idea. Selling tickets at a Casino Night! Wait until I see him…"

I gabbled something incoherent about what a lovely church service it had been, and how much I'd enjoyed my lunch, and what a marvellous hostess she was, and beat my retreat, leaving Father Donald to face the music alone.

Four

After several weeks in my idyllic hideaway, I began to feel familiar with my new environment. Gone were the mega-malls, the vast libraries, art galleries, concert halls, museums, the restaurants and theatres of my past. Gone also were Wal-Mart, Cineplex, Costco, The Bay, Blockbuster Video and Yakamoto's Take-out Sushi.

However, I soon found that the local ValuMart did supply my basic dietary needs, the Irving Gas Station did rent videos (albeit a little dated), and the library (in the basement of the Fire Hall) opened three afternoons a week. Take-out came from either Ralph's Pizza or Akbar's Donairs. Sit-down dining did not exist except at the Harbour View Motel, the sole restaurant in Cormorant Harbour—"fish and chips our specialty".

My life settled into a comfortable routine. In the mornings, I followed the example of the great writers, settling myself at the keyboard for several hours of work. Although the program people saw my writing as a cover story, it meant much more than that to me. For them, it represented a convenient way to explain my presence and lack of gainful employment. Truth to tell, I didn't need to be gainfully employed. The generous reward money for my information on the Bacciaglia gang, coupled with the conversion of my modest investments, kept me in reasonable comfort.

I recognized that I might never be published, given my circumstances, and even if by some miracle, my work did appear in print, I knew that any kudos it received would have to be anonymous. My face could never appear on any dustjacket, nor could I accept the Governor General's Award for Literature in person.

My afternoons were spent in more leisurely pursuits—long walks on the beach, shopping forays into the Harbour, the occasional visit to the library and the discovery of the dubious joys of gardening.

I no longer saw every shadow as a threat, or every person I met as a member of the Mob. I had replaced my earlier tendency to panic with a calm but vigilant watchfulness. I tried to obey the strictures of the Program to the letter. I still remembered the ominous tone in my agent's voice as she laid out the rules: "Whatever you do, don't draw attention to yourself. Don't rescue anyone from drowning, don't save any little old ladies from muggers, don't pull children from burning buildings, and never, ever, leap tall buildings at a single bound. Anonymity should be your watchword at all times. Try to blend in. Keep a low profile, that's crucial. It'll be years before the Mob forgets you, and even then, someone may be holding a personal grudge. If, for any reason, you suspect that your cover has been blown, get out and call me." Despite her anger with me regarding the lay readership incident, I knew she had my best interests at heart. They'd chosen my hideaway well. Although I'd seen a number of strange characters in my perambulations around Cormorant Harbour, I doubted any of them concealed a Mafia hitman.

My little cottage had become my home. Having always lived in high-rise apartments, I had never experienced the joys of home ownership. Now, I took pride in my abilities on the maintenance front. Despite Kevin Jollimore's disparaging remarks about my handyman skills, I found myself quite capable of mowing my own lawn and keeping the place tidy.

I saw far more of Kevin than I needed. Each day, he stopped by for one of his "neighbourly chats", which led up either to a blatant bid for work or a request for a "small loan". I always declined both, but that didn't deter his visits. Ricky continued to use my property as his own private path to the beach, and after several unsuccessful attempts at blocking his way, I gave up. I had yet to meet the elusive Arleen; however, her voice haunted my dreams at night and shattered my concentration several times a day. I hoped that one day I would be able to tune her out as successfully as Ricky and Kevin did.

Thank heavens, the older Jollimores were all late risers. Ricky vanished each morning on the school bus, but Kevin seldom appeared much before eleven, leaving my writing time undisturbed.

One morning as I sat in my study, a front room of the little cottage once designated as the spare bedroom, gazing out of the window in search of inspiration and finding little in the dirt road and shambles of the Jollimore establishment, I wondered again if I'd been too hasty in my decision to overlook the road rather than the ocean. However convinced I'd been that the beauty of the ocean would prove to be too much of a distraction, I couldn't help thinking that my present view might deter the muse within. I had tried writing out on the patio, but soon found that blackflies, an ever-present stiff westerly breeze and fog that would waft in without notice were more than even Hemingway would have been able to tolerate.

I made myself a pot of my special blend and took it outside, hoping that the caffeine and a stroll in the fresh breeze off the ocean would clear my brain. Twinkles joined me, tail held aloft, queen of all she surveyed.

"Howdy, neighbour!" As I rounded the corner of the cottage, I saw Kevin and a stranger sloping across the road towards me. Twinkles, in her usual way, melted into the shrubbery. It was only nine a.m. I couldn't imagine what would bring Kevin out of his bed at such an early hour. "Someone here wants to meet you."

I took in every detail of the stranger now standing on my patio and felt my heart lurch. Short and powerfully built, with a thick mustache and several days growth of whiskers obscuring most of his face, he had black, wiry hair that sprouted from under a greasy ball cap. I could see several gold chains entangled in the dark mat of hair on his barrel chest. Even the backs of his powerful hands and forearms were covered in hair. Aside from the hair, his short stature and massive shoulders gave him the appearance of a gorilla. His face sported a broken nose and one eye that wandered off to the left, so that I couldn't tell where he was looking.

I had seen his type before. Everything about him screamed "Mafia goon". Heaven knows, there'd been enough of them in the courtroom to recognize the species. He favoured me with a twisted smirk that revealed he'd lost a front tooth, no doubt in some previous life-and-death battle. I wondered how he'd latched onto Kevin Jollimore, and even more, how he'd found me.

I wanted to run, but where would I go? High tide covered the shingle beach. The stranger stood between me and the road. I thought about fleeing to my little cottage, but no door would be a barrier to him. If only I'd opted for a dog as my animal companion. A rottweiler or German shepherd might leap to my defense. With shaking hands, I put my coffee cup on the patio table, took a deep breath and resigned myself to whatever would happen next.

"This here's Arleen's brother, Clarence." Kevin introduced him with a proud grin. "Used to be a prize fighter. Good, too, until his last couple of bouts. Up from Lower Cormorant to give us a hand. I was tellin' him all about you. Says he's never met a computer whiz before."

I tried to cope with the sudden surge of relief that flooded my body. Not a hitman. Not a mobster. Not even a goon. Not here to do me harm. I swallowed hard and managed a weak smile. "How do you do...Mr...er...Clarence." A huge, hairy paw closed over my trembling fingers.

I disentangled my hand and tried once more to explain to Kevin my occupation. "Not a computer whiz, Kevin. I just use the computer for my writing."

"Whatever." Kevin dismissed my explanation. "Like I was saying, Clarence here is gonna give us a hand. Arleen wants to do a bit of redecorating, so we got to get stuff outta the house."

I drew a blank at the idea of Arleen redecorating, but if she did wish to give rein to some unsuspected Martha Steward tendencies, I couldn't for the life of me see what it had to do with me.

"So, we was wonderin' whether we could use your shed for storin' stuff. Just for a couple of weeks, eh?" Kevin looked hopeful.

I felt so relieved to realize that my worst nightmare of being discovered by my former adversaries had not materialized, that I would have agreed to anything.

"Oh, yes, well, of course. Why not? There's nothing much

in there at the moment. It's all yours. Go right ahead."

"C'mon, old son, let's get the stuff shifted. Arleen'll want to get going on her redecorating, eh?" I saw Kevin give Clarence a broad wink. A private joke, I decided.

I left them to it and headed inside to the kitchen to pour myself a fresh cup of coffee.

For the next hour, I watched Kevin and Clarence ferrying various items from the Jollimore residence to my shed. The eclectic nature of their burdens surprised me. Not the contents of a room as one might imagine for a redecorating project, but rather, a miscellany of esoteric items such as clothing, a television set, a microwave oven, various components of a VCR and CD system, a collection of hunting rifles and fishing equipment, some plates, a couple of pictures, a large family Bible and a photo album.

At last their labours ceased. They took their well-earned rest on the discarded freezer that graced the end of the Jollimore driveway, where they lounged bare-chested in the sun to enjoy a couple of bottles of beer. The sight fascinated me, and I found myself unable to decide which looked more repulsive: Clarence's furry front or the grey pudge of Kevin. An ear-shattering, "Kevin! Where the hell are you?" ended their idyll.

After the morning's excitement, the muse had left me, so I packed up my writing for the day. I decided my hair and beard needed a trim. Although the new beard had developed very well, I felt it now required professional attention. In Toronto, I had frequented Quentin's, a rather upscale salon in the downtown core that catered to business professionals. I knew I was vain about my hair, but unlike most men of my age who were battling receding hairlines, I still had the thick, wavy mane of my youth. I thought that the few silver strands in it gave me an air of distinction.

I had looked for a barber shop in Cormorant Harbour, and having seen none, resigned myself to a monthly trip to Halifax. However, St. Grimbald's organist, Boris Monk, a large, flamboyant individual given to hairy ties and baggy corduroy trousers, a man with an endless supply of local information, had recommended a woman called Sherri.

"All the local ladies go to her, but Sherri caters to the guys, too. Sets 'em up in a little room in back. Does a good job, too. I'd go to Sherri any time. Although," he continued as he fingered his thick, black beard, "nobody touches this baby but me."

Following Boris's instructions, I ventured into one of the small side streets in Cormorant Harbour. As he had said it would be, I found the large house trailer set back from the road. If Boris hadn't told me what to expect, I would never have assumed this to be a place of business. I hesitated before climbing the rickety wooden steps. I found it hard to imagine a man like Boris frequenting such an establishment. Taking a deep breath, I pushed open an old screen door, which screeched and slammed with a bang behind me. Inside, someone had transformed the narrow living room of the trailer into a hairdressing salon by painting everything in a most virulent shade of strawberry pink. Photos of various models with outrageous hair styles adorned the walls. Every horizontal surface was strewn with the paraphernalia of the beautician's art.

The small room was crowded. On my entrance, all activity ceased. A very large lady sat under one of the dryers against the wall. Another occupied the styling chair, her head bristling with brush rollers. The third, her head a mass of curls, sat in a wicker chair in the corner. Their eyes assessed me with curious stares.

"Hello." A younger woman, very pretty, with blonde hair teased into an impossible pouf on top of her head, turned off a small blow dryer as she came towards me. "You must be Mr. Trenchant. Boris said you might drop in. I'm Sherri."

I had a moment of shock as she spoke my name, then realized it wasn't a sign of possible danger. Of course she'd know me, since I was the only new face in Cormorant Harbour. "I'll just show you through to the back," she continued. "It's the bingo tonight, so I'm busy this morning, but it won't take long." The three customers continued to stare. I thought I recognized a couple of them from the church services at St. Grimbald's, but no names came to mind. I allowed Sherri to lead me through the main area, redolent of hair spray and shampoo, into a small cubbyhole off to one side.

This area, barely big enough to hold a styling chair, had been designed with the male customer in mind. The beige walls were soothing after the strident pink of the main salon, and here were adorned with masculine pictures of yachts, antique cars and horses. Sherri seated me in the styling chair, poured me a cup of coffee, then handed me a magazine to read. I felt trapped, but I didn't think I could bear to walk back through the assembled company and return another day. I cast a desultory glance at the magazine, *Body Builder*. My eyes were assailed with numerous semi-nude male bodies of unbelievable brawn and girth. I didn't need this reminder of my own unprepossessing 148 pounds, so I laid the magazine back on the counter. As I waited for Sherri, I noticed I could hear every word being spoken in the front salon. My ears pricked when I heard the name "Mildred". They had to be talking about Mildred Barkhouse.

"'Magine that Mildred taking over the Auxiliary the way she has. No one would run against her. Get on the wrong side of her, and you'll know it. A little more fluff on the top, please, Sherri. I do like a little height. Makes me look like I got some hair left up there." I thought the high-pitched, almost girlish voice must be coming from the lady in the styling chair.

I heard Sherri murmur some encouraging words. Another voice cut in, this one deep and gruff, obviously shouting over the sound of the hair dryer on her head. I had a memory of her in the choir at St. Grimbald's. Vi something…I thought. Father Donald's introductions, laced with extraneous information, made it difficult to get names straight. "Mildred Barkhouse is meaner than a wet cat. Looks like butter wouldn't melt in her mouth, but acts worse 'n weasel. I've known that woman for nearly sixty years, and she's always been the same. How poor Bev can live with her, I'll never know. Poor girl can't do anything right. She's no life of her own. Everyone knows that the only time she looked like getting away from her mother's clutches, Mildred scared the poor lad right out of town. Isn't that right, Etta Fay? And all the life Bev has is three afternoons a week stuck in the basement of the Fire Hall. It's a sin!"

I realized that they were talking about the librarian, a mousy slip of a woman with a whispery voice and persistent post-nasal drip. Now I had a name to match her face: Beverly Barkhouse.

"How's that?" I heard Sherri ask, no doubt holding up a mirror for her customer's approval.

"Just as long as it looks good for the bingo. Bert's calling the numbers tonight. It's been a year since his wife died. I figure he's ripe."

Ripe? I wondered.

"Bert! Oh, in your dreams, Bertha," the deep voice snorted.

"Even if he whispered sweet nothings in your ear, you wouldn't understand a word. Ever since he got those new teeth, it's like he's talking another language. You can't hardly understand a thing he says."

I had a moment of pity for the unwitting Bert. Little did he know what awaited him at tonight's game.

"And then there's that damn Casino Night! Mildred acts like it was all her own idea, when we all know that it was Phyllis George who brung it back from when she visited her daughter in Ontario." The gruff voice subsided as I heard the dryer turn off.

"You're done Bertha. Vi, hop into the chair." Sherri's head popped around the door to my little sanctuary. "I'll be with you in a moment, dear," she assured me.

"I don't think there's a soul likes the woman," the one they called Bertha continued.

I could hear the styling chair creak and presumed that Vi was taking her place. "Cyril Pye says she shouldabin drowned at birth, and he's her uncle. He says he knows fine well she snuck into the house after Grannie Pye died and helped herself to all his mother's good stuff. It's a wonder somebody ain't shoved her off the wharf before this. Why, leave a loaded gun on the table, and someone's gonna pick it up and shoot Mildred Barkhouse for sure."

"Vi! What a terrible thing to say." I noticed a decided lack of conviction in Sherri's voice.

"Come off it, Sherri!" The gruff voice rose. "Everybody knows Mildred's got you by the short 'n curlies. Owns everything in here, she does, and don't she let you know it every chance she gets. Told you you shoulda gone to the bank for the money to start up. Better pay interest to them than owe your soul to a woman like Mildred."

"Oh, now, Vi. Aunt Mildred's not that bad. It was good of her to lend me the money, and if she gets a little pushy by times, well, that's just her way."

Another genealogical piece fell into place. Mildred was not only the aunt of Kevin, but also of Sherri. I tried to imagine charming Sherri and the irascible Kev as brother and sister, but unless one of them had been switched at birth, it seemed more likely that they were cousins.

"She'll be at the bingo tonight, up to her old tricks," continued the harsh voice, now in full spate. "Sitting in Uncle Orville's lucky seat, and helping herself to Bertha's bingo candy, and jeering at me when I'm set and then don't win. And don't the woman have horseshoes up her bum—she always wins something. It just ain't fair. And when she cast her eye on Roy last week, I thought he'd die. You could hear him clear across the hall. 'For the love of God, I'll never win now that she's looked at me.' Everyone knows fine well the Fleets all believe they'll lose their luck if anyone talks to them or looks at them at the bingo. Just plain mean, Mildred is."

A third voice, thin and papery, which I could barely hear, cut in. "You know, I'd like to teach that Mildred a lesson. My poor Randy was never the same after she run him off. He was that stuck on Bev. Broke my poor boy's heart, she did. I hardly even hears from him since he ran off to Alberta. I'm lucky if I gets a card on Mother's Day. And no grandbabies, either. Says no other woman will satisfy him. Says he never wanted no one but Bev. I'd give anything to show Mildred that her sweet little act don't fool me none."

"Like what? Bash her with your bingo bag, Etta Fay? Poke her with your knitting needles?" Vi snorted as she laughed at her own joke.

"Well, there's more than one way to deal with someone

like Mildred Barkhouse. What goes around comes around. You just have to know how." I heard a malicious tone in the voice that caused a shiver to run over me. She sounded like someone I wouldn't want to meet in a dark alley.

"How's that look, Vi?" Sherri asked.

"Well, it's no better than a Brillo pad, I suppose, but that's not your fault, dear. The Hubleys always was a hairy bunch, but at least *my* hair don't need no teasing." I heard the chair creak again, followed by a flurry of goodbyes and the final slam of the screen door.

An hour later, I, too, left, well satisfied with Sherri's ministrations. Boris had been right; Sherri could hold her own with any of the stylists at Quentin's.

Later, as I sat on my patio well fortified with bug spray, a glass of sherry and a warm sweater, with Twinkles ensconced on my knee, I realized that the day had passed without my having written one word. However, I had an excuse. It had been a busy, if not fraught, day. First Kevin and Clarence, then the ladies at the salon. So many new faces. So much to think about.

I glanced at the shed, noting a large new padlock in place on the door. Strange for the Jollimores to be so protective of such an odd pile of belongings. I wondered about the progress of their redecorating project. Where had they stored the rest of the furniture? Something about the incident made me uneasy. I shook off the momentary discomfort and sipped my drink.

Twinkles stood up, stretched, turned around and settled back on my lap. I stroked her soft fur, but it didn't help. The many events of the day prevented my being lulled by the soothing qualities of my feline companion. I gave up and went inside to make myself a little dinner.

Five

The following day, an unexpected visitor again disturbed my writing time. I must admit that my heart sank when I saw Father Donald's little blue Toyota pull into the driveway. He had visited several times in the past few weeks, so I had come to know that regardless of the reason for his visit, it would last at least an hour. I resigned myself to setting aside my work in order to play host. Without Dorothy along with him to curb his intake, I could offer him some sustenance of the sweet variety, having laid in a few packages of the puffy chocolate and marshmallow concoctions that he loved.

In the past weeks, I had come to know him quite well. Aside from his proclivity for long-winded explanations and circumlocutions, his boundless enthusiasm for all things, both secular and spiritual, and his boyish good humour made him a popular figure in the community. Shut-ins, who looked forward to his visits, always welcomed him, knowing he was a bottomless well of local news. His bedside manner, although unconventional, seemed to have an uplifting effect on the spirits of those brought low by illness. You couldn't ask for a more assiduous rector or a more kindly pastor of his flock. What he lacked in intellect, he more than made up for with his energy. Although his sister Dorothy seemed a daunting figure to many, I thought her common sense and stability kept his feet on the ground.

This day, I could feel the excitement coming off him in waves as he pushed through the front door and preceded me into my small living room. This room, like all the other living rooms in the community, eschewed the view of the ocean in favour of a picture-window panorama of the road. Father Donald settled himself in his favourite chair, an overstuffed monstrosity, part of the suite ordered by the same nameless bureaucrat who had purchased the house. The entire house had been furnished in government beige, no doubt most of it coming from the pages of the Sears catalogue. As well, I doubted that the purchaser had ever seen the house. Since every item was overstuffed, oversized and overdecorated, I suspected that the buyer's selection reflected his own large size.

Twinkles leapt up and settled herself into Father Donald's capacious lap. Although shy with most strangers, she had formed an affinity with Father Donald which he reciprocated. I felt a pang when it occurred to me that she looked more at home on his lap than on mine.

"It's come!" he announced. "Not that I didn't think it would, but with the Bishop, I can never be too sure, although your credentials were impeccable, absolutely wonderful, in fact, even the Bishop said so, not that I think he actually checked them, that would seem as if he didn't believe you, well, not that anyone ever lies on their application, or not that I know of, after all, there's no reason to lie…" He rummaged through his battered brief case. "Here it is! Your certificate of lay readership in the Parish of Cormorant Harbour. You can start right away, well, not right away, you'll have to wait until Sunday, that is, if Sunday's all right for you, you won't need any training of course, although many do, in fact poor old Tom, our previous lay reader, had to take the course twice, most unfortunate, couldn't get the hang of the thing, probably his deafness had something to do with it, not that there's that much to learn, well, you know all about that, well, not all of it perhaps…"

"Cookie?" I said, a word that proved to be as effective as Dorothy's "Donald!". I had found the secret to turning off the flow.

"Oh! My! Chocolate mallows! My favourite!" I watched in fascination as he licked the chocolate off the top of the cookie, ate the marshmallow filling, and then popped the jam-covered biscuit bottom into his mouth whole. The ritual never ceased to amuse me. I handed him a steaming cup of my special blend of coffee, wincing as he stirred in several large spoonfuls of sugar and laced it with plenty of cream. He blew across the top surface, closed his eyes and sipped. "Oh my stars! Oh my soul! This is wonderful coffee. Not at all like Dorothy makes, not that Dorothy's coffee isn't good, well, certainly not as good as this, although I wouldn't want her to hear me say so, her being so touchy about the domestic side of things, and of course, I'd be the first to say that she's a wonderful cook, although…"

"Another cookie?" It worked again. I watched as he ate his way through several more cookies. I smiled as I realized that Dorothy was not going to be pleased anyway, whether he told her about the coffee or not. The combination of chocolate and caffeine would have Father Donald wound up tighter than a mainspring for the rest of the day. I topped up his cup.

Taking advantage of his full mouth, I moved the conversation to a topic that had not yet left my mind since yesterday's excursion to Sherri's. "How are plans progressing for the Casino Night?" I asked him, by way of preamble.

Father Donald bounced up and down in his chair as he launched into an enthusiastic description of the plans. "It's all coming into place. It's in the Fire Hall and the A.C.W. is lined up to cater and the casino equipment has been ordered from the City and Boris's friend Mattie is doing all the decorations and all of the firemen are going to dress up as Wild West gamblers with green eye shades and sleeve garters and fancy vests and I've already got mine and I was trying them on just this morning and I must say I do look so much the part and I'm sure that everyone is going to have a wonderful time and I know that it will raise a lot of money for our wonderful cause and I'm hoping…"

"Cookie?" I waited until Father Donald crammed the cookie into his mouth before I slipped in my next question. "Mrs. Barkhouse must be a great organizer," I suggested.

"Oh my stars! Wonderful! We're just chugging along in our little boat with Mildred's hand firmly on the tiller. Amazing how that woman gets thing done! She's a born leader, well, not that all leaders…"

I cut him off. He'd gone where I wanted him to be. "Mildred seems to be quite a powerhouse in the community," I began. "She must be very popular…?" I let the question hang.

"Oh, my soul! Popular? I suppose she is. Certainly she has no trouble getting everybody on board with her ideas. Well, not everybody, I suppose. I can think of one person who's not enthusiastic, although she is enthusiastic about most things, well, almost all things, she didn't care for the new choir gowns, not that we didn't need them, but it was Mildred who chose the turquoise, not a good colour, well, nothing wrong with it as a colour, it's certainly bright and cheerful, although Dorothy was quite right when she said that maroon wouldn't show the dirt, not that they get dirty, well, not muddy, unless of course we have a church parade and it's raining very hard, although I doubt we'd have a parade if it were raining…"

"Dorothy doesn't care for Mildred?" I cut in.

"Oh my soul! I hate to say it, but I am most grieved by the bad feelings between them. It all goes back to when we first arrived. In our previous parishes, Dorothy had always taken on the role and duties of the rector's wife, and I must say, executed them very well, despite the fact that she's only my sister. However, when we arrived at St. Grimbald's, Mildred was already firmly entrenched as the President of the A.C.W., a role usually reserved for the rector's wife. The previous rector had no wife, poor man, although perhaps 'poor' is a misleading word, since we are quite well paid now, really, not at all the way it once was, and indeed, he did have fewer expenses without a wife, I'm sure, although on the other hand, he would suffer from the lack of support and companionship that are so vital to the success of ministry…"

"More coffee?" Father Donald stopped long enough to hand me his cup. I endeavoured to get him back on track. "So, Mildred was already the president of the A.C.W.?" I asked.

"Oh yes, and she wasn't about to give it up. As she pointed out to Dorothy at their first meeting, Dorothy was in fact not the rector's wife, but only his sister. I'm afraid their relationship went downhill from that point. In fact, I said to Dorothy just last week that it was her Christian duty to be more forgiving in her attitude towards Mildred…" He paused and licked his lips. "I'm afraid she didn't take my little suggestion very well…" He took another large bite of a cookie and chewed thoughtfully. I felt it best not to ask for details.

"Your sister did seem a little upset about the Casino Night…." I prompted.

"Oh my stars! Oh my soul! A little upset? Dear Charles, she was beside herself with anger at Mildred. I had to give her two of her nerve pills, not that she takes them very often, just when she's feeling a little stressed, well, not a little stressed, she's usually a little stressed, but when she's extremely stressed, then she definitely needs them, I shouldn't say 'needs', sounds likes she's addicted or something, not that I know any real addicts, but I do think they are unable to do without their drugs, and I'm sure Dorothy could, that is, if she had to, although I wouldn't want to be there if she needed one of her nerve pills and didn't avail herself of them, having only experienced such a thing once in the past when her prescription ran out and indeed, it was not as dire as the police report made out…"

I let him ramble on as I digested the fact that my impression of Dorothy Peasgood as a rock of stability for Father Donald might be mistaken. Seeing that Father Donald had snagged the last cookie off the plate, I took it back to the kitchen for replenishment.

As I loaded half a dozen more of the chocolate cookies on the plate, I heard Father Donald shouting. "Oh my stars! A fire! A fire! Call 911!" Twinkles shot past me and disappeared into the bedroom.

I rushed into the living room to find Father Donald dancing up and down in front of the window, waving his arms "Charles! Your neighbour's house is on fire! I can see the smoke from here! Somebody do something!" I looked out the window. Sure enough, I could see a thin curl of smoke seeping out the front door of the Jollimore homestead. I dialed 911 and gave them the address.

Immediately, Father Donald's beeper began to emit the sounds I remembered from our last encounter with the fire department. "Oh shoot! What shall I do? I'm here, and the pumper is there. Oh my soul! By the time I go back and get it, it will be too late!" He rushed back and forth between the front door and the window.

"Can't someone else drive the fire truck?" I asked him.

"Well, yes, of course, we have several drivers, it's just that I'm next door, well, not today, but usually, and that's why they leave it to me, and now, I'm here, and they're there! Oh shoot!" Father Donald sounded close to tears with frustration.

"Let's go over and see what we can do," I suggested. "We can wait for the pumper there."

"What a wonderful suggestion. I have a fire extinguisher in my car. We all have, well not all, but all the volunteer fire fighters have, it's part of our kit, and perhaps we can do something. Come along, Charles. There's no time to waste."

I followed him out the front door. We lost a couple of precious seconds while he fumbled in the trunk of his car before producing a large, professional-looking fire extinguisher. I stayed well back from him, not wanting to be in the vicinity of any sudden heroics by Father Donald. In the back of my mind, I wondered if the contents of the fire extinguisher were in any way dangerous to humans. I thought that it might be a good idea not to get between Father Donald and the fire.

I stood in awe as Father Donald lumbered down the littered driveway, dodging the various impediments. With surprising efficiency, he threw his not inconsiderable weight against the front door, which fell open with a bang. It occurred to me that the caffeine and chocolate, combined with the adrenaline rush brought on by the situation, must have kicked in with a vengeance. I might have tried the door handle first, but I must admit, Father Donald's direct approach proved more effective. He'd been trained for just such an emergency. In seconds, I heard the roar of the fire extinguisher.

At this moment, the Four Cormorants Fire Department truck manoeuvered down the driveway, its siren wailing, followed by several pickup trucks filled with volunteer firefighters. The Jollimore collection of used vehicles, appliances and bedsprings were crushed and scattered before the onslaught. Hoses were unreeled and snaked across the unkempt lawn. Several men pulled out a ladder to place against the front of the house.

Before they could turn the pumper on, Father Donald appeared in the open doorway, waving his fire extinguisher in triumph. "No need, fellows," he called. "I put it out. Well, it looks out, and it was just a small fire, nothing at all really, a bunch of rags and some paint thinner that someone had left very carelessly in the front hall, spontaneous combustion, I suppose, quite surprising, although you only have to read the reports to know how often it happens, well, not that often, lightning being much more likely to strike, I believe…"

In obvious disappointment, the Cormorant crew began to reel in the hoses and stow the ladder. Those who had managed to put on their safety gear started to undress. A definite air of anticlimax hung over the scene.

Several other cars full of sightseers drove by, slowed down, looked, then drove on. I realized that a fire in Cormorant Harbour was a community event,

The appearance of a small van in the driveway caused a minor flurry of excitement among the firefighters. "Here's

Bev," said one. "I could use a cold drink. Hope she brought some sandwiches."

The men clustered around the open back doors of the van, where I could see Beverly Barkhouse handing out cans of pop.

"Oh, good," said Father Donald. "It's the Auxiliary Van. They always come to every fire with refreshments. Mildred has a beeper, too, and she makes sure that someone brings us a little something to keep us going." He grabbed two cans, offering one to me. When I declined, he slipped the second can in his pocket.

"Nobody home," said one fellow, who had done a quick search of the house. "Good thing, too. Those fumes can be pretty bad. Not much damage. Nothing a little redecorating won't cure."

From the rags and paint thinner Father Donald had found in the hallway, I could tell they'd already started redecorating. Kevin's carelessness did not surprise me. If it hadn't been for the quick actions of Father Donald, he might have lost his whole house to the fire. I congratulated myself that I had resisted Kevin's attempts to have me hire him as my handyman.

I heard the screech of brakes. Kevin arrived in his decrepit pickup truck, which he parked off to one side of the road. He and Clarence scrambled out and ran up the driveway.

"Hey, Kev. What's your hurry? Where's the fire?" yelled one of the lounging firefighters. The rest laughed at the old joke.

"Did you bring the marshmallows?" called another.

Kevin and Clarence stood in front of the house, a look of stunned amazement on their faces.

"It hasn't burned down?" Clarence stammered. "It's still all here?"

"Shut up!" Kevin hissed to Clarence. "What happened?"

he asked a nearby fire fighter.

"Some stuff you left in the hall caught fire. Paint rags is famous for doing that. 'Spontaneous confusion' they calls it. Lucky for you that Father Donald was on the spot. Called it right in and put it out afore we got here. Hardly scorched the walls. Won't notice a thing after a lick of paint."

Kevin looked shaken, and the depth of his emotion surprised me considering that nothing had been lost. It struck me that he must be very attached to his little abode, despite its outward appearance. He seemed at a loss for words, an unusual state for Kevin. He didn't even thank Father Donald for his heroic efforts.

"Gotta go and get Arleen," he muttered as he turned away from the house. "She's over at her Ma's. She's not going to be happy about this." He and Clarence made their way back to the truck, got in and drove away.

Father Donald and I waited until the last firefighter had left, then we, too, made our way back to my little house, stopping while Father Donald re-stowed the empty fire extinguisher. In the living room, Father Donald picked up his briefcase.

"Well, I must say, this has been much more exciting than I expected it would be, not that I didn't think a visit with you, Charles, wouldn't be exciting, well not exactly exciting, perhaps, but interesting at least, what with the news of the Bishop and all, but I never expected to be donning my firefighter's hat in your living room, well, not in your living room, since it was on the truck, but metaphorically speaking, I guess you could say that I am always on duty, as a firefighter, as well as in my ministerial capacity. Yes, that's me. Always on duty." He beamed at me, rocking back and forth on his heels. "Always on duty," he repeated.

"Thank heavens you *were* on duty," I told him.

"Otherwise, the Jollimores might have lost their house."

"Very careless of them. Even though we send out literature to all the homes in the area about fire safety…" He paused, looking thoughtful. "Perhaps we should have little seminars on fire safety. Something more interesting than a pamphlet, something with demonstrations, and real fires, although not real enough that anyone would be in danger, of course."

I could see that the idea appealed to him.

"And food. Refreshments that is. Make a real evening of it. Although an afternoon would be good, too. Maybe some games on fire safety for the little ones. I'm sure we'd get a big crowd out."

Somehow, I couldn't imagine Kevin Jollimore taking the family to a Fire Prevention Seminar.

Before I could say anything, Father Donald headed for the front door. "I must go," he said. "Dorothy will wonder what's happened. She always worries when she hears the fire sirens. And she's making fried chicken for lunch." He smacked his lips in anticipation. "I'll see you on Sunday in the vestry," he added.

"One thing, Father Donald." I felt a little awkward, but little had I thought I would once again be involved in church life. "I don't have any robes." I fumbled for an excuse. "They were supplied by my former parish, and so, of course, I left them with the church."

"Not a problem. Tom's passing has left St. Grimbald's with a spare set. It's going to be wonderful having you by my side."

"Wonderful!" That word did not spring to my mind when I thought about being part of Father Donald's own unique brand of liturgy. Interesting, or challenging, but not wonderful.

Six

On Saturday morning, Father Donald took me for a brief tour of the Parish of Cormorant Harbour. There were four churches. St. Grimbald's, known as the Parish Church, looked like a typical Maritime church, with painted white clapboard exterior, black trim and a slender steeple. It had the distinction of hosting the eleven o'clock service, while the others took turn and turnabout for morning and evening prayer.

St. Wulstan's, in Upper Cormorant, barely big enough to seat two men and a dog, sat against the side of a small hill. "They're all Catholics there," Father Donald confided to me as he drove through the village. "Hardly an Anglican left at all."

St. Elmo's in Lower Cormorant, known by the locals as the "Fisherman's Church", had a most striking stained glass window. Father Donald told me it depicted Jesus calming the waves. "One of our own parishioners did it," said Father Donald with pride as we stood in front of the brightly coloured rendering. I stuck to my usual response to art that went beyond my comfort level. "It's most interesting and colourful," I told him.

St. Finbar's in Cormorant Head presented an astounding edifice. It had been modelled after Winchester Cathedral in England, but the architects had overcome the dearth of dressed stone in the area by constructing it all of wood, painted to look like the real thing. Even the rounded pillars inside were marvels of *trompe l'oeil.* It sat on top of Cormorant Head, and as the largest building for miles around, formed a landmark for mariners. Father Donald explained that the church featured on all the nautical maps of the area. The fact that no more than six people ever attended a service didn't alter the determination of the community to keep it open and functioning.

During the course of the tour, Father Donald informed me that my duties as lay reader were to assist him at the eleven o'clock service at St. Grimbald's, as well as take one other service, either morning or afternoon, on the rotating schedule. Since my previous church had three services on Sunday and a mid-week one as well, this seemed a light load for me to assume.

The next day, I eased into my new role by helping Father Donald at the eleven o'clock service at St. Grimbald's, the Parish Church. Well before eleven, I presented myself at the vestry, where I found Father Donald and two young servers in the midst of preparations for the morning's service.

"I hope these robes will fit you, Charles." Father Donald rummaged through a miscellaneous assortment of gowns and vestments in the cupboard. He hauled out an alb, cincture and stole, saying, "I believe that Tom was somewhat larger than you, but I'm sure you can belt it up for the time being."

I threw the nightgown-like garment over my head, almost gagging at the pervasive odour of mildew and mothballs. The "fine white linen" alb, yellowed with age, hung in copious folds around my body. I wrapped the cincture—a somewhat grey and frayed rope—around my waist twice, then pulled up the extra fabric so that it hung over my midsection like a spare tire. The stole fit a much taller man, the ends brushing the tops of my shoes when I draped it around my neck.

Before the next wearing, I would have to engage the services of a seamstress to do some alterations. It didn't help that I heard muffled giggles from the two young servers who had positioned themselves in the farthest corner of the vestry. I fixed them with a stern eye until they subsided into proper decorum.

Meanwhile, Father Donald robed himself for the service. After watching him pirouette several times in the confined space in an attempt to get the cincture around himself, I understood why the servers had learned to stay well out of range.

"We start out in the choir room, Charles," he said. "With a little prayer, well not that little, but short enough for the occasion…with the choir. Then we all process into the church. Are we ready?" he asked.

"Don't forget your prayer book, Father Donald," said one of the servers, handing it to him.

"Oh my soul! Thank you."

"And your announcement sheet," said the other, handing the paper to him.

"And your hymn book," said the first one.

I wondered if Dorothy had trained the servers herself. At last we were ready. We slipped next door into a large room, where I found myself facing ten choir members, resplendent in the disputed turquoise robes. They reminded me of a flock of budgies. However, instead of the cheerful twittering of happy songbirds, I heard voices raised in anger.

The atmosphere was anything but spiritual.

"You don't have to shout at me, Mildred Barkhouse." I recognized the voice from my visit to Sherri's Salon, the same voice that had expressed a desire to "show" Mildred

Barkhouse; the thin, papery voice that had sent shivers up my spine. "I'm not deaf. I just want to make it clear that I have no intention whatsoever of baking cookies for this Casino Night scheme of yours, and I think it should have been brought up to the entire membership of the A.C.W. of St. Grimbald's for a vote before you so highhandedly involved us."

"Oh my stars! Oh my soul! Now ladies, this is not the time nor the place, not that there is any special time or place, but certainly, five to eleven on a Sunday morning in the church is probably the worst time and place for discussions of this nature, or of any other nature, come to that, since we must move along or we shall all be late, not that they can start without us, but…"

Mildred cut him off. "There's nothing to discuss. The decision has been made, and if certain persons don't want to be involved, then they can sit home with their knitting. As for the rest of us, we shall, as always, do our utmost to raise funds for St. Grimbald's, as we have done in the past."

Mildred chose to take the high road, but from the murderous look on Etta Fay's face, it occurred to me that it might be a very dangerous road to travel.

"Well, then, that's settled," said Father Donald. "In the name of the Father, and of the Son and of the Holy Ghost…" he gabbled. He was off, and so were we.

At the end of the service, a smattering of "amens" followed us down the aisle. As Father Donald passed Dorothy, she leaned out of her pew and smacked him on the leg with her purse. "Coffee!" she hissed.

"Whaa?" Father Donald halted. I glanced back. The procession straggled to a halt.

"Coffee Sunday!" she whispered in an urgent tone. "You forgot to mention it."

"Oh! Oh, shoot! Wait! Just a minute! Hold the phone, everybody. I forgot. It's coffee Sunday. Come on downstairs, coffee's on. Although, not just coffee, there's tea, too, although if you don't like coffee or tea, I don't know what you'll do."

We disrobed in the vestry, and I decided to take my robe with me, since I'd need to get it altered sometime during the next week.

Together, Father Donald and I descended the steep stairs to the dank, dark nether regions under the church, which the wardens and A.C.W. had tried to render habitable without much success. The sharp, heady tang of coffee overpowered the usual miasma of mildew and old hymn books. I used Father Donald as a battering ram to take me through the throng to the counter.

He'd already caught sight of a plate of butter tarts and was moving in on them like an elephant who'd spotted a bag of peanuts. Dorothy swept in on an intercept course. At the last moment, she scooped up the plate of tarts, favouring Father Donald with a triumphant glance before she disappeared into the kitchen.

"Shoot!" Father Donald sagged under the disappointment.

I stood in line to get a styrofoam cup of brown liquid poured from a huge urn, identified with red nail polish as "Coffee". It looked no different from the liquid from the urn marked "Tea". I had a moment's regret as I remembered the china mugs and glass coffee carafes of my old church. So often I had entreated them to find something more elegant, but never did I think that I would sink to styrofoam.

The crowd milling around the room also looked quite different from the Sunday congregation I had known. No pinstripe suits for the gentlemen or silk dresses for the ladies; here, polyester predominated for both sexes. Few men wore ties, and those that did had removed them at the last "amen". The majority of the women wore pants, although one or two sported more formal outfits, and one woman wore a hat. Most looked like they were out for a day's shopping at the mall in town rather than for a church service.

I felt a little out-of-place in my tailored grey Brooks Brothers suit, but I could not imagine wearing anything less on Sunday.

The coffee tasted as bad as it looked, but Father Donald sucked his up and went back for a refill. However, the redoubtable Dorothy stood guard, resplendent in a bright plaid skirt and vest that accentuated her height and girth. The guitar-shaped brooch that she always wore glittered on her ample bosom. Father Donald consoled himself with the only thing left on the plates, several crumbly digestive cookies.

"Never mind, Donald," said Dorothy. "You don't want to spoil your lunch. I've made a nice blueberry pie, and there's ice cream." I noticed that she had a half-eaten butter tart on her plate. She turned her attention to me. Her voice softened. "You were so splendid as lay reader, so spiritual, not at all like old Tom, deaf as a doorpost he was, and never sure where we were in the service, bumbling about up there. And when you read the Prayers of the People, it nearly brought a tear to my eye."

I demurred modestly, although several others had already commented on my performance.

"But that robe, Charles. It doesn't do you justice. Donald, you should have warned me beforehand, and I would have washed it at least." Father Donald quailed under her criticism.

"Well, Dottie, I did mention it, I'm sure I did, but you were busy, at least you seemed to be busy, and I tried to tell you, not that you weren't listening…"

"For heaven's sake, Donald, it's too late now. Charles, give it to me, and I'll see what I can do."

I saw Mildred Barkhouse, a vision in a shade of powder blue that matched her hair, bearing down upon us from the other side of the room.

"Oh, Mr. Trenchant!" she trilled. "What a lovely service! It's easy to see that you're most experienced in things ecclesiastical." She took my hand and held it. "Have you ever thought of becoming a priest yourself? Surely, you must have felt The Calling. The authority with which you read the prayers..."

I disengaged my hand. The atmosphere chilled as Mildred noticed Dorothy.

"I was just saying the same thing," said Dorothy, her voice edged with ice. "But what a pity about the gown. I'm surprised that the Altar Guild didn't think of it. It was your turn to prepare for the service, wasn't it?" She drove the point home. "I shall, of course, do something about it before next Sunday."

"Vestments are the responsibility of the A.C.W. If I had been properly informed, we certainly would have made sure that Mr. Trenchant's apparel was suitably prepared." Mildred glared at Father Donald.

"Well," he began. "I did mention it, but you were..."

"Give it to me, Mr. Trenchant," Mildred commanded. "I'll take care of it."

I held out the robe, but just as Mildred took it, Dorothy's hand shot out and forestalled the exchange. "I myself have already offered to wash and alter them for Charles." She took the robe in a firm grip.

"Get your hands off that robe, Dorothy Peasgood. It's an A.C.W. job, and I'm the A.C.W. in this church." Mildred's eyes had a dangerous glint.

"Well, the A.C.W. didn't do its job, and now it's up to me." Dorothy glowered down at her.

Mildred didn't flinch. She drew herself up to her full five-foot-one height, took a deep breath and hissed, "Nothing is up to you! Your problem is that you think you're better'n than the rest of us. You think you're the rector's wife. But you're not. In fact, you're not anybody's wife!" I saw Dorothy flush from the low blow as a mixture of rage and embarrassment crossed her face.

They had reached an impasse. The women glared at each other, their bosoms heaving. Neither would let go of the robe. Neither looked prepared to give an inch. Again, I had that David and Goliath feeling.

Father Donald watched the exchange with a growing expression of horror. "Now, Dottie. Now, Mildred. There's no need to be silly about this."

I winced. "Silly" had to be the worst possible choice of word. Two pairs of angry eyes turned on him. He looked like a deer caught in the headlights of an oncoming Mack truck. I stepped back.

Father Donald, a much braver soul than I, forged ahead, undeterred by their basilisk glares. "After all, Dottie, Mildred's right. It usually is the A.C.W.'s duty to take care of the vestments, although I generally take care of my own, at least, you do, Dottie, and a very good job you do, too, certainly you would have no trouble in taking care of Charles's little things, but I do think that we should probably stick with the traditions of this church, or of any church. Tradition is good!" He ended up on a hopeful note.

Dorothy Peasgood let go of the garments abruptly, shot Mildred a stare of pure dislike, graced me with a tight smile, and without another word, turned and left.

Somehow, I didn't think Father Donald would be getting blueberry pie or ice cream for lunch that day.

Seven

The Cormorant Harbour Library, situated in the basement of the Fire Hall, opened three afternoons a week, so I had learned to arrange my week accordingly. Wednesday afternoon proved impossible once I discovered that this day belonged to the junior school and the pre-school story time. Although I have no objection to children in principle, I find large groups of them to be distracting. That left me Tuesdays and Fridays for my reading pursuits.

The library itself bore no resemblance to the large city facility I had always frequented. I once had all the latest bestsellers at my disposal, but now I resigned myself to an endless diet of romances and westerns. However, I'd discovered that anything could be ordered from the central library, and would arrive at Cormorant Harbour in a matter of days. This meant that the librarian and I spent a good deal of time searching the database for the books I wanted both to further my research and feed my mind.

Now that I had a name for the lady, I saw Bev Barkhouse in quite a different light. Not only the epitome of the spinster librarian, from her mousy brown hair to her thick glasses, from her dowdy handknit sweaters to her sensible shoes, but also Mildred's downtrodden daughter. Our conversations were always punctuated by her endless sniffles and were often interrupted as she groped for a tissue to wipe her red-tipped nose. I suspected that the musty atmosphere of the Cormorant Harbour Library didn't help her condition.

Several times, it occurred to me that she might be quite attractive with a little bit of cosmetic enhancement and allergy medication. Her eyes were a startling shade of blue, and I must admit that I noticed she had quite a neat figure underneath her bulky clothing. I suspected that a day at the Cut 'n Curl Salon with her cousin Sherri would produce a whole new Beverly.

Bev had tried to make the library an inviting place, not easy in a cold and dank room under the Fire Hall. One small corner catered to children, and in another, she'd recycled an old easy chair with a bright reading lamp for the adults. The books were neatly arranged on the stacks; not a speck of dust blemished the shelves. However, the choking smell of mould did tend to detract from the bibliophile's experience.

On Tuesday morning, I received a telephone message that the latest books I had ordered were now in at the library. Right after lunch, I locked Twinkles in the house, a new habit I'd developed since I had returned home one day to discover Ricky Jollimore stalking her with a large piece of fishing net, the purpose for which I never did ascertain. I kept up a brisk pace as I walked into the Harbour, enjoying the warm sunshine, a welcome respite after four days of heavy fog. I noted the ease with which I walked the kilometre, something I would have found difficult in my former life.

As usual, I headed straight for Bev's desk but stopped when I saw her deep in conversation with another customer. Something about their demeanour made me think that they were engaged in a personal conversation, so I stepped back behind the large rack of westerns to give them some privacy. As I did so, a chill of recognition swept over me. Something about the woman with Bev seemed familiar. I made a space between two books in order to take a better look at her.

Her hair, long, dark and flowing down her back, tweaked a memory. The shape of her head, the way it tilted as she spoke, reminded me of someone. I closed my eyes and brought the image up into my brain. Another form superimposed itself over that of the woman before me—the form of Giorgio Bacciaglia's sister, Lucia, as I had last seen her, sitting directly behind the defendant's table in the courtroom. Never would I forget those dark, hate-filled eyes as I gave my testimony.

How could she be here in Cormorant Harbour? Surely not! I had to be mistaken. If only she'd turn around, I would know. I waited in a lather of impatience as the two women continued their conversation.

Although they were speaking in low tones, snatches drifted my way.

"I'm thirty-six years old, and this is my last chance…" I heard a note of desperation at odds with Bev's usual bland tones.

The murmured response sounded sympathetic, but I couldn't catch the words.

Bev continued. "All's I need is something to do the trick. Something strong. I can't wait much longer. You've got to help me."

"You know there's danger in this kind of solution. Things don't always turn out the way you expect them to…" The other woman's voice dropped to a whisper so that I couldn't hear the rest of her words.

I was stunned. It didn't sound like they were talking about me, but why else would Lucia Bacciaglia be here?

Bev's concerns sounded personal, and if I hadn't known

about her home situation, I'd have found it hard to believe what I thought I heard. Could she be trying to hire herself a Mafia hitwoman to get rid of Mildred?

Such a crazy idea couldn't be true. As usual, I'd let my imagination run away with me. My brief foray into the criminal underworld had warped my judgment.

Standing between *Buckskin Run* and *The Rustlers of West Fork*, I felt my hard-won sense of security slip from my grasp. If only I could be sure.

The woman with Bev was tall and slender, just like Lucia, with the shining black hair that flowed like lava to her waist, just like Lucia. She wore a long grey skirt of some gossamer material, and at first I thought her feet were bare, then realized she was wearing flimsy sandals. This was not like Lucia, whose black tailored business suit had brought a note of high fashion into the drab courtroom.

Any minute now she would turn away from Bev, and I would know. I shrank back into the shadows of the stacks. If she were Lucia, I couldn't let her see me.

"Charles!" The voice of Boris Monk, St. Grimbald's organist, boomed across the room. "What are you doing lurking back there?"

His voice startled me, so that at the crucial moment, I turned my head towards him instead of watching the woman. A swirl of grey skirts and black hair swept by me. I didn't see her face. The slam of the outside door told me she'd left the library. However, I still peeked around the edge of the stacks to make sure before I crept out of hiding.

"Here you are, Bev." I heard Boris dump a pile of books onto Bev's desk. "I'll take another half dozen of the usual. What have you and Charles been up to? He looks as if he's seen a ghost," Boris said in a teasing tone to Bev.

Bev's nose turned even pinker. "Oh, Mr. Monk. Don't be silly. You've been reading too many romances." She gestured at the pile on her desk.

"Not me, dear girl. They're for Mattie. Can't get enough of them. Finishes one, starts another." Boris held up several paperbacks with lurid covers. "Likes the bodice rippers best. Lots of lust!"

"Oh, you...!" Bev simpered. I could see she enjoyed Boris's light-hearted attention.

"Charles, if you're not in a hurry, let's go and grab a coffee at the Harbour View. I'd ask you to the house, but Mattie's on night shift this week. Still sleeping. Nurses work brutal hours, if you ask me. Twelve at a shot. Shift and shift about. Don't know how Mattie does it. Plays hell with the love life, too." He gave Bev a broad wink.

Bev ignored his comment. Instead she concentrated on checking out his pile of books, her cheeks as pink as her nose.

My head spun from the encounter with the unknown woman, my mind was still filled with the horrific possibility that my cover had been blown, but I managed to nod an assent.

Part of me longed to ask Bev about her visitor; another, more sensible side, urged caution. After all, I had overhead part of a very sinister conversation, and saying anything to her might make the situation worse. However, it occurred to me that Boris, who seemed to know everybody and everything, might be a source of further information about the mysterious woman.

The Harbour View Motel, a long white building in the middle of Wharf Street, overlooked the harbour. It had eight units which catered to travelling work crews for the roads and power departments, and the occasional tourist. The restaurant, an afterthought, formed an "ell" on one end the motel. It included a large dining room, a small bar and the motel office.

As we walked over, Boris gave me the lowdown on the proprietor of this establishment. "A German. Rudolf Von Clief. Everybody calls him Rudy. Came here eight years ago. Beautiful summer day. No fog for a change. Took one look around and bought the whole thing, lock, stock and barrel. Had an idea he could create a little bit of Bavaria right in the middle of Cormorant Harbour. Used to be a pastry chef, I understand. Didn't take long for him to figure it out. It it's not fried, the locals won't eat it. Poor fool. Been trying to unload the place ever since. Don't let his attitude put you off. Hates everyone. Hates Cormorant Harbour. Hates Nova Scotia. Hates Canadians. But the coffee's good."

Boris lived up to my expectations as a veritable fount of information.

We settled ourselves at a table overlooking the water. Aside from an elderly couple working their way through enormous mounds of fish and chips, we had the room to ourselves. As Boris had warned me, we were greeted with a grunt by a glowering "mine host", who accepted our orders in silence and disappeared into the kitchen.

Taking a deep breath, I tried to sound casual as I said, "I saw a woman at the library. I think she left just as you came in. Did you happen to notice her?"

"Nope. Didn't see anyone but you and Bev." He quirked an eyebrow at me. "Sounds like you're interested," he teased.

I felt myself flush. "No, no…" I said in alarm. I didn't need Boris deciding to play cupid. "Not at all. She's not my type," I added, wishing I hadn't opened up this particular can of worms. Now he'd be trying to match me up with some lonely woman in Cormorant Harbour.

My experiences with the opposite sex had always been somewhat disappointing, due no doubt to my own high standards and tendency towards perfectionism. Inevitably, all my past relationships had ended in disillusion and regret.

The closest I had come to matrimony was with a brief engagement to a colleague in another department of my old firm, a woman of elegance and refinement whose tastes mirrored my own. I have never understood the female's desire to rush into a relationship as important as marriage. I'd been quite happy to continue our mutual discovery of each other; however, after five years, Chloris had given me an ultimatum. I'd felt I had no choice but to decline.

From time to time, I regretted the demise of our friendship, but with the complications in my life since my unwitting involvement in the Bacciaglia case and my subsequent banishment to Nova Scotia under the Witness Protection Program, I had come to see what a blessing my single circumstances were. Having no family or close friends, my sudden disappearance had left no ripple on the world of my other life.

"I'm not ready for any entanglements right now," I said to Boris, determined to forestall his matchmaking propensities. "I guess you could say 'once burned; twice shy.'" I hoped that would hold him, but Boris pressed on undeterred.

"Bad experience, eh?" Boris said sympathetically. "Been there. Done that. Trust me—it's better to get back on the horse right away."

"I'm afraid I don't have your resilience, but I'll keep your advice in mind."

Before I was forced to give further details, we were interrupted by Rudy's arrival with steaming cups of coffee and plates with enormous slabs of apple strudel. He plunked them down on the table with another grunt, threw down half a dozen creamers, muttered, "Enjoy," and stamped back to his seat by the cash register.

I looked at my plate with apprehension.

"Dig in," commanded Boris. "Best damn strudel you ever tasted. Man's a genius with German pastry. Wasted in Cormorant Harbour. Most of 'em just order pie. Rudy buys them frozen from ValuMart in bulk. Next time, try the Black Forest Cake. Or the Bavarian Torte. Ambrosia!" He forked an enormous bite into his mouth while he continued talking. "Gotta take a piece home for Mattie. Gets mad as hell if I don't. Swear Mattie can smell it on my breath when I walk in."

I thought it more likely that Mattie could see, rather than smell, the evidence of Boris's feasting. The crumbs lodged in his full black beard and sprinkled down the front of his wine-coloured corduroy jacket were ample evidence of his visit to Rudy's restaurant.

I took a cautious sip of the coffee, expecting the usual Cormorant Harbour mud. Surprised, I took another sip. It tasted delicious. In fact, I rather thought it might be better than my own!

"Good, eh?" said Boris, seeing my appreciation. "Don't know where he gets the beans. Grinds them himself. Uses one of those European contraptions. Says it's wasted on Cormorant Harbour, but just won't lower himself to the gas station standards."

Having had one cup at The Irving, as the locals called it, I could see Rudy's point.

I applied myself to the excellent strudel and let Boris ramble on about local events. Inevitably, the conversation swung around to the upcoming Casino Night. Boris had been commandeered to play ragtime piano throughout the evening.

"Mattie's taking care of the decorations," he told me. "Damn genius at that kind of thing. Good at colour. Wait'll you see the Eagle's Nest. That's our place. Could win an award in one of those decorator magazines that Mattie's always reading. Having a ball with the Casino theme. Got all the firemen dressed up as gamblers. Gonna make the place look like a wild-west saloon." He wiped the last crumbs up off his plate, licking his fingers with great care. "Took some doing. Mildred had an idea for a Monte Carlo look. And usually, what Mildred wants, Mildred gets. But she didn't count on Mattie. Talk about gunfight at the O.K. Corral!" He swigged the last dregs of his coffee and waved the empty cup at Rudy. "Mattie won. Didn't surprise me. Haven't won a single fight myself in the past ten years."

Rudy ambled over. With a deep sigh, he refilled our cups and threw a half dozen more creamers down, ignoring the fact that both Boris and I took our coffee black.

I felt I had to comment on the strudel. "My compliments to the chef," I said. "That was excellent strudel!"

Rudy paused mid-turn and looked at me. "You're not from around here, are you?" he said in a thick accent. Before I could reply, he'd stomped back to his seat, where he resumed his contemplation of the wall.

I couldn't believe the afternoon had gone by so quickly after my trip to the library. I had planned to mow the lawn and vacuum through the cottage.

"I must go," I told Boris. "This has been delightful. But my lawn needs mowing again, and I have to do my chores in the afternoons, so I have the mornings free to write."

"You do all your own stuff?" Boris asked in surprise.

"Well, I had thought I might have to break down and hire Kevin Jollimore, my neighbour, to help me out, but after the fire, I have some serious doubts as to his ability to work safely."

"Jollimore? Oh, that's right. Had a little excitement out by your place, didn't you? His house caught on fire, I hear." Of course, Boris would have all the details.

"Fortunately, it wasn't serious. But I understand Kevin left paint rags and equipment in the hallway, and I couldn't bear to have that happen to me." Boris and I walked to the counter with our bills in hand. I wondered if one tipped the proprietor as one would the staff. I watched to see what Boris would do. Apparently not, since Boris pocketed his change and pushed open the door for me.

"You need a good man," continued Boris as we walked up the street to his car. "And someone to 'do' for you. Got ourselves a cleaning lady. Mattie hates to clean. And a yard man. Hate to mow, myself. Spend my whole damn summer off mowing the lawn. And shovelling snow in the winter. Hate getting up and having to shovel the driveway before I can head for the school. Tried to hire one of my students. Did a damn poor job! Found a husband and wife team. Annie and Oliver Fleet. Good workers. Cheap, too. Interested?"

I nodded my head. The chores I'd found so novel just a few weeks ago were now becoming onerous.

"I'll send Annie over to see you. She's one of Mildred Barkhouse's sisters. Different from her as night from day. Sherri, you know Sherri? Sherri's Cut 'n Curl? She's Annie's daughter."

My head spun. The genealogical complications of my new life were becoming more and more entangled.

Boris and I parted with the understanding that I would

visit the Eagle's Nest on Mattie's next off-duty day. I decided to walk home along the beach, since the afternoon had stayed warm and balmy. It took a little longer, but with the tide out, the exposed shingle made walking easy. At high tide, only large boulders remained.

When I'd first heard that my new home included beachfront, I'd imagined the white, sun-swept sands of Tahiti, or at least, the dunes and boardwalks of Wasaga Beach. However, the beaches around Cormorant Harbour were composed of shingle, rocks and boulders. A few sandy patches at low tide gave a brief illusion of holiday seaside swimming, but for the rest of the time, the tide rolled back and forth over the rocks with a soothing rattle.

As I crunched along the beach, the wind from the south stirred small wavelets that shimmered in the sunshine. Little birds on thin legs ran before me, while overhead the seagulls screamed in raucous abandon. The tangy low-tide smells of seaweed and salt wafted on the air. The beach soothed away any thoughts of the mystery woman.

I had just reached the old broken-down wharf behind my cottage, where I enjoyed the sound of the waves sloshing against its pilings, when I realized that I was not alone. At the end of the wharf, with their backs to me, two figures stood entwined.

I recognized Bev Barkhouse from the bright blue of the bulky hand-knit sweater that I had seen just an hour earlier. The other figure looked somewhat familiar. I racked my brains trying to place him. I didn't want to disturb them, so I crept up the path to Innisfree. It only took a moment to go through to my bedroom and pick up the binoculars I used for bird watching. I felt guilty prying into something that didn't concern me, but my curiosity overcame my distaste for spying. How could I resist Bev Barkhouse, the last person I would have expected to have an assignation, with a man on the end of my wharf? I bet even Boris didn't know about this!

As I adjusted the lenses, the figures sprang into focus. I knew why the man had seemed familiar.

It was Clarence, Kevin Jollimore's apelike brother-in-law.

It occurred to me that if Mildred disapproved of her nephew's marriage to Arleen, how much more would she object to her only daughter being involved with Arleen's brother, Clarence.

Perhaps Bev had already foreseen this difficulty. Her conversation with the mystery woman, its intensity and overtones of desperation, replayed itself in my mind. What *had* Bev been asking her to do?

Eight

Over the next week, I made numerous excuses to go into Cormorant Harbour in the hope that I would see the unknown woman. I even went to the library on Wednesday afternoon, where I endured several hours of Children's Craft Time, The Tiny Tots Puppet Show and Pre-Schoolers' Storytime. All to no avail, as if she had been a creature of my imagination and that moment of near-recognition in the Cormorant Harbour Library just a dream.

A growing discomfort with Bev Barkhouse added to my frustration. Our hitherto relaxed relationship now held a tension due to the suspicions aroused by my inadvertent eavesdropping in the library. As well, my guilty knowledge of her association with Clarence, brought about by my own compulsive curiosity, changed my perception of her from that of a demure librarian to one of a woman consumed by deceit and lust.

Trying to keep my own secrets without having to add Bev Barkhouse's clandestine activities meant I could not talk freely with her. In consequence, I found myself avoiding the long bibliophilic discussions I'd had with Bev in the past. Instead, I spent my time perusing the stacks as I waited in vain to see the mystery woman again.

I knew that a single glimpse of her face would settle the question: either I was in danger, or I wasn't. The woman was either Lucia Bacciaglia, Giorgio's sister, and my cover was blown, or she was just a friend of Bev's, and her identity was none of my business. Either way, I had to know for my own peace of mind. For the past week, my nights had been disturbed by violent dreams During the day, all my waking moments were filled with anxiety and unanswered questions. I couldn't eat, I couldn't write. Even Twinkles failed to soothe me.

My growing paranoia lead to an increased awareness of the need to be anonymous at all costs. To this end, I forced myself to take stock of my appearance. With some dismay, I realized that my natty attire made me stick out like a sore thumb. I decided to consult with Annie Fleet, the cleaning lady Boris had found for me. As well as an excellent housekeeper, she also proved to be a goldmine of information on everything local. On her advice, I visited a store called Bargain Harold's Clothing Emporium in Cormorant Harbour, the place where all the local men shopped. There I purchased several plaid shirts, two pairs of blue jeans and a peaked ball cap. With grim determination, I added a pair of grey velcro-tabbed running shoes, very similar to Father Donald's white monstrosities. A pair of sunglasses completed my new image. Thus disguised, I felt I could walk with impunity anywhere in the community.

It was imperative that I blend in since the annual Cormorant Harbour summer celebration—Harbour Day, held on the first Monday in August—loomed on my social calendar. Like many such events in the Maritimes, it provided a good excuse for the general populace to come together and enjoy the short summer season. As well, the locals hoped that some tourists might be lured from the South Shore and Cape Breton Island to our more remote and unpublicized area.

Whether or not tourists came, the residents of the four Cormorants (Upper, Lower, Harbour and Head) needed little prompting to enjoy the day's events.

It seemed certain to me that if the mystery woman remained in the area, she would attend at least one of the events. Large signs throughout Cormorant Harbour advertised the line-up of events. The day always kicked off with a Pancake Breakfast sponsored by the Masonic Lodge. The Harbour Day Parade, run by the Volunteer Fire Department followed the breakfast, backed up by the Lions Club Beer Garden. The Parade took place in the morning, but the Beer Garden ran all day. At noon, St. Grimbald's A.C.W. catered its famous Seafood Chowder Luncheon. Father Donald assured me that he had reserved seats for us at the second sitting.

If I didn't see her at any of these events, I hoped she might be the type to visit the Afternoon Craft Show in the Humbert Watts Memorial Arena.

If all else failed, I could attend the Chicken Supper Barbeque, a United Church tradition, at the baseball diamond. I'd seen the pits being prepared the day before. They were long greasy metal troughs filled with charcoal, covered with blackened mesh then laid on the dusty ground. I hoped that I would find the woman long before this event.

The crowning of Miss Harbour Day, a honour that was sought after by every young, nubile woman for miles around, followed the barbeque. "They can go on to Miss Eastern Shore," Father Donald told me, "and after that, Miss Nova Scotia, and after that, who knows... Miss Canada, I suppose. Even Miss World, although…"

The day always ended with a 'wonderful' (Father Donald's word) fireworks display sponsored by the Cormorant

Harbour Chamber of Commerce, held at the end of the government wharf, overlooking the water.

Surely she would be at one of these events. In my mind, I decided that if I didn't see her at Harbour Day, I could presume that she no longer lurked in the area and posed no threat to my life.

Early on Harbour Day, I made my way to the Masonic Hall for the kick-off pancake breakfast, feeling confident in my new disguise and the anonymity it gave me. No one could know how my heart pounded in anticipation, or that my nerves were stretched to the breaking point. I looked just like any other happy-go-lucky fair goer in Cormorant Harbour, intent on nothing but a day of enjoyment.

A large tent had been erected in front of the Masonic Hall. Inside the tent, a battalion of Masons manned the electric frying pans, connected by a myriad of extension cords to some inside power source. Already, I could see that the pans were busy, filled with golden disks of batter swimming in oil. A number of picnic tables covered in sheets of white paper were placed around the inside periphery of the tent. The line-up at the serving tables stretched to the doorway.

I stood in line, unaware of my surroundings, intent on searching for the woman.

"Charles! How wonderful! There, Dottie, I told you that Charles would come. Not that there was any reason that you wouldn't come, Charles, but Dottie thought it might not be your kind of occasion, and I said, that if there was anything going on in Cormorant Harbour, you'd be there, or at least, you'd want to be there, not that there would be anywhere else you would be, and…"

"Donald! You're holding up the line." Dottie turned and

smiled at me. "How nice to see you, Charles." I saw her smile waver as she took in my new jeans and shirt. "Well," she said, "you certainly look different."

I didn't hear a compliment in her voice. I had a pang of regret for what would have been my chosen attire: blue blazer and flannels. However, looking around the tent reassured me that I had made the right decision. I looked like all the other men, except for Father Donald.

Father Donald resembled a huge over-inflated beach ball, the illusion heightened by the striking orange and yellow striped shorts and pistachio green T-shirt he had on. His thongs squeaked in protest at every step.

"Dottie's idea," he beamed, holding out the hems of his shorts and looking down at himself in satisfaction. "Well, not really her idea, but she encouraged me to dress coolly, that is, as coolly as you can dress on a day like this…"

"I did not suggest shorts," said Dottie. "Or those ridiculous things you have on your feet! I certainly hope you're planning to change before the luncheon. Will you be at the parade, Charles? Donald is driving the fire truck, of course," she explained, "and I will be on the St. Grimbald's float with Boris and the choir. I'm so sorry we weren't able to persuade you to join us."

Indeed, I had been tempted to accept the invitation to be part of the St. Grimbald's float until Boris told me that the CBC always sent a camera crew to Harbour Day, meaning that I might be on the local television news. Boris revelled in this kind of publicity for his choir, but I knew that if my face were to be in the public gaze, I could be in danger. I had declined, stating that my propensity to motion sickness might mar the day for the St. Grimbald's choir.

"Just two pancakes for Father Donald!" Dorothy

commanded the servers. "And one sausage. He's already had breakfast and doesn't need any more."

"Oh shoot! Dottie, it's a holiday. And it's pancakes. My favourite." His protest made no difference. He watched glumly as two small pancakes and a wizened overcooked sausage were dumped onto his plate.

Father Donald and I followed Dorothy to a picnic table on the far side of the tent. The heavy smell of hot grease and sausages along with that of old tent canvas, overheated bodies and crushed grass created a noxious atmosphere in the enclosed, airless space. I began to feel queasy.

The breakfast before me didn't help: three thick pancakes surrounded by four charbroiled sausages, all awash in a lake of butter. The syrup jugs, well used by previous diners, sat in sticky puddles of golden goo on the paper cloth. A styrofoam cup of what purported to be orange juice, but which in fact was a brightly coloured, highly sweetened, powdered drink, completed the repast. Father Donald took two cups, I noticed. Coffee urns loomed in one corner, but I had no intention of inflicting their contents on my sensitive stomach.

We seated ourselves on the rickety benches. Father Donald ate with gusto. I noticed that Dorothy made good inroads on her hefty serving. When she wasn't looking, I exchanged my untouched plate for Father Donald's empty one. He shot me a grateful glance and dug in.

"It's wonderful to have you here, Charles," he said between bites. "I'm so glad you're part of our little St. Grimbald's family. And a lay reader, too. So many of the lay readers are much older, you know, not that there's anything wrong with being older, but it does make it difficult to bridge the generation gap, although I like to think that I'm able to relate to everyone, well, not everyone, there are always a few people that are more difficult, not that there are people like this at St. Grimbald's, of course, but you, Charles, you're not just a lay reader. I like to think of you as my friend." This last he gulped out, looking abashed. He forked a huge portion of pancake into his mouth to cover his emotion.

I was touched. Up until this moment, I hadn't thought much about the impact my presence had made on Cormorant Harbour or St. Grimbald's. I'd been using them as a convenient hiding place, a stepping stone to somewhere more conducive to my tastes and lifestyle. Now, I realized that in the short time I'd been there, I'd become a part of this community and the lives of some people. However, if the mystery woman turned out to be who I feared she was, then my disappearance would be swift and irrevocable. I wouldn't even be able to say goodbye. For the first time, I realized that I *wanted* to stay here and make it my home.

Until I had settled the matter of Lucia Bacciaglia in my mind, I couldn't let my guard down. I cast furtive glances around the tent, and in a heart-stopping moment, I saw her. Mumbling an excuse, I left Father Donald and Dorothy mopping up their plates and slipped away, following the elusive glimpse of long black hair. My heart thudded in my chest. I swallowed with difficulty as my mouth went dry. The early morning coffee I had consumed at home sat like lead in the pit of my stomach. I could feel perspiration trickle in a damp trail between my shoulder blades. I pushed through the throng and found myself outside the tent. Here, the air seemed marginally cooler than inside. I looked around in desperation, but it was too late. I had lost her!

"Are you all right, Charles? Dottie thought you looked a little pale," said Father Donald, who had followed me outside.

"I'm fine, Father Donald. Just not used to such a heavy

breakfast. And it is warm." I pulled out my handkerchief to wipe my brow.

"Well, then, that's good. I'm off to the parade now, well not to the parade, that hasn't started yet, but I have to meet the boys at the fire hall and get the truck ready, not that it isn't ready, it's always ready, well, almost always, that is if we haven't drained it for cleaning, but we always pump water right back in so it's always ready..." He paused. He'd come full circle. "So, I'm off then..." he finished.

I decided to head down to the Harbour View Motel, where I could get a decent cup of coffee and maybe even a slice of apple strudel while I composed myself before the parade started. Who knows? Perhaps the woman would be on one of the floats. Or she might be at the restaurant. Or in the crowds watching the parade. Wherever she had disappeared to, I meant to find her.

After two cups of Rudy's restorative brew, I felt ready to face anything. From the size of the crowds gathering on Cormorant Harbour's main street, the parade highlighted the day. I managed to find a spot on the shady side of the street. I soon wished I'd thought to bring along a lawn chair, as most of the others had done. In fact, several people had coolers with cold drinks and various comestibles brought for a family group. I watched with fascination as a large lady in bright pink shorts and matching halter top dispensed can after can of orange soda to an endless stream of overexcited children while exhorting each one, "Now stand still and drink that." Each child dashed off with a can clutched in its fist.

Although my view would be blocked by the people standing in front of me, I had chosen not to position myself at the front edge of the roadway, since I didn't want to be where I might be inadvertently picked up by a stray camera shot. As well, I wasn't here to watch the parade; I was here to watch for *her*.

"Howdy, neighbour!" Kevin Jollimore, trailed by Ricky and Clarence, stopped next to me. Ricky's face disappeared behind the huge cone of cotton candy, which he pulled off in big sticky chunks and stuffed into his grubby mouth. I stepped back.

Clarence gave me a brief nod in greeting and with a "see you later, Kev," headed away from us and crossed the street.

"So, you're here for the parade, eh?" said Kevin. "We always comes early. I bring the boy to get himself stocked up on candies. Better'n Hallowe'en. The firemen throw out buckets of candy. We just stay close to the pumper. Arleen didn't come. She can't stand to be out in the heat. It makes her feet swell up something terrible, and then she's a bear for the rest of the day. Hell for us all. I'll tell you when her feet are swolled."

It struck me as far too much information, so I nodded without comment.

"We always stay right up until the fireworks. After that, there's a big party at Clarence's in Lower Cormorant. Probably won't get home tonight, so don't wait up for us." He slapped my shoulder in bonhomie. "See you around. Don't do anything I wouldn't do." He and Ricky headed off up the street, no doubt to position themselves near the pumper.

The first notes of the Cormorant Harbour Consolidated High School Marching Band and Drum Corps sounded on the air, causing a general stir of excitement in the crowd lining the street. From my vantage point, I had glimpses of the various floats and flower bedecked cars that passed. The band, loud, if not musical, lead the parade, followed by the Cormorant Harbour Volunteer Fire Department's entire fleet. I saw Father Donald ensconced behind the wheel of the lead vehicle, where he energetically sounded the siren and bell at every opportunity. When he caught sight of me, he honked the huge air horn with glee and waved. I noticed he still wore his "cool" garments, which looked incongruous beneath the official fire helmet on his head.

As Kevin had said, the firemen dispensed continuing largesse in the form of lollipops and various wrapped candies.

Several floats went by, most of which were large flatbed trucks with themes depicted by helium-filled balloons, cardboard cutouts, tissue paper rosettes, and one pretty girl in a long dress with a sash across her shoulder surrounded by a crowd of attendants, all waving to the crowd. So far, none of them included the woman, nor could I see her in the crowds around us.

The St. Grimbald's group had made their float from a large flatbed wagon drawn by a tractor. The float depicted St. Grimbald's church interior with paper stained glass windows, in front of which Boris played his accordion while the assembled choir in their colourful robes warbled "Onward Christian Soldiers", singing out with more gusto than grace. The two young servers tossed caramels off the back of the float. I felt a twinge of disappointment when I realized how splendid I would have looked in my newly-altered robes.

"Are you enjoying the parade?" I hadn't noticed that Bev Barkhouse had joined me.

"Umm…er…yes." I said. "Most colourful and interesting. Not at all what I expected, having only seen parades on television before."

Bev looked shocked. "Never been to a parade before? Didn't your parents take you to the Santa Claus parade when you were a kid?"

"Oh, dear. No. My parents were quite old when I came

along. I was a bit of a surprise, I suspect, and they were already set in their ways. They tended to take me to museums if they wanted to give me a treat."

I stopped talking and mentally kicked myself yet again. I kept forgetting that my true life differed radically from my current life. The most innocent question could lead me down avenues that were now closed to me forever. In actual fact, my father had been a university professor, an intellectual whose specialty of Mediaeval Literature did not lend itself to such childish pursuits as parades. My mother, on the other hand, a political activist, spent her time writing endless letters to the editor and volunteering for the local New Democratic Party. It had made for a somewhat unusual childhood, peppered with forays to the Royal Ontario Museum and the Legislative Buildings, and not much else in between. Being an only child, I had never experienced the camaraderie of brothers and sisters and the give-and-take of family life. My parents tended to treat me as another adult in our home, and as a result, I found myself to be a loner when it came to school life. With great relief I had left academia to take up my place in the business world.

"Museums! Are there lots in Ottawa?"

"Umm…er. Yes." It seemed a safe answer.

Bev didn't pursue the subject any further. She stood on tiptoe and gazed fixedly, not at the parade, but at something on the other side of the street. I heard her sharp intake of breath.

"Oh, no!" she said. "I can't bear it! Damn, damn, damn!"

I was shocked. I had never seen her exhibit so much emotion. I tried to follow her gaze, but saw nothing amiss.

"What is it?" I asked. "What's happened? Are you all right?"

To my horror, she burst into noisy sobs as she threw herself against my shoulder. "I knew this would happen. He couldn't wait forever. And I felt him losing interest."

I looked across the street again. This time, I saw Clarence with his arm around a large, bosomy blonde woman. They made a striking couple. Clarence looked like a pirate newly escaped from the ship's brig, and his companion, her overblown charms encased in skintight leopard print pants and skimpy halter top, complemented his hairy darkness. Poor Bev! It looked as though Clarence had forsaken her for greener pastures.

I attempted to comfort her by patting her back and making soothing noises, but truth to tell, other than Chloris during her discreet farewell, no woman had ever shed tears on my chest before. I lacked experience in this department.

Bev groped in her pocket, where she found an already-soggy tissue. She blew her nose noisily, wiped her eyes and pulled herself together.

"Oh, Mr. Trenchant. You must think I'm terrible. I'm sorry to fall apart all over you like this. It's not like me, but I just can't bear it. My last chance at happiness, and I can see it slipping away." For a moment, her tears threatened to overwhelm her again.

I murmured something encouraging, knowing I couldn't let her suspect that I knew the reason for her grief: the despicable Clarence had been playing fast and loose with her affections.

Bev thanked me again and then said, "You'll have to excuse me. I must go. I've to got to find a friend. She's the only one who can help me now."

I knew she meant the mystery woman. Before I could ask Bev where she was going, she disappeared into the dispersing crowds around us. I realized that the parade was over.

Nine

I made my way to the Fishermen's Hall for my luncheon date with Father Donald. On the way, the sight of our RCMP Constable being escorted to the PTA's Mock Jail transfixed me. I suspected his colleagues had paid to have him incarcerated, and now he would have to wait until someone bailed him out. My heart started to pound as I imagined the Bacciaglias in their prison. How did they feel behind the bars of the Kingston Penitentiary? Did they still think of me as a part of their downfall? Was my name still on some hitman's list? Had they indeed sent Lucia to finish me off, or were they waiting patiently to wreak a personal revenge once the Parole Board released them back into the world?

A cloud passed over the sun. I shivered as the day darkened for a brief moment.

"Yoo hoo! Charles!" Father Donald bounced up and down on the steps of the Fishermen's Hall, waving in my direction. "Over here!" I noticed that he had obeyed Dottie's command and now wore khaki pants with a short sleeved shirt and clerical collar. However, he still had on the thongs that she had so abhorred. I joined him, and we were bustled inside with the group which had been waiting for the doors to open for the second sitting. It occurred to me that I should have arrived earlier so that I could peruse the faces of those leaving from the first sitting.

As the heat of the hall hit me, I wondered how the older women in the A.C.W. were holding up. They were on their second full lunch sitting, and already a hundred people had been served under primitive conditions. Looking around the hall, I hated to think what it must be like in the small, cramped kitchen at the far end. I noticed several women mopping their streaming faces on their aprons while some others tried to aim a small fan at the general throng. I recognized many of the women. Mildred Barkhouse was in charge of the operation. Like a sergeant major in the field of battle, she marshalled the forces, ready for the next charge. I saw no sign of Dorothy and presumed that Mildred had relegated her to kitchen duties.

I looked around the hall, hoping to catch a sight of my mystery woman. I didn't see her among the long rows of folding tables, covered with the ubiquitous white paper, now rather the worse for wear after the first sitting. The tables were laden with baskets of rolls, dishes of butter pats, bowls with sugar packets and creamers, and various plates of pickles and relishes. Paper napkins dotted the tables surfaces, covering the irreparable stains and damage left by previous diners.

I allowed myself to relax. The appetizing aroma of seafood caused my mouth to water. I decided to put my fears and my search on hold in order to take advantage of this respite.

The A.C.W. had set up the hall so that in order to reach the dining tables, one had to run a gauntlet of raffles and draws for various prizes, ranging from a box of groceries (out of which I could see several heads of celery protruding), to an ornate arrangement of gilded paper flowers (which Father Donald told me that the choir members had made from old hymn book pages), to a large, lumpy afghan in shades of green and maroon (an annual offering from the busy needles of Etta Fay), to a finely carved duck decoy.

Father Donald liked the decoy so much that he bought several books of tickets. "It's made by Basil Myers," he said. "He does wonderful birds. Woodpeckers and jays and chickadees and all kinds of birds, although I understand he does horses, too, and even dogs, although I'm not really an animal lover, not that I don't like animals, it's just that Dottie would never put up with all the bother, not that they're all a bother, some are quite clean, I understand, dogs that is, not horses, although those little miniature horses they have nowadays probably aren't that messy…"

I managed to make it to our table without purchasing any tickets. With my luck, I'd *win*.

Boris and Sherri were seated opposite us.

"Mattie's working nights. Again," sighed Boris. "Third year in a row. Always misses the whole damn thing. This time, I brought a date." He grinned at Sherri. "Best looking lady in the place."

I had to admit that Sherri looked most fetching in a blue summer dress that complimented her tanned shoulders and blonde hair, which today she wore down. I had not, as yet, met Boris's housemate, but even so, I couldn't help but wonder if Mattie would be pleased to see Boris so enjoying himself with Sherri.

"With or without, or beef barley?" the woman at my elbow demanded. I looked to Boris for translation.

"Seafood chowder, with or without lobster and scallops. Some are allergic to shellfish. Or there's beef barley soup," Boris explained. "Chowder with for me, Gladys. With. My lovely companion will have the beef barley. Right, Sherri?"

"With for me," said Father Donald, as he buttered several buns in anticipation of the meal. "Although the beef barley is good, too, although the whole idea of coming to a seafood chowder luncheon is to eat the chowder, although on the other hand, one can get chowder almost anywhere, but then, it wouldn't be Laura's chowder, would it?"

Gladys didn't even blink. She'd come up against Father Donald before.

"I'll take with, too," I told her, wondering what gastronomic disaster lay ahead.

Within minutes, four large styrofoam tubs of the sort used in a take-out deli arrived, brimming with chowder and soup. The table fell silent as we plunged our plastic spoons into the steaming broth.

One sip, and I knew heaven. Never had I tasted a better seafood chowder. Not the thick, lumpy wallpaper paste concoction I had expected, but a rich, buttery broth filled with large chunks of lobster and fish, thickened with small cubes of potatoes and seasoned with celery, onions and carrots.

Our group lapsed into silence until the last drop had disappeared from our bowls. Without waiting for coffee, Father Donald bounced up. "Must get my dessert," he said, "before all the good ones are gone."

I decided to allow the soup to settle before going on to the dessert tables. Boris and Sherri remained with me.

"Nathan did really well on his finals," said Boris to Sherri. "Is he all set for Dalhousie?"

"Yes, but he's having trouble getting a decent summer job. University's an expensive business." She saw the perplexed look on my face. "Nathan is my son. Eighteen last April. He just graduated from high school. I can't believe how fast the years have gone."

It surprised me that someone as young as Sherri could be the mother of a grown boy. Without thinking, I glanced at her left hand and saw no ring there.

Sherri laughed and waved her hand at me. "Nope. No ring! He took off the moment he found out Nathan was on the way. We were only seventeen, so I can't really blame him. Trouble is, he could get out of it, and I couldn't. But I've never regretted Nathan." This last she said fiercely. Boris squeezed her hand in sympathy.

I felt my face flush. "Oh, dear…I'm terribly sorry," I began.

"There's no need to be sorry, Charles. I stopped being sorry a long time ago. It's been a struggle being a single mom, but it was worth every tear to see my Nathan doing so well. He'll be the first in our family to finish high school, much less go to university." She sighed. "I never realized how expensive it was going to be, even with a couple of scholarships, but we'll do it, Nathan and I. We've had lots of practice in making ends meet."

I felt a wave of admiration for Sherri. How brave she'd been, and how steadfast in her unwavering support and devotion to her son. I'd never thought of the financial difficulties single parents faced. Of course, I'd read stories in the newspapers of the poverty-stricken lives of women left to fend for themselves, but I'd never met anyone like Sherri. My own life had never been fraught with financial considerations. Having two professional parents, both with good incomes, I had gone on to university with no thought of the cost. In fact, I hadn't even needed to have summer jobs, although I did do some clerking in a brokerage house for the experience. The position I'd held in my old firm had brought me modest financial rewards, and along with my inheritance from my parents, I had always lived quite well.

Even when adversity had struck, forcing me to give up my comfortable life, the substantial reward for my cooperation in the Bacciaglia case made my current life quite luxurious in comparison to that of most people in Cormorant Harbour.

Before I could say anything further, Father Donald returned, clutching a large piece of lemon meringue pie. "There's so many to choose from," he mourned. "I was really torn between carrot cake or lemon meringue pie, which Dottie never makes, not liking the meringue, well, it's not the meringue, so much as cooking it, not that she cooks it, it just needs browning, I believe, but that seems to be a problem for Dottie, having burned several, although I'm not sure it was really Dottie's fault, what with the stove in the rectory being so old, well not that old, but old in terms of appliances…"

"Coffee?" Etta Fay, our coffee server, waved a pot in front of him, speaking the magic word.

She filled our cups. Against my better judgement, I took a sip. It was bitter, thick and almost cold.

Leaving the tepid coffee, Boris, Sherri and I wandered over to the dessert tables. I looked for a piece of carrot cake with the intention of giving it to Father Donald. At that moment, Bev Barkhouse ran into the room and came to a halt next to us, her eyes searching around the room.

"Beverly Barkhouse! Where have you been? You were supposed to be here at eleven thirty sharp!" Mildred marched out of the kitchen with a tray full of dessert plates. I saw Bev's face pale as she quailed before Mildred's onslaught. "Get into the kitchen right now. I've had to reassign Etta Fay to your post, and God knows she's pretty useless with a coffee pot. Only thing she can handle is knitting needles, and she's not much good at that either, if that afghan is any indication." She said this just as Etta Fay herself passed by. Mildred must have seen her and made the disparaging remark on purpose.

Etta Fay's face darkened with anger. "I'll have you know that people ask me to knit for them. I'm known as a professional crafter."

"Well, you may be a professional something, but knitter you aren't," Mildred shot back.

I hastily backed away from the group. Just in time, too, because Etta Fay lifted the coffee pot she was carrying and dumped the contents over Mildred's head. Mildred shrieked, dropping the tray of desserts which hit the floor with a crash. Bits of crockery, cream, cake, chocolate, pie crust and icing scattered in all directions.

"Take that, you miserable old bitch!" Etta Fay hissed. "I'm sick to death of your mean mouth. If it wasn't for you, my boy and Bev would be giving me grandbabies by now. As it is, I'm only thankful he doesn't have to put up with you as a mother-in-law." Etta Fay threw down the coffee pot, splashing the last dregs on the debris of fallen desserts. "You can pour your own coffee. I quit! And I quit the A.C.W., too. God take the lot of you!" Etta Fay pulled off her apron, threw it on the floor and stamped out.

Bev ran after her.

By now, every eye in the hall turned to Mildred. I saw Father Donald half rise from his seat, and then, seeming to realize that discretion might be the better part of valour, sat back down again and returned to his pie.

After a second of shocked silence, Boris burst into hearty guffaws. "Well, Mildred. Baptized with coffee. She sure told you!"

Sherri started to giggle, at first surreptitiously, but soon she had lost control, joining Boris in helpless laughter. The laughter spread across the crowded hall.

Under the coffee grounds still dripping off her hair and

face, Mildred blanched white with fury. She rounded on Boris, her eyes snapping with anger, her voice full of venom. "Don't you dare laugh at me, you… you…pervert!"

It seemed an odd choice of epithet to me.

Boris continued to laugh heartily. Mildred didn't intimidate him.

Mildred drew in a deep breath and turned to Sherri. "Think it's funny, do you? Laughing at me. After all I've done for you and that bastard of yours. Well, we'll just see how funny it is when I call in your loan. Then who'll be laughing? You owe me, girl, and I want every penny back. Maybe you've forgotten why the bank wouldn't give you the money in the first place to start your pitiful little business, but I haven't."

Sherri's laughter stopped abruptly. She sagged back against me. For a moment, she seemed to be fainting. "Get me out of here, please," she gasped.

I helped her out the side door, where we sank down on the wooden steps. Sherri leaned against my shoulder, sobbing. "What a fool I was, losing it like that. I know you can't laugh at Aunt Mildred. If only I hadn't got involved with her money. But it seemed the only way out at the time." Her sobs deepened.

"Well, I'm sure the bank will cover you now that you've got a viable business," I said, trying to comfort her, aware of her head pressed against my chest. For the second time today, a young woman had availed herself of my shoulder to cry on.

"You don't understand. It's not that easy. There's something…" Her voice trailed off. She stood up. "I've got to think. I can't let her do this to me. Not now. Not with Nathan finally on his way. Thanks for everything." She kissed me on the cheek. I sat for several moments in a daze.

Finally, I pulled myself together. The time had come to concentrate on my primary purpose for being at Harbour Day. After six hours of sun and crowds, I had not found the mystery woman. I looked down at the wreckage of my jeans and shirt, now splashed with coffee and desserts and damp with tear stains. I realized that I couldn't go looking as I did to the Craft Fair, where I had planned to continue my search. I decided I might be able to make repairs in the washroom.

Inside the hall, all had returned to normal, as if nothing had ever happened. Two ladies were clearing up the last vestiges of the dropped desserts, while someone else plied the coffee pot between the tables. Mildred had vanished, but I noticed that Dorothy Peasgood had taken charge of operations. I stopped by the dessert table, where I picked up a fresh piece of carrot cake. I made my way back to where Father Donald sat, deep in conversation with the diner on his right.

"Oh, Charles! Carrot cake! My favourite! How kind of you. Are you sure you don't want it?" I waited for some mention of Mildred's debacle, but Father Donald simply pulled the plate towards him and tucked in.

I left him to it. In the washroom, I sponged off the worst of the damage. Certainly, my new clothes were much more forgiving of the kind of wear and tear that Cormorant Harbour dished out than my usual blazer and flannels would have been.

The day was half spent. Apart from one questionable sighting at the Masonic Breakfast, my attempts to find the mystery woman had failed. However, the Craft Show at the Humbert Watts Memorial Arena still remained.

Ten

I found her next to a display of plastic cross-stitch toilet-roll covers. From the long, black hair to the flowing grey skirt and the flimsy sandals, I recognized the woman I had seen with Bev in the library. She leaned across the table, deep in conversation with the proprietor.

I positioned myself so that I would see her when she moved, but she wouldn't see me. She ended her conversation and glided past me. I held my breath. As she turned her head, our eyes met. I realized she was not Lucia Bacciaglia. But she was the most delectable, delightful, desirable woman I had ever seen. My heart fluttered in my chest. I couldn't catch my breath. A mixture of tumultuous emotions, emotions I had never experienced before—euphoria, rapture, elation—washed over me. I felt as if I had fallen into the deep well of her dark mysterious eyes. A faint scent of her perfume, musky and enticing, hung on the air as she passed by.

"Zerena!" Bev Barkhouse dashed out from a side aisle and grabbed the woman's slender arm. "I've been looking all over for you! Have you got the stuff? I've *got* to have it. I can't wait!" She and the woman she had called Zerena disappeared behind a stall holding a display of driftwood clocks.

I stood slack-mouthed, drained and exhausted. The surge of unfamiliar emotions gave way to an overwhelming weariness.

The United Church Barbeque and the Fireworks Display

would have to proceed without me. I just wanted to be safe in my little home, alone to think, to relive that moment when our eyes had met. For now, the danger of being hunted down like some helpless animal did not loom large in my life. What tomorrow would bring, I did not know. I did, however, know that my life had been changed forever.

Once in the sanctuary of Innisfree, I stripped off my disguise, took a long, cool shower and slipped into my robe. With Twinkles on my lap and a glass of sherry in my hand, I sat on the patio, where I contemplated my world: the ocean, the sky, the cottage and Zerena. I mouthed her name. Zerena.

I made myself a light supper, a small salad and an omelette, washed up the few dishes, found myself a good book and retired to the sounds of distant fireworks. I fell asleep in minutes.

I awoke in a daze of confusion. I had no idea of the time, but I felt as if I'd slept for some hours. In the darkness of my room, I could see the growing light of dawn creeping in from around the blind. It took me a moment to pinpoint what it had awakened me. Ear-piercing cat wails from the living room snapped me alert. I jumped from my bed in an instant, imagining Twinkles trapped or suffering from some dire feline ailment.

In the beginning, I had cared little for this creature who had now become a mainstay of my new existence. I felt that she reciprocated my own growing affection for her and that our relationship had reached a point where I couldn't imagine my life without her.

I raced to the living room with my heart in my mouth, dreading what I would find. However, I found no blood or mayhem, only Twinkles marching back and forth along the window sill, her tail twitching, emitting the loud wails that had wakened me. I could see nothing wrong with her.

I peered out into the early dawn greyness, looking for the source of her anxiety. Perhaps a fox or a stray dog had crossed the lawn. Nothing moved. Then a flicker of light in the Jollimore house, caught my attention. At first I thought it could be a reflection of the sunrise in the window but then realized that the sun had not yet risen.

With disbelief, I identified the light as fire. The Jollimore house was on fire! Again! I rushed to the front door and flung it open. The unmistakable odour of smoke hung in the still air.

At first, I wanted to rush across the road in order to warn the occupants, but I remembered that Kevin and the family would still be in Lower Cormorant. I turned, grabbed the telephone, and with shaking hands dialed 911.

The operator kept me on the line for some time even after she had ascertained the nature of the call. As I hung up, the first pick-up truck screeched to a halt on the road. Seconds later, I heard the wail of the sirens, then all hell broke loose. Pick-up trucks, cars, ATVs, plus emergency vehicles, the Auxiliary van, the RCMP cruiser and an ambulance all crowded both the roadside and the Jollimore driveway. Amid the shouts that rang out on the still morning air, I could hear the rasp of fire hoses and the rattle of ladders.

I got dressed, shut Twinkles into the bedroom and headed over to see if I could help.

The Four Cormorants Volunteer Fire Department swung into their routine, working with surprising efficiency and organization. Within minutes, the front door fell down, again, and two firefighters hauled a long hose into the house. From the amount of smoke seeping out of the house, I feared that the Jollimores would lose it all this time.

Despite the early hour, quite a few onlookers already lined the road, craning their necks for a good view. The Auxiliary Van opened for business, while the ambulance stood by for any casualties. Firefighters ran back and forth with an air of purpose, unreeling hoses, cranking up the pumper truck and positioning ladders against the side of the house. I saw Father Donald leaning against the pumper, pulling on his fireman's boots. I smiled when I noticed the bottoms of his striped pyjamas peeking from under his long black slicker. He must have come straight from his bed without bothering to change.

I could hear shouts from inside the Jollimore house, followed by the front window exploding outwards with a crash. A large chesterfield tumbled out through the gaping hole. Two chairs, an end table and a scorched rug joined it on the front lawn. With a cry of triumph, those outside doused the burning articles.

"That's got it!" said one fellow, wiping his brow. "Any more in there, Fred?"

"Nope!" A face appeared in the gap where the window had been. "I reckon we got it all. Not too much damage in here, considering. Just water to mop up. Some soot and smoke, too."

I stood with the rest of the crew looking at the charred chesterfield. A considerable audience of onlookers had joined us. I recognized quite a few faces, including Sherri's. We all watched a few stray wisps of smoke rise from the remains.

"Probably dropped a cigarette between the cushions," said one firefighter.

"Happens all the time," said another. "Smoulders for hours and then—whoosh! Up she goes."

One of the Auxiliary volunteers handed me a cup of coffee. I took it without thinking.

"Oh my stars! Oh my soul! What a fortuitous thing that you were up, Charles." From out of a face besmirched with soot, Father Donald's eyes gleamed with excitement. He chewed on a very large cookie. "Could have been much worse, not that this isn't bad enough, although you can always replace a chesterfield, well, not this one, I suppose, it being quite an old one, though not an antique exactly, although I suppose some might find it charming in its vintage, but not now, at least, I doubt it will ever be serviceable again…"

"I wasn't up, Father Donald. In fact, I was sound asleep, but Twinkles woke me," I told him.

"She must have sensed that something was amiss, well, not necessarily amiss, but certainly not quite right. Animals have that ability, you know. I certainly expect the Jollimores will be buying her more than one little can of special cat food," said Father Donald. "In fact, I wouldn't be surprised if they gave her a whole haddock!" He beamed. "I should think this would be a wonderful story for the paper. 'Cat saves house'." He looked at me with an air of expectancy.

"No, no! It wasn't anything like that. She was just meowing to go out, and I happened to get up and see the fire," I said, trying to nip Father Donald's enthusiasm in the bud. I had to avoid notoriety of any kind.

"Well, then, *you're* the hero!" said Father Donald.

'No! No!" I protested. I felt a desperate note creep into my voice. I had to get him off the hero track. "As I said, it wasn't like that at all. No heroes. Nothing special. Just doing my civic duty. Anyone would do the same." I backed away, with the intention of beating a quick retreat to Innisfree. Out of sight, out of mind, I hoped.

My foot entangled in one of the loops of fire hose. Before

I could react, I felt myself falling. I tried to catch myself, aware that I had a cup of hot coffee in my hand. With a wrench, I twisted sideways. My ankle turned with an excruciating stab of pain that took my breath away. The cup fell from my grasp.

"Oh my stars! Oh my soul! Charles! Are you all right?" Father Donald's cry attracted the attention of the two nearby paramedics, who had been lounging against the unneeded ambulance, watching the fun. In moments, they were with me, probing my painful ankle with skillful fingers.

"Looks like it might be broke," said one. "It's swelling up something fierce. Better get you to the hospital."

I detected a note of satisfaction in his voice. The trip wouldn't be wasted after all. Before I could protest, I found myself on a stretcher. The doors of the ambulance slammed shut behind me.

A few minutes later, the attendants wheeled me into the Cormorant Harbour Memorial Hospital. Real emergencies were taken by ambulance or helicopter into the city, but for small accidents such as mine, the local doctor was on call.

The paramedics transferred me onto a gurney, then left me in the treatment room while they went off to do their paperwork. By now, I could feel the growing pain in my ankle.

"Let's see what we have here," said a cheerful voice. A young man in hospital greens came from behind the screen. He smiled at me. "Looks like you're the only casualty of the fire. Jollimore's, wasn't it?"

I nodded then winced as he began to probe my tender ankle.

"Let's get some ice on this and get you along for an X-ray. I don't think it's too bad, but we'd better make sure. Either way, you'll have to keep off it for a day or two."

"Thank you, Doctor," I said.

"No, not doctor." The young man laughed. "I'm a nurse. And you're Charles Trenchant, aren't you? Boris has told me all about you."

I looked at him, wondering how he knew Boris.

"I'm Matthew Williams, 'Mattie' to most people." He pointed to the badge on his pocket.

I took a good look at him. Before me stood Boris's Mattie, quite tall, very handsome, with wavy blonde hair. My head reeled as I tried to take in the implications of this astounding new knowledge. Several things fell into place, including Mildred's unpleasant remark to Boris at the Chowder Luncheon.

"How do you do," I said, holding out my hand. "Boris has told me all about you, too," I said. Except for one small detail, I thought.

I spent the next hour being X-rayed and examined, but in the end, the doctor, a matronly woman from Upper Cormorant, confirmed I had sprained the ankle.

"I'll give you a ride home," said Mattie, as he helped the doctor tape up my ankle. "Boris will be here in a few minutes to pick me up. It's the end of my shift." Mattie wheeled me out to the parking lot, already bathed in the morning sunshine.

Boris waited in the car. He didn't seem surprised to see me. I supposed the Jollimore fire must be old news to him by now.

Mattie and Boris were just manoeuvring me into the back seat of their car when another car drew alongside us and parked. Mildred and Bev Barkhouse were both dressed in the flowery blue smocks of the Hospital Auxiliary Volunteers. Bev looked pale and washed-out, the experiences of the previous day written on her tired face, a noticeable contrast to Mildred's air of energetic efficiency.

"Oh, Mr. Trenchant! Are you all right?" Bev asked, as they got out. "Mother and I are just here to open up the Auxiliary Gift Shop. It's our turn today."

"Nothing at all. Just a little sprain. Thank you for asking." I winced as I swung the throbbing leg into the car.

"Mr. Trenchant, I *am* surprised at the company that you keep." Mildred's eyes flickered over Boris and Mattie with disdain.

"Hi, Bev," said Boris, ignoring Mildred. "Stuck as chauffeur again?"

Before Bev could reply, Mildred turned to Mattie. "Oh, Mr. Williams, I want to speak to you," she said in a saccharine sweet voice. She looked at her watch. "I only have a moment, so I'll be brief." She smiled, a small sinister smile, much like the one she'd bestowed on Dorothy Peasgood before she'd dropped the bombshell about Father Donald's involvement in Casino Night. "We've decided to change the theme for the Casino Night. It will be as I originally planned, a Monte Carlo evening. So much more tasteful than a Wild West Theme, don't you agree?"

I could see that her words had stunned Mattie. Boris had told me of the hours of work he'd put into the event, now all lost.

"Changing the theme?" Mattie stuttered. "But it's all set. I've hired the props and costumes from the city. And all the backdrops have been painted. Not to mention the musicians —Boris has had them practicing for weeks. You just can't change it now. It's too late."

I caught a glimpse of pure malice in her eye.

"You seem to forget that I'm the President of the Auxiliary, and as such, I have the responsibility of making sure that everything is done in the most acceptable manner possible. When you first volunteered to help, I didn't realize the full implications of your involvement with our group." She turned as if to leave.

"Just a moment!" Boris shot out a hand. She pulled herself away.

"Don't you dare touch me!" she said, glaring at him.

"What do you mean, 'full implications'?" Boris asked, his voice low and angry.

"It would be more suitable if the planning were done by a member of the Auxiliary, someone reliable, and not an outsider, such as your friend here. Especially given the circumstances. One must be so careful these days when public money is involved. And a person in my position must avoid the appearance of condoning *certain* activities." Mildred flecked a speck of imaginary dust off her sleeve.

"Oh, Mother!" Bev squeaked, her hands pressed against her flaming cheeks. "Don't say such horrible things!"

"They aren't horrible things, dear—they are the truth. And I feel it is my duty to speak out. Now, we must hurry, or we'll be late." She took Bev's arm and turned her towards the hospital entrance.

"You miserable old cow!" Boris's voice shook with rage. I shrunk back in the seat. Mildred didn't move an inch. "You're just doing this to get even with me. Couldn't stand me laughing at you. Where do you get off? After all Mattie's work. Voluntary, too. Did it just for the community. Like he does his job here at the hospital. Damn lucky to have him! What do you do? Make everyone miserable. Hound Sherri. Bully Bev."

Bev gasped in horror. "Oh, Boris! Oh, Mattie..." she said. "I can't bear it!" With a cry of pure misery, she wrenched herself out of her mother's grasp and stumbled across the parking lot, where she disappeared around the corner of the building.

"Now see what you've done!" Mildred turned and faced Boris. "You've upset poor Bev."

"Upset Bev? My God! If that woman doesn't have a nervous breakdown soon, I'll be surprised. Having to sneak around at her age, like some little teenager hiding a boyfriend from her parents—that's what I call upsetting."

I realized that Boris had let the cat out of the bag. I should have known that he'd be in on all the secrets in Cormorant Harbour, even Bev's secret love affair with Clarence. I trembled to think what Mildred would do with this information.

Mildred's mouth dropped open before it tightened into a thin line. "I don't need you to tell me about my daughter. Bev has always been a good girl and does what I tell her." A small fleck of spittle appeared on her lip. "You and your pretty boy. Your 'partner'. Your... your..." Words failed her. Her lip curled. For a second, I could see her genteel mask slipping, but then she drew in a deep breath. With a visible effort, she pulled herself together. "How dare someone like you cast aspersions on my daughter. You're not fit to be a teacher, and as for him, why I wouldn't let him lay a finger on me if I was dying. We don't need people like you in Cormorant Harbour. And I'm going to make sure that everyone knows what kind of people you are."

"You're a poisonous old bitch, and you can go to hell!" Boris roared back at her. He slammed my car door shut, pushed Mattie into the front seat and got behind the wheel. With a grinding of gears and a spray of gravel, he spun out of the parking lot, leaving Mildred glaring after him.

We drove in grim silence. Mattie chewed his lip. Every now and then, Boris would reach over and pat his hand.

"Like to kill that woman," Boris said through clenched

teeth. He caught my eye in the rear view mirror. "Told Mattie not to get involved with her. Did it anyway. Now look where it's got him. Bloody old cow."

The grimness of the scene drove me to silence. Now that I knew about Mattie, I realized how discreet Boris had always been. I couldn't imagine anyone being offended by their relationship. It was no one's business but their own. I felt sorry for Mattie and sympathized with Boris. Just the thought of how Mildred Barkhouse had treated Mattie brought a wave of anger. I agreed with Boris. Mildred had thrown Mattie off the Decorating Committee to get back at Boris for laughing at her. I could understand just how dangerous and ugly Mildred could be when someone thwarted her wishes or offended her in any way. I hoped that Sherri and Bev wouldn't also fall prey to her anger.

I sighed with the realization that none of it had anything to do with me. My ankle throbbed. My head ached. I was tired. I just wanted to go home.

Eleven

I barely remembered Boris helping me into bed, Mattie beside him propping my ankle up on a soft pillow. I swallowed the proffered painkillers and fell into a deep, dreamless sleep. The sound of the key in the lock followed by the opening of the front door woke me. Twinkles jumped off the bed, using my legs as a platform. I gasped as a stab of pain shot through my ankle.

Annie Fleet's cheerful voice filled the hall as she greeted the cat. "Well, hello, Pussykins. Your Uncle Boris sent me over to see your Daddy." I winced. She always spoke to the cat in baby talk. "Poor Daddy has a sore ankle, and you're a hungry Pussykins, aren't you? 'Never rains but it pours.' Bet you haven't had a bite to eat all day, poor baby. Let Auntie Annie find you some dinner." I found it hard to believe that she was Mildred Barkhouse's sister. "Would you like a cup of tea, my dear?" she called through to me. "And a little bit of something to eat perhaps?"

"Yes, please," I called back. I felt an incredible sense of relief. Thank God Boris had asked Annie to drop by, even though it wasn't one of her regular days.

Annie bustled in to set the tray on my bedside table. She straightened the blankets on the bed and plumped my pillows. How different from the time I'd had my appendix removed in Toronto. Then, I'd been forced to make do with a local homemaker for a few days. She'd been a large woman with no interest in anything other than the contents of my refrigerator and the continuing saga of her favourite soap opera on my television.

Having Annie around disconcerted me though, since she could have been Mildred's twin in size, shape and general features. However, Mildred and Annie's resemblance ran only skin deep, since Annie tended to favour T-shirts with mottos such as "I'd rather be playing bingo", stretch pants and the ubiquitous velcro-tabbed running shoes, rather than Mildred's coordinated ensembles, complete with hat and gloves. Since Annie always wore a headscarf over lumpy protrusions I took to be hair curlers, I had no idea if she also had Mildred's styled blue curls.

They were as unalike as any two people could be when it came to disposition and temperament. Annie was one of those easygoing women who take life as it comes, relying on time-worn adages to get her through any crisis.

"Do you need to go to the little boys' room?" she asked. "Can I give you a hand?"

"No! No!" I said, startled. "I can manage *that*." When I returned, my ankle felt as if someone were beating it with a hammer. I sank back into my bed with a sigh of relief.

"'Every cloud has a silver lining," she now told me. "This will give you a chance to have a nice rest while you work on your book without any interruptions. I've told my other customers they'll have to take care of themselves for the next day or two, until you're up and about again." She settled the tray on my lap. "Now you eat every bit. You must keep your strength up. I'll be in the kitchen if you need me. Just shout."

She left me with a bowl of excellent soup and my thoughts.

The faint odour of smoke that still hung in the air turned my thoughts to last night's fire. How fortunate that Twinkles had wakened me. If she hadn't, no doubt the Jollimores would be returning to a blackened shell. I hoped they hadn't got too far with their redecorating. It would be so disheartening to have to begin again. For one uncharitable moment, I savoured the idea of their having to live elsewhere, perhaps re-locate for an indefinite period.

From there, my thoughts swung to my meeting with Mattie at the hospital, and I remembered my surprise when I'd discovered that Boris's friend was a man. I thought back to the times that Boris had mentioned him and wondered why I had been surprised. Mattie seemed such a kind soul, so caring and gentle. Mildred Barkhouse's spiteful attitude towards him didn't make sense. It occurred to me that she had cut off her nose to spite her face by dumping Mattie from the Casino Night, since my instinct told me that Mattie's plans would have been far better than whatever Mildred could now drum up.

I doubted Mildred would now be welcome in Boris's choir. Poor Father Donald. How would he handle this looming personnel problem? He had no idea what lay ahead if Mildred insisted on staying in the choir. No doubt Boris would leave, and St. Grimbald's would never be the same. Boris's irreverent personal style did not make him popular among the older members, but even they could not refute his musical contribution to St. Grimbald's services. Finding an easy way out for Father Donald would be difficult since Mildred was a life member, and Boris just paid help. Whatever the final solution, factions for each side would develop within the congregation. I hoped my ankle would give me a good excuse to stay away until the dust settled.

I wondered what Mildred would do about Bev's clandestine love life. Poor Boris. He was probably kicking himself a thousand times for spilling the beans and landing Bev in even more trouble with her mother. At least no one knew that *I* had any idea what had been going on between Bev and Clarence. I wanted to keep it that way.

And the mystery lady? She remained an enigma. What did Bev want from her? And for whom? And why?

Zerena, Bev had called her. The image of her arose before my eyes again. Now that I knew that she wasn't Lucia Bacciaglia, I felt free to contemplate her attractiveness—the long dark hair, the graceful hands, the luminous eyes. I felt a little flutter of my heart. I thought I might ask Boris about her, now that I had a name to give him.

"Zerena," I whispered. The name lingered on my tongue.

Thoughts of Bev led me to thoughts of Sherri. I wondered what kind of hold Mildred had over her. I knew that Sherri owed Mildred money for her hairdressing business, but it seemed logical to me that Sherri should go to the bank and negotiate a loan. She had her business; she had her clientele. What more would she need? How terrible for her to be under Mildred's thumb for all those years. Since Annie spoke so proudly of her daughter and adored Nathan, her grandson, I wondered why she and Ollie hadn't helped Sherri out themselves.

Sherri had been so distraught yesterday. I remembered the feel of her in my arms, her faint perfume in my nostrils and her silky hair brushing against my cheek. I wondered why she had never married. But then there are those who remain faithful to their first loves, although the way she had spoken about Nathan's father belied this idea. Sherri certainly presented another enigma.

I sighed. Nothing I could do would change anything.

However, there were braver souls than I in Cormorant Harbour. Despite myself, I felt a smile creep onto my lips. Who would have thought that little Etta Fay, she of the knitting needles and whispery voice, would have taken such drastic action. I chuckled. Mildred had been a sight after Etta Fay had baptized her in coffee. Etta Fay might look like a frail little old lady, but I remembered the menace I'd heard in her voice at Sherri's. Dumping the coffee on Mildred looked like nothing more than a spur-of-the-moment reaction. I thought that Mildred had gotten off lightly. No doubt this wouldn't be the end of their feud. Etta Fay's long-term bitterness over her son Randy and the lack of grandchildren seemed to drive her hatred. I reminded myself to remain on pleasant terms with Etta Fay for my own safety's sake. I didn't see her as a woman who would ever forgive or forget.

The efficient way in which Dorothy Peasgood took command of the Chowder Luncheon after Mildred's debacle made me realize how galling it must be for her to play second fiddle to Mildred. She had the skills to be a powerhouse in her own right, albeit a stifled powerhouse. But for how long? This might be the beginning of the end of Mildred's reign, since Dorothy could take advantage of the situation to wreak havoc on Mildred's position in the church.

I began to feel a small headache at the back of my eyes. Too many people; too much thinking; too few answers. I cleared my head and settled back to enjoy the soup.

Twelve

L ook who's here!" said Annie. I must have dozed a little because I hadn't heard the doorbell. "It's Boris."

"How's the ankle?" Boris said as he plunked himself down on the edge of my bed. Annie rescued my tray just in time. Brought you some stuff." He opened up a plastic grocery bag. "Thermo-pack from Mattie. Put it in the freezer or the microwave. Whichever feels better." He laid the pack on the bedside table. "Grapes. Good for you." He popped a couple in his mouth and laid the enormous bunch next to the pack. "Chocolates. Even better for you." A box of chocolates joined the growing pile. "Crossword puzzles. Cryptic. Good to keep the old brain going. Mattie loves 'em. Can't do 'em myself." He drew out a book. "That should do you." He smiled in satisfaction and broke off another small bunch of the grapes. "Seedless. Easier. No seeds in the bed," he told me with a wink.

"Do you want a cup of tea, Boris?" Annie called from the kitchen. "I'm just brewing up a pot."

"Thanks," Boris hollered. My headache returned and ratcheted up a notch.

"Cookie?" Annie hollered back.

"Don't mind if I do."

"Chocolate or peanut butter."

"Both!"

"Oh, you!"

Boris pulled himself into a more comfortable position. I winced as the mattress shifted under his weight. He took off his jacket and threw it over the end of the bed, settling in for a visit.

"So, how's the ankle?" he asked again. Before I could reply, Annie brought in the tea tray.

"Here you are, then," she said, handing him a cup of tea and a plate with several cookies. "Mind you don't spill on Charles's nice duvet." She put my cup of tea on the bedside table, now crowded with gifts. "Oh, look at all the nice things Boris has brought you," she said. "'Pennies from heaven!' Mmmm. Grapes." She popped a couple in her mouth. "I'll just take these and give them a rinse. And a muscle bag— Ollie had one of these when he hurt his shoulder. I'll put it in the freezer, and you can use it later. Oooh! Chocolates."

"Here, have some," said Boris, whipping off the cellophane wrapper and opening the box.

"Don't mind if I do," said Annie. "Oooh! Chocolate covered cherries." She selected two from the tray. "One for now and one for later," she said.

"Take another," said Boris, helping himself.

"I'll put them in the fridge," said Annie, covering the box. "It's a bit warm in here, and they'll get sticky."

So far, I hadn't said a word, eaten a grape, or sampled a chocolate.

"So, how's the ankle?" said Boris yet again. "Still sore, eh?" He answered for himself. "Won't be long until you're up and about. Not broken, after all." He chewed on the last cookie. "Hope all that crap with Mildred this morning didn't upset you. Just because she's pissed off with me, she takes it out on Mattie. Typical! Hope the whole Casino Night goes up in flames. Monte Carlo! In Cormorant Harbour! Suppose she's going to wear her diamonds." Boris snorted in derision. "Bloody woman! After all the work Mattie put in. Hours of it. Lot of the stuff had a deposit on it. I'm sending her a bill. She can explain to the Auxiliary why they have to pay for something they didn't get. And she'd better not bring her ugly mug to my choir again! Going to tell Peasgood that it's her or me! United Church has been after me for months—ever since their organist kicked the bucket."

I wondered if Father Donald knew about the treacherous advances of the United Church.

Boris shifted again on the bed. His voice dropped to a grim note, "She better hope she's never brought into Emergency when Mattie's on duty, that's all I can say. Or that she doesn't run into me one night in a dark alley."

He slurped up the last of his tea, stood up and put his jacket on. "Ah well, mustn't tire you out," he said. "Too much socializing isn't good for you. Need your rest. I'll give your love to Mattie." With a wave and hollered "Goodbye Annie" in the direction of the kitchen, he left, banging the door behind him.

Although I hadn't said a word, I felt as if I'd been in a conversational marathon. Boris always had that effect on me. His personality, tiring at the best of times, overwhelmed me in my present state. I shook out a couple of Tylenol from the bottle on my bedside table and swallowed them with the dregs of my tea. I settled back against my pillows. In the time of the appendix, there'd been no visitors.

The doorbell rang. I heard Annie's footsteps in the hall, and a cheery, "Do come in! He's just in here. I know he'll be pleased to see you. No, no, not sleeping. Sitting up and alert, he is. Boris was just here cheering him up. You go on in, Bev dear."

Bev Barkhouse appeared in the doorway of the bedroom, looking around with a hesitant air. "I've brought you some books," she said. "Some light reading while you're laid up." She opened a plastic grocery bag and laid three books on my bedside table. The lurid cover of the top book told me they were not my usual fare. "*The Mulgrove Mystery of the Crypt,*" I read. "Thank you," I managed, looking as grateful as I could muster. "Just what I need. It was so kind of you to think of me," I added. "Please sit down. Shall I ask Annie to get you some tea?"

"Oh, no, no. I can't stay. I have to go. I…I'm…meeting someone," she gulped out. I took a close look at her for the first time. Bev's eyes were swollen and red-rimmed from crying. I presumed that her day hadn't improved since this morning's dust-up.

"How are you?" I asked. "Everything all right?" I didn't know what else to say. I couldn't come out and ask her point blank about her mother's reaction to Clarence, since as far as Bev knew, the affair remained a secret. For a moment, I wished Boris were still there. He would have pried the information out of her in seconds.

"Everything's going to be fine," she said with an edge of desperation in her voice. She licked her lips. "I just wanted to apologize for Mother's behaviour this morning. I hope you weren't too upset by it. Sometimes, she gets carried away and says things that she doesn't really mean." Her words lacked conviction.

I wanted to reply "Your mother says exactly what she wants to say!" I murmured something conciliatory instead.

"So, just as long as it's all right, and you know she didn't mean to offend you personally. Charles…she likes you. Thinks you're a real gentleman. We all do. Like you, that is."

Her face flamed bright pink as she fumbled for a handkerchief. Dabbing at her nose, she backed towards the door. "I should go. As long as you're all right. Don't worry, everything's fine. I know what I have to do." She drew a long breath and straightened her shoulders. "It's something I should have done a long time ago." With a tight smile, she walked out of the bedroom.

"Oh, hello, Father Peasgood. Hello, Miss Peasgood! I'm just leaving, but I'm sure he'll be pleased to see you," I heard Bev say from the hallway.

I found myself praying for patience, unsure that I could handle Father Donald's enthusiasm, much less Dorothy's overpowering bedside manner.

"Here they are," said Annie, ushering them into my bedroom. "Two ministering angels come to 'soothe the fevered brow'."

A large double bed, two dressers, the bedside table and an overstuffed armchair, all in the massive pseudo-colonial style that I had always disliked, crammed my bedroom. Now, with the two Peasgoods in the room, I began to feel a definite sense of claustrophobia.

"I'll bring tea, shall I? And some cookies?" suggested Annie, ever the soul of hospitality.

"Oh, yes, that would be wonderful!" said Father Donald.

"No thank you, Annie," said Dorothy. "We've just had lunch."

"Oh, shoot," said Father Donald, his face falling.

Annie shrugged and left the room.

Dorothy ensconced herself in the chair, smoothing out the skirt of her rose-patterned dress. Her trademark guitar pin glittered on the wide lacy collar. Father Donald, dressed in his "visiting" suit, the black clericals and white running shoes in which I'd first seen him, plumped down on the side of the bed. My ankle gave a sickening throb as the bed lurched.

"Well then, how's the patient?" said Father Donald, peering at me. "It's lucky your ankle wasn't broken. I had a broken arm once when I fell out of my treehouse, well, it wasn't so much a treehouse as a platform in a tree, although I called it my treehouse, being only nine, or was it ten? Dorothy, do you remember?"

"Oh for heaven's sake, Donald. Charles has no interest in your broken arm, much less your treehouse. And you were eight." Dorothy reached over and patted my arm. "I've brought you some of my matrimonial cake, as my mother always called it." She gave me a small, meaningful smile. "Date squares," she explained as she pulled out a package from the plastic grocery bag at her side. She put it on my bedside table, pushing aside Bev's light reading and setting the package on top of Boris's puzzle book. "I hope you'll like them. They're my specialty."

Father Donald reached across to open the package, only to be checked by a sharp smack on his hand from Dorothy. "Those are for Charles," she said.

"Oh shoot," said Father Donald, his face falling even further.

I noticed that Father Donald lacked his usual ebullience. If anything, he gave the impression of being somewhat down in the mouth. I wondered what could have reduced him to this state. Word of the battle royal between Boris and Mildred could surely not have reached his ears yet.

"How are you, Father Donald?" I asked him. "Have you got over the excitement of the fire?"

"He's got a lot more excitement than a fire to think

about," said Dorothy. "He's heard from the Bishop." An ominous note to her voice caused my heart to miss a beat.

"The Bishop?" I said. My mouth went dry. Had the Bishop checked on my credentials, talked to a fellow Bishop perhaps, visited some church in Ottawa—oh God! Was my cover blown? If only I hadn't started down this slippery slope of lay readership in Cormorant Harbour. I tried not to let my face show the alarm I felt.

"Yes. Just as I predicted, Donald should never have become involved with this ridiculous Casino Night affair. Not at all fitting. Not in his position. I knew the Bishop would be upset." She said, a smug smile touching her lips.

I felt a wave of relief wash over me. Thank God. Father Donald was in trouble, not *me*. I was still safe.

"Someone felt it necessary to inform the Bishop of the goings-on here in the Parish of Cormorant Harbour. Such things as the A.C.W. catering a gambling party, and the rector actually taking tainted money from those who attend." Dorothy settled back into the chair. I could see her enjoyment of the moment. "I suspect that Etta Fay may have had something to do with it. And it's all Mildred's own fault. Rushing ahead willy-nilly without anybody's say-so." She ran her fingertips over the rhinestones in her brooch. The smile still played on her lips. "Of course, it's all come to an end now. The A.C.W. will not be involved, and neither will Donald. And I doubt that Mildred will be the President of the A.C.W. for much longer. In fact, I'm going to insist on a special meeting to consider her resignation," she ended on a triumphant note.

I could sense Annie listening in the hallway. The news would be all over the four Cormorants within hours.

"Now, now, Dottie," Father Donald began. "Don't get all

worked up. You've already had one of your pills today, and you know what the doctor said, and especially after the last time, although I know that wasn't your fault, well, perhaps not all your fault, what with the pharmacy being closed on Remembrance Day, and a good thing, since I believe we should all pause and remember, but it did mean you were without your pills, and that's not a good thing, although, it would be nice if you were able to give them up, well, perhaps not give them up, but simply cut down, although…"

His voice trailed off under a gimlet stare from Dorothy. Her mouth thinned out into a hard line. "I'm sure Charles doesn't need to hear any of this, Donald. We mustn't tire him out." She rose and gathered her things. "Come along. We still have to visit the nursing home."

Father Donald rose at once. He shook my hand with much less than his usual enthusiasm. "Well, I certainly hope you'll be up and about soon. Of course, I won't expect you to be on duty on Sunday." He heaved a deep sigh. "Things won't be the same without you, and the choir is singing a special anthem this week."

"I doubt that there'll be any special music on Sunday, not if Mildred plans to sing in the choir," I said without thinking. The words just slipped out. I could have cut out my own tongue. How could I be so stupid? I kept forgetting that I couldn't afford to relax my guard for even a moment.

The Peasgoods stopped in mid stride. Both turned and looked at me open-mouthed.

"What do you mean, Charles?" asked Dorothy, ever the interrogator.

"Oh, well, umm," I floundered. "Boris…er, Mattie…um. Casino Night. A bit of an argument with Mildred. Nothing really." I tried to brush off my faux pas.

Dorothy pounced. "Mildred! I might have known! That woman's got her nose in everybody's business. She's a trouble-making busybody."

"Now, Dottie. We must remember to be Christian in our attitude towards others," Father Donald began.

"Christian! Mildred! The two words don't go together." Dorothy's voice rose several notches. Bright spots of colour flamed on each cheek, matching the roses on her dress. She clutched her handbag to her chest. I hoped Father Donald had some of her pills on hand, or we might be in for a repeat of whatever had happened on some better-forgotten Remembrance Day in their last parish. "The woman is evil. Malicious. Now she's upset poor Boris and wrecked the choir. She must be stopped. Somebody has to do something." Her eyes glittered. "And if no one else has the courage to do it, I will." She drew herself up, took Father Donald's arm and marched him out of the room.

I fell back on my pillows, exhausted by the Peasgood visit.

Before I could close my eyes, the doorbell rang again. I wondered if I could feign sleep. However, when I heard Sherri's voice in the hallway, I brightened at the prospect of a visit from her.

"Would you like tea, dear?" Annie asked her daughter.

"No, no thanks, Mom. I'm not staying. I've got to get back and give Gladdy a perm. I just dropped by to see how Charles is doing." She came over to the bed and pecked me on the cheek. "Hi, Charles. How's the ankle?"

I smelled a light waft of her perfume and noticed her casual T-shirt and jeans. I thought how much nicer she looked in a dress, but realized she must have come straight from the shop to see me.

"I'm fine," I told her. "Just a little stiff and sore. Mattie says I'll be my old self in a day or two."

"I've brought you some magazines from the shop," she said, opening up a plastic grocery bag. She dropped several on the bed. I could see brawny men on ATVs holding large fish on the cover of the top one.

"How thoughtful," I said. "I didn't have a chance to finish this one when I was at the shop."

"It's the least I can do after you let me bawl all over your shirt yesterday. I don't know what came over me. I don't usually lose it like that. I guess the whole 'empty nest thing' is getting to me. I can't imagine having Nathan gone. And then there's all the expense and the worry of having him in Halifax by himself. And then...Aunt Mildred's being so nasty. It was just too much." She looked away from me.

I didn't know what to say. Everything in me wanted to be her knight in shining armour, to rescue her from the dragon Mildred, but I didn't understand her problem or how I could help without becoming involved. I was frustrated by my sense of helplessness and impotency, stuck in this bed, a powerless observer. In order to obey the strictures of the program, I had to keep a very low profile in the community. Judging from the number of visitors I'd received, I hadn't been very successful. Never before had I been so involved with so many people in so little time.

While I floundered for a suitable response, Sherri bent again to kiss my cheek. "Well," she said. "I've got to run. I'm helping Nathan pack. He's found a summer job in Dartmouth, and he has to be there by tomorrow morning. Take care of yourself. See you soon."

I heard her call, "Bye, Mom", from the hall as she left. My bedroom seemed cold and empty without her.

I felt tears gather in the corners of my eyes. What had

seemed such a straightforward proposition: take on a new name, a new life and live in anonymity in a community where I knew no one, had become an untenable situation.

"Don't get involved, Eric," my agent had said. "Involvement always puts you in danger of disclosure, no matter how hard you try. It shouldn't be difficult for you to do. Just live the way you've always lived—privately and conservatively." She'd even smiled at me. "It's lucky you don't have a slew of friends and family to worry about. This will be easier for you than most."

My heart clenched. If this was her idea of easy, I hated to think what other people went through. I didn't want to be anonymous. I didn't want to remain uninvolved. I didn't want to live the way I'd always lived.

I wanted to live like Charles Trenchant would live. As a respected, even loved, member of the Cormorant Harbour community, he would be involved in the lives of the people around him; he would involve himself in their concerns; he would be a rock of dependability during their times of adversity, not just a shoulder to cry on, but a friend and counsellor whom they could trust.

He wouldn't be anything like Eric Spratt.

Thirteen

I spent a restless night. Not just the throbbing of my ankle, but the turmoil in my brain, or perhaps, to be more accurate, in my heart, kept me from sleep. For hours, I swung between two poles: that of complete surrender to my growing desire to become involved with the people in my new life and that of strict adherence to the rules I'd agreed to abide by in exchange for the safety of this new life.

With the dawn came resolution: I would be a model Witness Protection Program participant, behaving in a manner that would satisfy the sternest strictures of my Agent. She would be proud of me. I'd realized giving way to maudlin sentiment would only expose me to the danger of disclosure. Eric Spratt had lived a satisfactory life in his own private, unencumbered way. Charles Trenchant could do the same.

I could now hobble on my ankle, so later in the morning, Annie suggested that I might like to take my coffee on the patio. After a great deal of fetching of books, afghan, sunglasses, sweater, coffee and cookies, followed by enthusiastic pillow plumping, she left me in peace at last. Twinkles jumped up onto my lap, where she settled down for a nap. I settled back to enjoy one of those rare perfect seaside days—clear skies, warm sun, gentle ocean and rose-scented air. I lay back in the lawn chair, luxuriating in a sense of well-being engendered by Annie's loving attentions.

My new resolve and emotional equilibrium were disturbed when Annie arrived with the morning mail. Along with the usual flyers and junk mail, I found half a dozen get-well cards from various members of St. Grimbald's. The Peasgoods had spread the word of my indisposition. Although I felt gratified that people cared about me, I also felt a rising alarm. I had been right to take stock of my situation. I had become too involved. Again, I cursed that moment of weakness when I had exposed myself by boasting to the Peasgoods of my former association with the church. Everything to date stemmed from that revelation of my lay readership experience. "Pride goeth before a fall," I reminded myself, sounding like Annie. Nevertheless, I began to wonder if I could use the ankle as an excuse to withdraw from active duty in the Parish of Cormorant Harbour.

"Howdy neighbour! Didn't expect to see you. Thought you was laid up." Kevin and Ricky appeared on the path that their continual use had made across my lawn to my wharf. They each carried a bucket and fishing rod. At the sound of Kevin's voice, Twinkles disappeared into the bushes. "You go on down, Ricky. I'll stay and cheer Charlie up a bit. Here, take some cookies." Kevin helped himself to my cookies, giving a couple to Ricky, who ran off down the path, stuffing them in his mouth as he went.

Dropping his bucket and rod on the patio, Kevin slumped down in the other lawn chair, ready to visit. If anything, Kevin Jollimore looked even more disreputable than usual. He hadn't shaved, and he wore the same clothes he'd had on at the Harbour Day Parade.

"Oh, it's you." Annie's head appeared around the kitchen door. "I heard voices. Suppose you want coffee, too."

"Three sugars, Aunt Annie. Double cream," Kevin

reminded her. "And some cookies," he called out. "Charlie's eaten most of these."

"Anything else, Your Highness?" Annie sniffed and disappeared into the kitchen.

"I guess you've been pretty busy, cleaning up after the fire," I said, resigning myself to the visit.

"Goddam mess, pardon my French, you'd think them firefighters would clean up after themselves when they was done. Water everywhere! Soot on the ceiling. Helluva thing! Arleen's nerves have been taken some bad. Thought me and the boy'd get out for a bit till she calmed down." He reached out a hand and took the cup of coffee Annie proffered to him. "Thanks, Auntie. Got the cookies?"

Annie put a tin on the patio table and pried off the lid. "Here's three," she said. "You don't need no more. 'Give you an inch and you'll take a mile', and I haven't got any more baked up yet for Mr. Trenchant." She put the lid back on.

"Ahh, gimme a break, Auntie. I ain't had any breakfast yet. Whole damn house is smokey. What a mess. Wrecked the couch, too. Besides breaking my window, them fellas tramped mud and water all through the place, and that's got Arleen in a twist." Kevin shoved a cookie in his mouth.

"Are you complaining about the fire department?" Annie said in a sharp tone. "Talk about 'biting the hand that feeds you'. They saved your house twice now. And it was all your fault they had come out. Any fool knows you don't leave paint rags lying around, and I suppose it was your Arleen what dropped the cigarette down the back of the couch. You'd think 'Once bitten; twice shy', and you'd be more careful after that first time. Some folks never learn. You should be down on your knees thanking your lucky stars that you still have a roof over your head." She turned on her heel and marched back into the house. I gathered that although Kevin might be Mildred's favourite nephew, Annie did not share her sister's feelings for him.

"Yes, it was fortunate that the fire department were able to get here so quickly," I said. "Before the fire took hold. If it wasn't for Twinkles, I would have slept through the whole thing."

"Twinkles? Isn't that your cat?" Kevin asked, looking around him.

"Yes. She woke me up. The fire had hardly started. It would have been much worse if I hadn't been able to call the fire department right away." I waited for him to say something complimentary about Twinkles.

"I knew black cats was unlucky." Kev blew across the top of his cup then took a long swallow of his coffee. "Goddam cat should mind its own business," he muttered. "Better not let Arleen know. She don't like that cat already."

His attitude surprised me. I had expected at least a word of praise or thanks for both Twinkles and myself. Instead, I got the impression that Kevin felt annoyed with both of us. Perhaps dealing with the aftermath of the fire had taken the edge off his gratitude.

"I suppose you and Arleen have a lot of cleaning up to do," I said, trying to sound sympathetic. "And you'll have to replace the window and buy some new furniture."

"Helluva mess," he repeated.

"Wasn't it fortunate that you and the family were at Clarence's for the night? How dreadful if any of you had been hurt. Are you going to try to live in the house while you do the clean-up?" I asked.

"Nah! Clarence don't mind if we stay awhile. We was fixing on doing that anyway." His eyes shifted away from me, and for a moment he looked uneasy. "Gives Arleen a bit of a break, and her Ma's just next door."

"Kevin!" The Voice reverberated across the still air. "Where the hell are you? If you think I'm staying in this dump, you've got another think coming. You get your ass back here now!"

Kevin jumped and looked guilty. "Oops! She's found me. Gotta go. She's worse if I don't. We're going back to Clarence's, and she's chompin' at the bit." He slurped down the rest of his coffee, scooped the remaining cookies from the plate into his pocket and stood up.

"Ricky!" he hollered. "Time to go!" Ricky came running from the wharf.

"Kevin!" The Voice ratcheted up several decibels. "Now!"

"Holy shit, woman. I can only go so fast. I'm coming!" Kevin hollered back.

"Mind your language, Kevin!" Annie's voice floated out the open kitchen window. "Your mother didn't raise you to talk like that!"

"Oh, hell," Kevin mumbled to me. "Two of 'em on my ass. Trust me, Charlie, you're better off without a woman in your life. They're only noise and trouble." He and Ricky shambled off across the lawn. Moments later, I heard their old pick-up drive away.

I settled back in my chair, thinking that a nap in the sunshine might be in order. However, Ollie, Annie's husband, taking advantage of the warm day, arrived to cut the grass, which up until now had been too wet with dew to mow.

I lay back and enjoyed the somnolent sound of the lawnmower and the smell of fresh-cut grass. Thanks to Boris, I didn't have to do anything to produce this bliss. Annie and Ollie Fleet had proved to be treasures beyond counting.

"Do you got a key to the shed?" Ollie's voice at my elbow roused me from my daydreaming.

Ollie was a little man of indeterminate age, with a perpetual frown and a propensity for pessimism and foul language. He had two speeds: dead slow and stop. It amazed me that he always managed to get the job done.

"I sees you got a sickle in there hanging on the wall, and I figures I'll cut back them effin' weeds by the driveway." He thumbed off his cap and scratched the sparse hairs on top of his head.

I roused myself and tried to figure out what Ollie meant. "The shed?" I frowned. "Is it locked?"

"'Course it's locked. Effin' great padlock on it. Think you'd got the goddam crown jewels inside, 'stead that bunch of junk I saw through the window. What you'd be wanting with all that, I don't know. Take it to the dump for you, iffen you'd like. Wouldn't take but one load in my truck. Only charge you fer the gas. Then you could put your mower in there where it belongs, 'stead of leavin' it rustin' out in the woodshed where it won't be no effin' use to you come next year." As usual, once Ollie got started on a subject, he didn't let it go. "No way to treat a good mower. Needs a goddam proper roof, it does."

Then I remembered Kevin and Clarence locking the shed behind them after they'd loaded in the Jollimore belongings.

"I don't have a key," I told Ollie. "The stuff belongs to Kevin, and he put the lock on. You'll have to ask him."

"Kevin! That effin' blowhard!" Ollie grunted the name in disgust. "That fella's a waste of skin, iffen you ask me. Never done a goddam lick of work in his life. Spoiled rotten, he was. Annie's sister Mona, his mother, always let him do whatever he wanted. And Mildred's no better. Always givin' him money, here and there. Says she's put him in her goddam will, too. Dumb old bitch! She's probably worth mor'n a few thousand. Should be leavin' it all to poor Bev, not to that sack of shit across the road. I don't have no time for the goddam fella and never did. And what's he wantin' your good shed for, anyway? Got a effin' shed of his own, ain't he?"

"Well, Kevin told me that Arleen wanted to do a little decorating, so he asked to borrow my shed to store a few things in. I guess his shed was already full. Anyway, it's not a problem. There wasn't much stuff. Just a few family things. A big Bible, some photo albums, the microwave, the television…things like that." Even as I said it, I began to feel a growing wave of uneasiness clench my stomach. I hadn't given the shed another thought, but now it occurred to me, as it had at the time, that Kevin had an unusual collection of items to store.

"Arleen goddam decorating! The lazy cow wouldn't lift her goddam bum up off the effin' couch except to get another beer out of the fridge. She can't even sweep the goddam floor, much less paint a wall! My son—you've been shit on good and proper. I thought them goddam fires was funny, but now I sees the lay of the land, I know what he's up to. Mr. Trenchant, that goddam Kevin's got you buried in it up to your neck."

"Buried in what?" I asked, a dawning suspicion beginning to bloom across my brain. That vague feeling I'd had right at the beginning became more of a certainty. Kevin must be setting up one of Dorothy Peasgood's "lucky strikes". I felt sure of it! Worse, he'd made me an accessory after the fact. Would they take into account that I had been responsible for calling in the fires on both of the occasions, or would it look like I had bungled my part in the plot, and called them in too early? Oh, god! It would mean investigations, inquiries and people poking into my business. I had to stop Kevin

130

somehow. If he tried again, it would be the end. And I had to get Kevin to move his stuff out of my shed!

"Buried in shit!" Ollie answered my question with a note of grim satisfaction in his voice. The prophet of doom had spoken. "Iffen I was you, I'd get that goddam stuff off my property right quick." He left me to my turbulent thoughts and went back to his lawnmower.

I lay back in the chair, my brain in a turmoil. With a groan of despair, I tried to think my way out of the dangerous situation my own stupidity had landed me in. Anyone else would have been suspicious of what Kevin Jollimore was doing, but I, a lamb to the slaughter, an innocent abroad, felt a rising anger. I had been used in a low and deceitful way. Perfidy, I whispered to myself.

And here I sat, helpless, chained to my chair, unable to drive, unable to do anything about it until the feckless Kevin returned home from Clarence's. I prayed that Kevin didn't have another lucky strike in the offing.

I no longer felt the beauty of the day around me. I called to Annie, and she helped me back indoors, where she settled me on the couch and brought me a lunch I couldn't eat.

"There's no use crying over spilt milk," she told me as tutted over my untouched tray. Ollie must have filled her in on Kevin's schemes and my gullibility.

"What's done is done. It'll all look better in the morning. You weren't to know. Kevin's always been a lazy lad, looking for the easy way out. Anything to avoid hard work. I keep telling Mildred not to give the boy money—it just encourages him. And she keeps promising him something in her will. 'Course, it's likely only promises, but Kevin don't know that. Keeps him at her beck and call, 'stead of settling down and taking care of his family proper like a man should." She sniffed in disapproval of the whole affair and took the tray out to the kitchen.

I'd had enough of Kevin Jollimore for one day. I could tell from Annie's tone that the diatribe would go on all afternoon if I let it. Weariness overwhelmed me. My ankle hurt. I wanted to be alone.

"Why don't you and Ollie take the afternoon off?" I said to Annie when she returned with my tea. "I'm fine now. I can manage by myself. I'm just going to lie here and nap."

"Are you sure? Ollie was talking of going over to Truro for some car parts…"

"Absolutely sure. You go on with Ollie. I'll be fine. I'll see you in the morning."

She looked doubtful but at my insistence agreed that I could be left alone.

"There's a cold plate in the fridge for your supper," she told me. "Ollie and I are off now, and I'll be back in the morning. If you need anything, just call."

"Thanks, Annie. Leave the front door unlocked. People seem to be popping in and out all over the place, and I don't want to have to get up any more than I have to. I'll lock up before I go to bed." I told her.

The house seemed lonely without her comforting presence. Even Twinkles seemed restless, moving from the couch to the chair and back to the couch, unable to settle. My own uneasiness had affected her placid disposition, so close had we grown.

The doorbell rang, jarring the silence.

"Come in," I shouted. "It's not locked." As I said this, I wondered at my own bravado. For all I knew, a contingent of Mafia goons could be on my doorstep. I didn't care. I'd sunk too low to be concerned about my personal safety at this point. I had a moment of guilt as I thought how shocked my agent would be if she knew I had left the door unlocked, ready to invite in an unknown person or persons. I would never be a satisfactory program client. All my good resolutions of the night before were just so many broken promises.

"Hello?" I heard a low and musical voice, one I did not recognize.

"I'm in here," I said, wondering who my visitor could be.

As she came through the doorway, I felt as if I'd been hit by a fist in my solar plexus, knocking the breath out of me. It was her! Zerena! The mystery woman. Here. In my living room. I stared at her, my mouth hanging open, too surprised to speak.

"Hello," she said again. She smiled. As her eyes met mine, I fell again into their dark depths. Like a stone dropped into a bottomless well, I plummeted into a vortex of emotion. I felt a deep resonance within, a stirring unlike anything I'd ever experienced before, not even in my most intimate moments with Chloris. My heart pounded, my palms were sweaty, my breath caught in my throat. I tried to struggle to my feet.

"No. No. Don't get up. My name's Zerena. Bev sent me over to see you." She came across the room, stretched out a graceful arm, and with a cool hand on my chest, gently pressed me back onto the pillows.

Her touch, her nearness, the exotic perfume that swirled around her, filled my senses.

"Bev sent you?" I managed to croak.

"Yes. She told me about your ankle. I've brought you some salve." She pulled a small container out of the canvas bag she carried over her shoulder and placed the jar on the coffee table. "It's wonderful for sprains."

"Salve?" I said, feeling as if my world had been turned upside down. Even in my altered state, I could see Twinkles insinuating herself around Zerena's slender ankles, purring and rubbing them in feline ecstasy. I envied the cat.

"Yes. I'm a herbalist," Zerena said. I thought her voice sounded like golden temple bells on still air. "I make all kinds of natural remedies. Shall I put it on for you?"

"Put it on?" My voice rose to a squeak. The room became much smaller and very warm.

"Yes," she said. "I'm also a masseuse. I'm sure I can help you." In one fluid movement, she tossed her shawl onto the chair and knelt down beside me. Her dark hair fell forward, screening her face from me. She bent over my ankle. Inch by inch, she began to peel off my sock.

My mouth went dry.

With great care, she unwound the elastic bandage. I lay back, unable to move, unable to speak, unable to think. I didn't want this feeling to stop.

"Well," she said. "This doesn't look too bad." She screwed the cap off of the jar. I felt cool ointment on my throbbing ankle, then, the touch of her gentle fingers, probing and rubbing my skin.

I closed my eyes, giving myself up to her healing caresses. Time stood still. The ugly room with its oppressive furniture melted away. Only the touch of her hands remained.

"There," she said, rocking back on her heels as she put the lid back on the jar. "That should do it." The moment ended. She began to gather her things together as if to leave. I wanted to keep her with me.

"You're a herbalist," I said, searching for a way to prolong her visit.

"Yes," she replied, and to my relief, sat down in the chair.

"Have you been doing this for very long?" It was a fatuous question. "Um…er…I mean, is this your business? Do you have a store?"

"Good heavens, no!" She laughed, and the temple bells again rang in the room. "I work at home, in Cormorant Head. I live out at the end of Cliff Lane in my grandmother's old homestead. I came back two years ago when she died so I could set up my business in the house. It's mostly mail order through the internet. My website gets up to a thousand hits a day."

I couldn't imagine this exotic creature as a prosaic businesswoman. I pictured her in a small, dark shop or in the kitchen of a tumbledown cottage, but not in front of a computer.

"My grandmother was known as the Cormorant Head witch!" She laughed again. "I'm afraid the locals have passed the title on to me. People are always coming to my door for love potions and the like. You'd be surprised at what people think I can do for them—make someone fall in love with them or bring back a straying lover. I don't mind. It's kind of fun, and I can usually come up with something that will satisfy them without doing any real harm."

I gaped at her. Not only was she not Lucia Bacciaglia, she wasn't a conspirator with Bev. Of course! That's why Bev was asking for Zerena's help. Not to knock off Mildred, but to entice Clarence.

"You're from away?" I managed to ask.

"Yes. From Toronto. All my father's family are there. They're Italian." She looked directly at me as she said this. I felt a chill wash over me. Was she trying to give me a message? Her dark eyes were unreadable.

I didn't dare question her further. An Italian! From

Toronto! Had someone sent Zerena to see me? Someone other than poor innocent Bev? Could all this be part of a grand plot, with me as a dupe once more?

"But I'm here now," she continued, "and I don't imagine I'll go back to Toronto." She paused and gave me that same dark, enigmatic look. "And what about you? Where are you from?"

My shock made me careless. "Tor…er…Ottawa!" I groaned inwardly in despair. I still couldn't keep my story straight in a crisis. And this *was* a crisis. How much did Zerena already know? I took a deep breath as I began to trot out my story. I knew it sounded rehearsed, but it took all my concentration to keep my voice from trembling.

"A writer! How fascinating? What are you writing, may I ask?"

Until this moment, no one had ever asked me that question.

"Um, er…a novel!" I gasped out. "About a man on a river trip. Comparing it to the metaphysical world, to exploring our id and ego, how we are all linked with the forces of nature and our exploration of the universe is simply our exploration of our internal selves…it's difficult to explain."

"How interesting." Zerena looked like she meant it.

"It'll be some time before it's ready for a publisher." In truth, the novel had started out well, but I was bogged down on the second chapter.

"I must go," she said, standing up. A hint of her perfume wafted on the air. She put her bag over her shoulder. Again our eyes met. I felt that familiar sinking, falling, plummeting sensation in the pit of my stomach. "It's been so nice meeting you. I'll leave you the salve for your ankle." She smiled. "This one's a sample, but the next pot will cost you."

She picked up her shawl and started for the door.

Part of me wanted to ensure that she would come back, but part of me feared that she would. My indecision halted any words in my mouth, so that I could only nod. I forced myself to swallow the lump of fear in my throat. I had to find out whether she was more than she seemed.

"Will I see you again?" I blurted out.

She stopped in the doorway and turned to me with a smile. Her hair swung forward so that I couldn't see her eyes. "Oh, yes," she said, "you most assuredly will." The door closed behind her with a soft click.

My heart soared at the thought of seeing her again. Yet, in the pit of my stomach, I felt a growing knot of doubt and fear as I replayed her last words over and over in my mind.

Fourteen

I spent the next couple of days watching in vain for the Jollimores' return. Every vehicle that went by brought me to the window. When it wasn't Kevin's truck, my heart would start to pound, wondering if this vehicle belonged to the authorities, coming to check on the contents of my shed. Only when it passed by did I relax. I didn't think that Ollie would take the story to the authorities, but I had little confidence in the discretion of Kevin and Clarence themselves, considering how often they came close to giving the game away to me by their careless remarks and inappropriate reactions. Soon, more people than Ollie would put two and two together and come up with a lucky strike.

I didn't care about the lucky strike; I wanted Kevin to remove the evidence of his criminal activities from *my* shed. Until then, I knew that I would not rest.

On Thursday afternoon, as I continued my vigil at the office window, I began to notice something strange. Twice, a large black SUV drove by, slowing down as it passed the house. I couldn't see anybody through the tinted windows, but it didn't look like a local vehicle. Such an expensive automobile would have been noticeable in an area given to beaten-up pick-up trucks and second-hand economy-sized rust buckets.

On the third pass, the vehicle pulled into the Jollimore

driveway, and two men got out. They were dressed in dark suits, most unusual for Cormorant Harbour. The larger man wore wraparound sunglasses, so I couldn't see his face. The other, small, wiry and dark, gestured towards my house as they got out. They stood for several minutes, looking around them. I began to feel a gnawing sense of unease. The larger man pulled out a camera and took several photos.

I drew back from the window, hoping they hadn't seen me. Why were they taking pictures of my house? To my horror, they opened the gate and started down my front path.

At this point, a dreadful suspicion began to arise in me. What better front for Mafia hitmen sent to investigate me than to pose as some kind of legitimate investigators of the Jollimore fires? The more I thought about it, the more sense it made. Who else would drive a large black SUV with tinted windows? Who else would travel in pairs, wearing suits and sunglasses? My heart skipped a beat. Who else would have the tools of their trade in a brief case?

In a panic, I limped hurriedly to the back of the house, thinking I might run out the back door. But they would see me leaving! I would have to hide. But where?

The heavy furniture cramming every room left little space for me to conceal myself. Then I remembered the large wardrobe in my bedroom. I slammed open the doors, burrowed between my suits, concealing myself behind the rack of clothing. I held my breath. I could hear nothing except the pounding of my blood in my ears.

The shrill tone of the doorbell told me that my instinct to hide had been a good one. I'd concealed myself just in time. I had to stay calm, stay quiet and stay put until they went away.

To my horror, I heard a scratching on the door of the wardrobe. Twinkles! The scratching increased. Soon, she added plaintive mewlings which became louder as she realized that I didn't intent to let her into my sanctuary.

"Go away!" I hissed, but the sound of my voice encouraged her to make louder efforts. I eased open the door, reached out a desperate arm and scooped Twinkles into the wardrobe with me.

The doorbell rang *again.*

I froze. Twinkles squirmed in my convulsive grip. I put her down whereupon she began to scratch and mew at the inside of the door. Now she wanted out.

"Stop it! Stop it at once!" I hissed in a fever of apprehension. I didn't dare open the door to let her out.

The doorbell rang again. I held my breath, willing them to give up. Then I heard loud knocking on the back door. They were more determined than any Jehovah's Witness had ever been.

"Hello? Anybody home?" The voice came from the kitchen. They were inside! I cowered in the wardrobe. Twinkles started to mew with increasing volume, no doubt thinking that visitors meant food. I threw a jacket over her, so that I could bundle her squirming body in my arms in order to keep her quiet.

"Funny, I thought I saw someone at the window, but I guess nobody's home," I heard a gruff voice say. Did I detect an Italian accent? I couldn't really hear from the muffled confines of my hiding place. "We'll come back another time."

After what seemed like hours, I heard the back door slam. I remained still and quiet for some time longer, clutching the struggling Twinkles to my chest. When at last I deemed it safe, I crawled from the wardrobe, hot and dishevelled. I released Twinkles, who stalked off with her tail in the air. I knew it would be hours before she forgave me for the undignified treatment.

With shaking hands, I made myself a cup of tea. Carrying the cup with me into the living room, I sank back onto the couch, trying to take stock of the situation. Everywhere I looked, I saw danger. Danger from the Jollimore's belongings in my shed. Danger from the unknown visitors at my door.

A thought struck me. It had only been a matter of days since Zerena had sat in this very room with me. Had she told these goons where I lived?

My tea grew cold in the cup as I contemplated the ramifications of my suspicions. I wondered whether I should call my Agent. I thought this could rate as one of the emergency situations she meant when she told me to call her.

I realized that all of this could well be a figment of my overactive imagination. Paranoia, perhaps, from my obsession with preserving my anonymity. With a grim smile, I reminded myself that sometimes even paranoids are being watched.

I let out a deep sigh as I came to the conclusion, once again, that I must withdraw from all public scrutiny. I would become as reclusive as a hermit, as silent as a Trappist monk, as unapproachable as a porcupine. Indeed, I would begin to use my not inconsiderable intellect to out-think these goons. Eric Spratt might have run off with his tail between his legs, but not Charles Trenchant.

I sat down with my note pad to make a list.

One. I would resign as lay reader at St. Grimbald's. I felt a pang as I wrote it down, but it had to be done. I knew Father Donald's disappointment would have to take second place to preserving my safety. Resigning as lay reader would no doubt take care of my association with Boris, too.

Two. I would avoid Zerena at all costs. If she called, I

wouldn't answer. If she came, I would hide in the wardrobe again if necessary. Anything to keep her at a distance. Even as I wrote this down, my heart sank. I shook my head, telling myself that it must be done, despite the hours I'd spent thinking of her touch, her perfume, her presence at my side and the sound of her voice.

Three. No more long chats with Bev in the library. I had become far too involved with Bev and her life. From this point on, I would patronize the main library when I went into Dartmouth.

Four. Find myself a gentleman's hairdresser in town. I needed to put distance between myself and Sherri. Her problems were not mine.

Five. The Fleets. Here, I paused. What to do with Annie and Ollie? The sensible thing would be to let them go. However, I thought of the full cookie tin in the cupboard, and the clipped grass around the house, and the gleaming shine on the floors, and I thought again. No, perhaps if I just kept my distance, kept the relationship on a professional footing, that of an employer and his employees, I might not have to let the Fleets go.

I read through the list again. A wave of depression washed over me. I wondered if I'd be able to follow through on the plan.

I must have fallen into a deep sleep after the emotional ups and downs of the previous day. I didn't wake up until I heard Annie's arrival. She came into the bedroom with a breakfast tray. In my defeated state, I accepted the gesture with gratitude.

"It's a good day to stay in bed," she told me, pulling back the curtains. "There's not much to rush up for out there. Just more rain and fog. Forecast says we're in for thunderstorms tomorrow. Bad weather right through till Sunday."

The day matched my mood—grey and gloomy. I picked up the list which I had put on my bedside table. As I sipped my tea, I began to formulate a plan of action. My first priority would have to be to see Father Donald. I knew that I would have a week's grace due to my ankle, but I felt I must tell him straight out that I wouldn't be returning to St. Grimbald's as his lay reader. What excuse could I use?

I continued to mull over the problem as I showered and dressed. No ready answers came to my mind. Short of citing something as drastic as a "crisis of faith", I couldn't think of any reason why I would want to quit.

In the middle of clipping my beard, now a healthy, glossy Van Dyke of admirable proportions, an idea hit me. I would tell Father Donald that I had been watching an evangelical program on television during my convalescence, one affiliated with the Baptist Church, and that the message had so affected me that I had come to realize the shallowness of my faith, and that I hoped to renew myself by joining the local Baptists, involving myself in their particular brand of Christianity, in which I would be one of the flock and no longer part of the establishment.

I looked at myself in the mirror. How low would I need to go in order to maintain my own security? Lying to my priest about matters of faith seemed to be the bottom of the pit, but I had no choice. If I were to quit, I thought it would break Father Donald's heart. This way, I knew that his kindness would overcome his disappointment. He would rejoice with me in my new-found religious convictions.

I decided to phone Father Donald in order to set up a private appointment with him. Dorothy told me that he was away for the day, but would be home that evening. We agreed that I would come by about seven o'clock.

In our normal routine, Annie and I paused for coffee about mid-morning, sitting at the kitchen table together, where we would be joined by Ollie. I wondered if I should avoid the familiarity of the kitchen-table coffee klatsch in order to establish the more formal employer-employee relationship that I had determined necessary for my safety. However, my courage failed me when I came into the kitchen to see that Annie had already set out our cups. I sank down into my accustomed place, promising myself that I would say something next time.

Annie poured my coffee as she filled my plate with several freshly-baked cookies. "There," she said. "Cinnamon-raisin. Ollie's favourite. Pity he's not here, but there's not much he can do outside in this weather." She took a long sip from her cup. "Ahh! Nothing like that first cup of the day. So," she said, "are you going to the Casino Night tomorrow?"

"Tomorrow? Is it Casino Night already?" Somehow, I hadn't realized that the date for the great occasion had come round. If I planned to fulfill my own resolution to remain apart, I couldn't go to Casino Night. I felt a pang. I had been looking forward to the event.

"No. I don't think so," I told Annie. "My ankle, you know."

"Oh, don't worry about that," Annie replied. "They've got handicap access at the Fire Hall, and besides, it's all on one level."

I sank back into silence, taking refuge in another cookie.

"It's all a mess since Mildred took over the decorating," Annie said. "I thought that nice boy Mattie was doing a fine job, but no, Mildred has to go and change it all at the last minute. People is some upset by her ideas, I'll tell you. None of the fellas wants to have to wear tuxedos. They was much happier with the vests and shirts. And if you ask me, there's something silly about trying to 'make a silk purse out of a sow's ear'. A fire hall is just not the place for a Monte Carlo Casino with all them fancy chandeliers and gold mirrors and flowers, and such. Mildred's on her high horse, as usual. She always did have big ideas, figuring she was better than everybody else. This time, I think she's bit off more than she can chew." She took a bite from a cookie, chewing in silence for a moment. "Now, we's all got to go and help do the decorating tonight," she continued. "There's three rooms if you counts the bar, and they's all got to be done up like a high-class casino." Annie brushed some cookie crumbs from the front of her dress. "Don't even know if I'm going to go, either. I don't have no fancy dress to wear, and Ollie won't want to put on a tie. Only wears 'em to funerals and weddings."

I must admit I felt a sense of vindication for Mattie. Somehow, I couldn't see the male residents of the four Cormorants arriving at the Fire Hall in anything more than the ubiquitous jeans and plaid shirts, which would have been in keeping with Mattie's Wild West theme, but would look ridiculous in the middle of Mildred's Monte Carlo.

"Well, the 'proof of the pudding is in the eating'," Annie said. "We'll just have to wait and see how it all turns out. 'Handsome is as handsome does'. Though if you ask me, it's going to be a disaster, and Mildred's riding for a fall." She ended up with a note of satisfaction in her voice.

I grunted a noncommittal reply.

"'Course, with the A.C.W. out of the picture, what with the Bishop being all upset and everything, they's got to find someone else to cater the food. Mattie was going to have chili and baked beans with homemade bread, something that people could get their teeth into, but Mildred's gone all silly, wanting them little 'horsey-doovers' and things on sticks, and thinking people will be satisfied with no more than a bite of cheese and bit of meat on a cracker. She was even thinking of having no beer, it being 'low class', but once she discovered there wasn't a bottle of wine in the place, and it costing so much more to bring in, and then nobody drinking it, why she backed off that idea. Proper thing, too." She poured us both fresh cups of coffee.

So far, my lack of response had made no difference to Annie.

"So, she's got Kev lined up with that n'er-do-well Clarence to bring in some extra beer for the night, and then she decides to get a bunch of those 'cooler' things that the young people like. Of course, with all her changes, it was too late to get them at the local liquor store, so Kev and Clarence has gone with Ollie into the city to get the 'coolers'. At least she had enough sense not to send those two in on their own. They'd bootleg the booze long before they got back to Cormorant Harbour. Ollie'l keep them in line." She paused to sip her coffee.

I felt constrained to say something. "Does that mean Kevin will be around?"

"Yes. He'll be bringing the supplies over to the Fire Hall tonight."

I wondered if I could waylay him. I would stop by after my interview with Father Donald and tell Kevin to remove his belongings from my shed at once. By tomorrow, two of the biggest stumbling blocks to my peace of mine—my lay readership and my shed—would be taken care of. I had been wise not to cut myself off from Annie's endless fount of information. Perhaps I should reconsider cancelling the coffee times with her.

"Had a bit of excitement yesterday," she continued. "Billy

Barnes stopped by to see me and Ollie. This used to be his family homestead, you know, and we was always close to his Mom and Dad. Hadn't seen him for years. He was asking after the old place, and I told him all about you."

There lay the problem. They were all talking all about me. How could I maintain the anonymity I needed in order to survive if everybody in Cormorant Harbour felt free to discuss me with any stranger who happened by their doors. I had been too open, too trusting, too willing to share my life with them. No more. Starting tonight, a new Charles Trenchant would be born, a man so reclusive that there would be nothing to talk about.

Annie chatted on about her old acquaintance, but I had ceased to listen, lost in my own thoughts about the coming interview with Father Donald. In some ways, I felt I was back at the beginning of my time in Cormorant Harbour, when I still needed to remember the facts and figures about my new identity. Now, I had to remember that the convivial friend of all, the spiritual lay reader of their church, and the benevolent employer and neighbour no longer existed.

Fifteen

I dreaded my upcoming interview with Father Donald. With some trepidation, I set out for the rectory on Friday evening. The day had been muggy and hot, with a lowering, thundery feeling in the air. The ocean glittered white under the hazy sun. Even as I walked, I could see the thunderheads, shot with heat lightning, building up in the west.

I walked gingerly along the road, favouring my ankle a bit, although it was much better, due no doubt to Zerena's professional ministrations. I rehearsed what I would say to Father Donald. Even to my own ears, my excuse for leaving St. Grimbald's sounded improbable, but try as I might, I couldn't come up with anything better. I hoped that Father Donald wouldn't get into the spirit of the thing and rush off to the Baptist pastor with the good news of a new convert. Unlike most ministers who might take umbrage at the thought of a key parishioner going over to the competition, his only concern would be for my happiness. He didn't know that I had no intention of darkening the doors of the Baptist church, or of any church in Cormorant Harbour. The thought made me feel even more guilty.

"Are You Lonesome Tonight?" the doorbell chimed at the rectory. Prophetic, perhaps?

"Do come in, Charles," said Dorothy. "Donald will be with you in a moment. He just ran over to the church with the supplies he picked up from the cathedral today." As she stepped aside, her guitar brooch glittered in the hall lights. Elvis watched us move into the living room.

I avoided the horsehair sofa, opting for a less hazardous seat on the piano bench. Dorothy sat down, smoothing the folds of her pleated skirt. She cleared her throat, preparatory to beginning the usual inquisition.

"How is your ankle? You seem to be getting around very well."

"Fine, thank you." I wished Father Donald would hurry up.

"How is the writing going?"

"Very well," I said, dismayed at my new ability to lie with such ease.

"Have you seen the Jollimores? Are they working on their house?"

"No."

A small silence ensued, broken by an ominous roll of thunder. Dorothy rose to the challenge.

"I do think we shall have a storm. It's been quite hot all day, hasn't it?"

"Yes, quite." The old Charles would have been very forthcoming, but the new Charles kept his own counsel.

"Will we see you in church on Sunday, not as lay reader, of course…?"

"I don't know."

Dorothy took a deep breath.

"And your cat, how is she?"

"Twinkles is fine, thank you."

At this moment, we heard the back door slam. Father Donald rushed into the room, mouthing various apologies for being late. Both Dorothy and I stood up to greet him. I don't know which one of us felt more relief at his entrance.

"Well, I'll just leave you two to chat," said Dorothy. "Perhaps we can have a nice cup of tea when you're done." I knew that my departure from my usual sociable self had aroused Dorothy's suspicions. As she walked by me, she put her hand on my arm, squeezing it as if to encourage me. "I'm sure you'll feel better after a nice chat with Donald, Charles. It always amazes me how many people have said that after a chat with Donald they feel as if they have another perspective on their little problems," she said, dismissing my concerns.

"Well, Charles," said Father Donald, settling down in Dorothy's chair. Before he could say any more, "Are You Lonesome Tonight?" announced another arrival on the rectory doorstep. I hoped it was no one I knew, since I didn't think I could deal with small talk much longer. Dorothy had emptied my reserves of noncommittal responses. As well, I could feel my resolve wavering, because the story I'd prepared in my mind for Father Donald seemed thinner by the moment.

"Donald. It's Boris. Shall I ask him to come back later?" Dorothy stood in the doorway of the living room, with Boris at her side.

We were trapped.

"No, no. Come on in, Boris. You don't mind, do you, Charles? We can continue with our little talk later." Father Donald waved Boris to the sofa. I noticed that Dorothy continued to stand in the doorway.

Boris plunked himself down on the sofa, oblivious to its treacherous qualities. "Don't worry. Won't take long. Hello, Charles. Glad you're here. Might as well hear about it from the horse's mouth."

Boris' voice sounded grim, and I noticed that he looked more dishevelled than usual. He'd been running his hands through his hair and his beard, both of which stood on end.

A bright flush suffused his face, though with anger or excitement, I couldn't tell.

"That's it! I'm done! No more Mr. Nice Organist at St. Grimbald's!" Boris leapt right to the point. "I'm going over to the United Church!"

Father Donald's mouth dropped open.

My heart went out to Father Donald. Little did he know that he would have to deal with not one, but two, deserters tonight.

"The United Church? Reverend Eaton's church? Pamela Eaton's church?" Father Donald seemed to be having difficulty in grasping Boris's announcement.

"Yup! Been after me for months. Finally gave in. Can't take it any longer. It was her or me." Having said his bit, Boris slumped back on the couch. Another roll of thunder shook the room.

"Her? Her, who?"

"Mildred Barkhouse—that's who! Bloody old cow! Oops, sorry Father. But she is. Should be shot. Oops, sorry again. I'm just upset." Boris didn't look sorry. He looked as if he'd like to do the deed himself.

"But, Boris, you can't leave. There's the special anthem on Sunday, and I know that the choir has been practicing for ages, well, not ages, but for some weeks, or at least, many hours, and they're all eager to sing, well, as eager as they ever are, which is more eager than most choirs, some being quite unenthusiastic about their small roles in the church service, although I wouldn't want you to think that your role is small, Boris, on the contrary, it's very important, in fact, one might call it pivotal, what with me being totally unmusical and we don't really want Dottie to feel that she must take up the musical torch, what with all the other things she has to do, it would be too stressful, and I can't imagine St. Grimbald's without you. You can't leave! For the United Church! They don't deserve you!" Tears sprang to Father Donald's eyes. I wondered how he would handle my news?

Dorothy had remained in the doorway throughout the scene.

"Mildred Barkhouse! I might have known." She crossed the room and sat down beside Boris. "How dreadful for you," she said, patting his knee. "Whatever has she done now?"

Boris's eyes flashed fire. "Long story. Too sordid to tell. Suffice to say, she hurt Mattie's feelings. Insulted me. Threatened us both. Unforgivable. Then had the nerve to turn up at *my* choir practice. Caused a real ruckus. No choice for me but to throw in the towel. Otherwise, she'll wreak havoc on this church. Split it right down the middle. Don't want to go. Like St. Grimbald's, admire you and Dorothy, enjoy working with Charles. Have no other choice." He ran his hands through his beard with a distracted air.

"Now, Boris, dear, I'm sure we can come up with some other solution to the problem. Frankly, I'd rather see Mildred out the door than you." I noted an edge of excitement in Dorothy's voice. If anyone would champion Boris's cause, it would be Dorothy, primed to turn on her arch rival.

However, I knew that it wouldn't be that simple. Any resolution to the problem would create a schism within the little parish. I had never been on the receiving end of Mildred's particular brand of nastiness, and if I hadn't known Sherri, Bev and Boris, I might have found myself siding with those parishioners who thought her to be a wonderful organizer and faithful supporter of the church.

"Yes! Yes! Dottie's right. There must be a better solution. Charles is here, so let's all put our heads together and see what we can come up with. Perhaps a word of prayer will help…" He bowed his head, preparatory to launching into an impassioned plea to a higher power.

"Are You Lonesome Tonight?" forestalled his opening words.

"Oh, shoot! Now, who? Dottie, will you get that?"

Dorothy bustled to the front door. We could hear a babble of voices echoing in the hall. It sounded like half Cormorant Harbour waited on the rectory doorstep.

Etta Fay burst into the front room, followed by a young woman wearing a clerical collar which looked incongruous with her blue jeans. Her sweatshirt proclaimed "Save the Seals". I'd never met her but decided that she must be the Reverend Pamela Eaton of the United Church. Behind her stood a large, florid man dressed in a black suit with a string tie, clutching a big, black Bible to his chest like a shield. I could see a number of people crowding into the hall. Some were carrying placards. Dorothy tried in vain to shut the door, but they continued to pour in.

"Etta Fay! Reverend Eaton! Reverend Quoil!" Father Donald stood up, his face creased in puzzlement. "Oh, dear. Have I missed the Ministerial Meeting again?"

"Brother Peasgood, you've missed a lot more than a Ministerial Meeting. That's why we're here." The large man advanced on Father Donald until they were almost toe-to-toe. "Sin and perdition are afoot in our community, and one of your sheep is leading the innocent lambs astray. I hold you spiritually responsible, 'for if a man know not how to rule his own house, how shall he take care of the church of God?', 1 Timothy 3:5, And verse 8: 'Likewise must the deacons be grave, not doubletongued, not given to much wine, not greedy of filthy lucre.'" He paused, tossing back his thick white mane, a practiced move, made even more dramatic by the peal of thunder that accompanied it.

"Oh, give it a rest, Quoil. We haven't got all night to listen to you parade chapter and verse. Let's get down to business."

Reverend Eaton, although younger by several decades, elbowed him aside.

"'But I suffer not a woman to teach, nor to usurp authority over a man, but to be in silence'. 1 Timothy 3:12. Reverend Quoil waved his Bible under her nose. "The Word of God," he announced, "tells us all we need to know."

The two glared at each other. Etta Fay took advantage of the impasse. "It's the gambling, Father Donald. It's not right. And the drinking, too. Mildred Barkhouse has got to be stopped. It's a shame on our church that she's the one who is running this disgraceful thing."

The crowd in the hall murmured in agreement. A wave of "Amens" and "Preach it sister", interspersed with "Yes, yes", "Right on", and "You're right" backed up her words. They waved their placards in righteous enthusiasm. I read several of the scrawled messages. "Down with Gambling!", "Sin no More!", "No Casino Night!", "Prepare to meet Thy God!" Dorothy leaped in front of her Elvis poster, no doubt trying to protect it from the waving signs.

"Some of us are going to march on the Fire Hall. They're all in there, decorating for tomorrow night." Etta Fay waved her arm in the direction of the crowd in the hall. I could see several of her cronies, including the ladies I'd first met at Sherri's. This did not bode well for Father Donald. Others in his congregation shared Etta Fay's opposition to Casino Night.

"They are preparing the Den of Iniquity for the night of debauchery to come," Reverend Quoil said in a sepulchral voice, the tone more suitable for a pulpit than the Peasgood living room. "I have rallied my Baptist brethren to come with me, and as Jesus did in the temple, we will cast out the money-changers."

The penny dropped. I identified him as the Reverend

Quoil, the Baptist minister of the congregation that I had been prepared to adopt as my own. I sent up a prayer of thanksgiving that I had not yet had an opportunity to use my feeble excuse on Father Donald. Just the thought of being under the spiritual guidance of this Bible-thumping, chauvinistic anachronism made my blood run cold. I'd have to think up another excuse to leave St. Grimbald's.

"Oh, let's not get into all this religious hoo-ha," Reverend Eaton snapped. "The point is, Donald, they're drinking and they're gambling. Both of which are the biggest social problems in our society today. We need to be the conscience of our community, to stand firm on issues that affect all of us. It is our duty to…"

Reverend Quoil cut her off in mid sentence. "Brother Peasgood, I'm calling on you to join with the sons of light to battle this evil among us. Together, we'll march into the camp of the enemy and the Gates of Hell shall not prevail before us."

In the hall, the crowd began to sing "Onward Christian Soldiers."

Reverend Eaton grimaced in disgust. "Oh, for heaven's sake!" she said. "Are we going to have to listen to that noise all night? I really don't see the place of music and hymns in the social fabric of the church in the modern world. It's positively mediaeval."

I saw Boris's face fall. His enthusiasm for joining the United Church had sunk to the same low point as my own had for joining the Baptists.

Throughout, Father Donald had been standing as if pole-axed, looking at each speaker with open-mouthed amazement. Several times, he turned to Dorothy for support, but her involvement with the crowd pressing forward in the hall kept her occupied.

"'So, then, because thou art lukewarm and neither cold nor hot, I will spew thee out of my mouth'. Revelation 3:16. The Lord is calling you, Brother Peasgood. Are you with us or not?"

"Umm, er…" Father Donald managed. "Well, yes. Indeed. Oh my stars! Oh my soul! Shoot!"

He sounded pretty lukewarm to me, but it seemed to be all that Reverend Quoil needed. With a loud, "Forward, Brethren." He clutched Father Donald's arm and led him through the cheering crowd in the hall, who had now switched to a boisterous "We Shall Overcome".

Soon, only Boris, Dorothy and I were left in the rectory.

"C'mon, you two," said Boris. "Let's go. Wouldn't miss this for the world. Better'n a front row seat at a Las Vegas prize fight."

Dorothy patted her hair back in place, straightened the poster on the wall and turned to us, her face a mask of self-righteous triumph. "Indeed," she said. "We must be there to support Donald. Come along, Charles."

She took my elbow in a firm grasp, and I found myself being propelled down the steps and onto the sidewalk. By now, the thunder rolled in continuous waves, although no rain fell. Brilliant flashes of lightning lit up the night sky. The heat and humidity, greater now than earlier in the day, felt overwhelming. I longed for the storm to break, even if it meant a soaking on the walk home.

The procession straggled across the firehall parking lot, the crowd continuing to swell, no doubt joined by most of Cormorant Harbour who didn't want to miss the fun.

I might have extricated myself from Dorothy's grasp and melted away into the crowd, but I saw Kevin Jollimore's truck parked at the back of the building. This reminded me of the next item on my list. At last I could tell him to get everything out of my shed. With this resolve, I moved forward with the crowd.

Sixteen

The Four Cormorants Fire Hall, a long, low building, with the front half given over to the garages and equipment of the fire department, had the back half partitioned off into several small meeting rooms around one large, central room which featured a bar. A door on the side of the building led through a short hallway into this room and the meeting areas. A separate entrance on the back wall of the building gave access to the kitchen.

The crowd streamed past the large garage doors on the front, continued down the side of the building to the meeting area. Reverend Eaton's youth had given her an edge over Reverend Quoil and the reluctant Rather Donald so that she had sprinted ahead of them to lead the crowd, still singing and waving placards, into the main room.

By the time Boris, Dorothy and I brought up the rear, the decorating activities had come to a halt under the onslaught of the protesters. Mildred's decorating crew, holding festoons of silver garlands, flashy mirrors, gaming wheels and balloons glared at Reverend Quoil's self-styled "army of God". The good Reverend lost no time in launching into a sermon on the evils of gambling and the demon rum, his deep voice booming around the room. Reverend Eaton and her supporters were busy handing out pamphlets, no doubt a product of some government study on the social ramifications of alcohol consumption and gambling. The decorating crew either tore these up into small pieces or threw them back at the distributors. Loud altercations began to break out around the room as the decorators realized they were under attack. In one corner, several people joined in a scuffle as two protesters began to pull down the crêpe paper streamers festooned over the bar. Mildred, alerted by the commotion, charged in from the kitchen area, waving a broom, scattering protesters left and right.

"Get out! Get out!" she screamed. "What do you think you're doing? Get out!"

She took several swats at Reverend Quoil, who deflected them with his Bible, not missing a beat in his sermonizing.

Unaware of the drama unfolding in the main room, a disembodied voice kept repeating, "Testing, testing, One, two, three. Testing," over the loudspeakers.

"Turn that goddam thing off," Ollie shouted from his position on one of the ladders.

Ollie's profanity spiralled Reverend Quoil into a frenzy of righteous wrath. "'O generation of vipers, who hath warned you to flee from the wrath to come? Bring forth, therefore, fruits meet for repentance.' Matthew 3, verses 7 and 8." The continuing peals of thunder and flashes of lightning gave a prophetic aura to his rantings.

I looked to see what had happened to Father Donald, and I saw that he'd taken advantage of Reverend Quoil's distraction to edge towards the laden refreshment table set up for the workers.

Boris chortled in my ear. "Wish I had a camcorder," he said. "*America's Funniest Home Videos* ain't got nothing on this. God, wish Mattie was here. He'd love every minute."

By this time, the two sides had ranged themselves into opposing lines in the middle of the room, with Mildred in the forefront of her crew, and the Reverends Quoil and Eaton and Etta Fay with the "army of God" facing them.

Dorothy dropped my arm and marched to the front of the lines, where she stood shoulder-to-shoulder with Etta Fay and eye-to-eye with Mildred Barkhouse. I began to surreptitiously sidle around the two groups, hoping to make my way to the kitchen area, where I thought I might find Kevin.

Before I reached the doorway, a loud crash came from the kitchen, followed by the unmistakable tones of The Voice. "Kevin! You careless son of a bitch. That's a whole case of beer on the floor!"

The Voice stunned the room into a momentary silence. Even Reverend Quoil stuttered to a halt.

"Oh, my God. The effin' beer," muttered Ollie. "I shouldna left those two goddam boobies unload it alone." He climbed down his ladder and headed for the kitchen.

Mildred turned on her heel. "I don't have time for this nonsense," she declared as she walked away. "There's work to be done, and nothing you say or do will make any difference. Casino Night will go on as planned," she threw out over her shoulder. "Now, if you'll excuse me, I'm needed in the kitchen."

With Mildred's exit, the crowd broke up into small clusters of people who continued to argue amongst themselves. Reverend Quoil and Reverend Eaton trailed after Mildred, followed by several others, including Dorothy, Etta Fay and Boris. They all swept past me into the kitchen, and I joined them, still hoping to catch up with Kevin. The odour of spilled beer hung on the air.

I got stuck behind Dorothy and Boris, whose combined bulks blocked the doorway, so I couldn't see into the kitchen. A screech from Mildred cut over the babble of the crowd and echoed across the room.

"You worthless scum!" she screamed. "Get your filthy hands off my daughter! I know all about you Hubleys and your tricks."

Although I could still see nothing of the kitchen, I surmised from her words that Mildred had found Clarence and Bev together.

"Beverly may be naïve enough to believe that you want her, but I know better," Mildred continued, acid dripping from her voice. "You're just after her for the money she'll have when I'm gone. God knows—there's no other reason for a sex-mad animal like you to sniff around her. We all know you're getting it regular from that little slut you're shacked up with."

Frustration overwhelmed me when I realized I couldn't see the happenings in the kitchen. Even on tiptoe, Dorothy's height forestalled any chance of a view.

"Mother!" I recognized Bev's voice, filled with anguish. "How could you? Clarence, tell her it isn't true."

"Don't bother with your Hubley lies!" Mildred cut in. "Just because your whore of a sister managed to trap Kevin doesn't mean that you'll get away with the same thing."

A collective gasp rose from the crowd. I heard Dorothy suck in her breath, though whether with shock or delight, I couldn't tell.

"Oh, ho!" whispered Boris. "The game's afoot!"

"Now you just wait a goddam minute!" The Voice reverberated on the air. Even though I knew the scene had nothing to do with me, I still cringed at the venom in her voice. "Who are you calling a 'whore'?"

I heard several sniggers from the crowd behind me.

Mildred's voice rose, cold as ice. "I told Kevin eight years ago that you were nothing but a piece of Hubley trash, and I haven't changed my mind."

A resounding slap followed these words. Bev screamed.

Several people tried to push past me, but we were all blocked from the kitchen.

"Right on!" said Boris, punching the air with his fist. "Wanted to do that myself a few times."

"Oh, shit, Arleen! Now you've done it," I heard Kevin say.

"Screw you and your whole goddam family!" The Voice replied. The back door slammed with a resounding thud.

"'As a jewel of gold in a swine's snout, so is a fair woman that is without discretion.' Proverbs 11, verse 22." The sanctimonious voice rose above the babble of the crowd.

"Oh, shut up, Quoil," snapped Reverend Eaton.

Dorothy turned back to me. "Don't look, Charles," she admonished. "Women brawling in public. It's too disgraceful." Despite her words, I noted the look of satisfaction on her face, betraying her pleasure in the scene.

I took advantage of Dorothy's movement to thrust my way between them. I found myself looking at Mildred. She sat on the floor amidst the broken beer bottles, her skirt rucked up about her thighs, her hair uncharacteristically mussed. A large puddle of beer, edged with foam, seeped out from around her. On her cheek flared a bright red welt, the shape of the fingers of her assailant's hand. It stood out against the chalky white of her face. Sherri knelt beside her.

Clarence and Beverly attempted to help her up.

"Get your hands off me," she snarled at them. "I don't need anyone's help." With some difficulty, she grabbed the edge of the counter to pull herself upright. Avoiding the eyes of the avid onlookers, she straightened her beer-stained skirt and patted her hair into place.

Drawing in a deep breath, she turned to the two reverends. "You're my witnesses," she said. "You saw what happened. She assaulted me. I'm going to bring charges against her."

"I'm sorry, Sister Barkhouse, I will not be a party to a lawsuit. 'Dare any of you, having a matter against another, go to law before the unjust, and not before the saints?' First Corinthians 6, verse 1. It is against my principles." Reverend Quoil spun around, the crowd parted before him like the Red Sea to Moses as he stalked out of the kitchen.

"Get back here, Quoil." Reverend Eaton went after him. "Put your money where your mouth is," I heard her say. Their voices rose in argument from the other room.

"Now, Auntie," Kevin began. "You can't do that. We don't have no money for anything legal."

"No, and you never will have, either," Mildred snapped. "If you think I'm leaving any of my money to you to spend on that slut, you've got another think coming. First thing Monday morning, I'm going to my lawyer and having my will changed. We'll see how long Arleen hangs around once she knows there's no money in the offing. And that goes for you, too, Beverly. Clarence won't be wasting any more time on you, either. I'm leaving all my money to St. Grimbald's."

"Oh my stars!" I heard Father Donald mutter behind me. His face appeared between Dorothy and Boris who still filled the doorway.

"Mother! You can't," Bev wailed. She tried to take Mildred's hand, but Mildred snatched it away.

"I can and I will. I've looked after you all these years, putting a roof over your head and food on your plate, and this is the thanks I get." Mildred folded her arms and glared at Beverly. "Sneaking off behind my back to consort with trash like Clarence Hubley. Just like you did with Randy Izzard, and if it wasn't for me, you'd be stuck with his little bastard."

Beverly's face blanched. She gasped. For a moment, I thought she might faint. Sherri put her arm around her cousin.

Mildred continued, her voice cold and hard. "All these years, never a word of reproach for all the suffering you've put me through." For a brief moment, I saw an expression of regret cross Mildred's face. Had she realized that she'd gone too far?

Etta Fay, who had been watching the whole scene with avid attention, turned white. She pushed past Beverly and Sherri, grabbed the front of Mildred's dress and demanded: "What did you say about my Randy? There was a baby? Nobody ever told me nothing about any baby. What did you do with my grandbaby?" I saw her eyes bright with tears.

Mildred shook herself free from Etta Fay's grasping fingers. "A grandbastard you mean. Maybe Ollie and Annie didn't care about Sherri bringing a bastard in their family, but I have higher standards than that. There's no way I would let my Beverly marry someone like your precious Randy." Mildred's voice rose in righteous indignation. "Didn't even have a proper job. Couldn't support his ownself, much less my Beverly. No doubt he thought he'd live off my money. Well, I showed him!" She pushed Etta Fay away. "No point bringing a baby into that kind of mess. That's what I told Beverly then, and that's what I still believe."

Etta Fay swung around to face Bev. "A baby, Bev? Why didn't you tell me?" she asked in a quavering voice.

"Oh, Mrs. Izzard, I'm so sorry," Bev sobbed. "Mother wouldn't let me tell you about the baby, and Randy had already left for Calgary. I didn't know what to do."

Etta Fay groped for a chair. She slumped down at the table, her face blank and slack with the shock of Mildred's revelation.

Dorothy's voice cut through the general babble that had arisen with Mildred's sudden airing of the family's dirty laundry. Her eyes glittered. "Poor Mildred. I'm afraid this has all been too much for her. I did think that taking on the duties of such a large event at her age might prove to be an onerous task, especially with so many people being against it," she told the group.

With a small smile of commiseration, she turned to Beverly. "I'm sure your mother never meant to let your dreadful secret out, dear, since it reflects so badly upon herself. I hope you will find it in your heart to forgive her. After all, she is your mother, and although she may be labouring under mental stress at the moment, with some professional help, she will be her old self again. Under the circumstances, I'm sure you'll all agree that it might be best if Casino Night were cancelled." She fingered her brooch and continued. "Mildred, dear, Donald and I will be only too happy to take you along to the hospital. They can check out that nasty blow you received and give you a little something to calm your nerves."

An enormous flash of lightning, followed by an ominous roll of thunder shook the room. The electric lights flickered, went out, and then came back on.

"How dare you!" Mildred screeched. She threw herself at Dorothy, fingers curved into talons as if to scratch out Dorothy's eyes. Dorothy stepped back in alarm, and only the quick thinking of Sherri who threw her arms around her aunt prevented Mildred from reaching her target.

"Oh my stars! Oh my soul! Dottie! You stepped on my foot." Father Donald leapt about on one leg. Boris moved aside as Father Donald lurched towards him. Father Donald hobbled across the kitchen and collapsed in a chair at the table.

"Oh my soul. I hope it isn't broken," he said, looking at Dorothy. "I won't be able to drive Mildred to the hospital, although I'm sure you could drive, Dorothy, that is if you're not too upset, although it isn't far and you have had your pill today, haven't you?"

"Shut up, Donald." Dorothy snapped at him.

Father Donald lapsed into a hurt silence, rubbing his foot as he looked around the room for sympathy. When none was forthcoming, he fished in his pocket for a mint, popped it in his mouth and sucked it with gusto.

Mildred wrenched herself out of Sherri's grip. "Get your hands off of me, young lady. You're just as bad as the rest of them. Taking, taking and taking from me, with never a word of thanks or gratitude for all I've done. Well, I'm through with you, too. I want my money, and I want it Monday. If not, I'm going to report you."

Sherri fell back with a gasp. "Oh, Auntie. Please don't…" she began.

"Now, Mildred. You don't want to be doing that," said Ollie. He came and stood beside his daughter. "She hasn't done nothing to you."

Mildred ignored both of them and swung back towards Dorothy. Boris immediately placed his bulk in front of Dorothy, as if to protect her.

"Get out of my way, you pervert," Mildred hissed. She kicked out and landed a sharp blow on his shins. "I'm not finished with you yet."

Boris gasped in pain and hopped over to join Father Donald at the table, who offered him a mint.

Mildred thrust her face within inches of Dorothy's nose. "How dare you?" she repeated. "Telling everyone that I'm crazy. Well, all I can say is that it takes one to know one. Maybe other people here think that you're the wonderful, upright sister of our rector, but I know the whole story. My cousin Norma Jean is the clerk in the Seal Cove RCMP office. She told me all about you and what happened there. No wonder the bishop moved you out of that parish."

I saw Dorothy go rigid, her face flushing a painful red. Father Donald stood up in alarm. He started to cough violently, no doubt having swallowed his mint. Boris pounded his back.

Dorothy cleared her throat hard several times. Her chest heaved. "What happened in Seal Cove is none of your business, Mildred Barkhouse," she said, underlining her words with jabs of her forefinger in Mildred's face. "You say one word, your cousin is out of a job, and you'll be in court. I'll sue you for slander. You may be able to push everybody else around, but not me. I'm not one of your minions, nor am I a member of your miserable family. You can't bully me!" This last she said with bravado, pulling herself to her full height and towering over Mildred.

Mildred laughed in scorn. "You can't sue me! What you did is common knowledge in Seal Harbour. Everybody there knows what you did. After all, half the community was there when it happened."

The room fell silent. Even I held my breath, waiting for the next revelation.

Before Mildred could open her mouth, the cacophony of the fire siren, which howled from the front fire hall, split the air. A dozen beepers began to sound. In moments, the people around me sprang into action, all thoughts of the impending revelation forgotten as volunteer firefighters ran for the trucks. Father Donald limped after them.

"It's at Kevin Jollimore's house!" a voice yelled from the doorway.

"Not again!" said a second voice.

"Not tonight!" said Clarence. "It's not supposed to be tonight. Oh, shit. Arleen'll kill us."

"Shut up, Clarence," snarled Kevin.

Several people sniggered. I heard Ollie snort.

"Get the food from the refreshment table," Mildred ordered, back in command. "Sherri, take the coffee pots and the sandwiches. Beverly, bring the van around." Both women dropped into their automatic auxiliary modes as they hastened to obey.

Etta Fay stood up, a look of grim determination crossing her face.

"Mildred," she began, "I have to talk to you."

"Not now!" snapped Mildred. "Besides, there's nothing to talk about." Without even a glance at Etta Fay, she headed out of the room, shouting orders as she went.

Etta Fay turned to Ollie. "I need a ride," she told him. "Are you going out to the fire?"

"Yup. Car's out back. Let's go. Don't want to miss nothing." Ollie hustled Annie and Etta Fay through the door.

"C'mon, Dorothy. You, too, Charles. Let's go see the action. Maybe Kev got it right this time." Boris herded us out of the kitchen. Dorothy seemed too spent to protest. As for me, I knew that whatever the outcome of Kevin's latest fire, the damning evidence lay in my shed, and no one would ever believe that I'd played no part in the lucky strike plot.

I hadn't been able to speak to Kevin, nor had I spoken to Father Donald. Nothing had changed. Even now, Boris and Dorothy, two people I had planned to avoid, herded me along with them. I seemed doomed to be involved in this community.

I would have to be proactive. As soon as Boris dropped me off at Innisfree, I would pack a small suitcase, and Twinkles and I would go to Halifax. How long we would stay there depended solely on the outcome of the Jollimore fire.

In minutes, the hall cleared, with nothing more left to show for the evening's mayhem than the abandoned placards on the floor, and the spilled beer in the kitchen.

Seventeen

We pulled up behind the phalanx of vehicles and parked in Lupin Loop. It looked to me as if everyone in Cormorant Harbour had turned out for the show. Lightning flashed in the dark sky as the thunder continued to roll overhead.

This time, any hope that the fire would create minimal damage on the Jollimore shack died before the huge flames leaping up into the sky. We could feel the heat of the fire on our faces as we clambered out of the car. The thick black smoke roiling up into the air filled our lungs.

A great gasp went up from the crowd as part of the roof caved in, sending up a huge fountain of sparks. I could hear people shouting and saw them dodging back and forth, trying to avoid the falling embers. Streams of water blasted the sides of the building, their arcs illuminated against the sky by the flames. If anything, the fire grew more fierce, causing several firefighters to pull back to safety. I looked for Father Donald but couldn't distinguish him from the rest of the crew in their bulky safety gear.

The fire held Dorothy and Boris's attention, so I took the opportunity to edge back towards my house. I'd pack, get Twinkles and be gone before anyone would miss me. To my horror, I saw two firemen directing a stream of water onto my roof. My God! My house was on fire, too! Twinkles! My heart stopped.

I tried to push past my gate, but Ollie and one of the local constabulary stopped me.

"Twinkles!" I gasped. "My cat! She's inside."

"Don't worry, Mr. Trenchant," said Ollie. "Everything's under control."

"The fire hose is just a precautionary measure with all those sparks flying," the constable explained. "If there's any real danger of your house going up, we'll send someone in for your cat." He patted my shoulder as if to reassure me. "Just stay out here on the road until things calm down a bit."

"Annie 'n me'll be in tomorrow to clean up the mess. Don't you worry none about that." Ollie looked at the shed and back to me. "We'll get it all cleared out for you," he said, with a sideways glance at the constable. "Get rid of a lot of old junk you don't need while we're at it."

I found myself trying *not* to look at my shed. If only a stray spark would land there, all my arson troubles would be over.

I wandered back over to Boris and Dorothy and rejoined the crowd of onlookers.

"I can't think why I let you persuade me to come along, Boris," Dorothy said. "I generally try not to think about Donald's fires. I do hope he knows what he's doing. It looks very dangerous to me. I should have stayed at home. Whatever was I thinking?" Dorothy walked away from us. "I don't want to watch. I shall go and wait in the car," she called back to us.

"Poor old Dorothy," said Boris. "Terrible business with Mildred." He smirked as he winked at me. "Must be 'all shook up', eh? Wonder what Mildred was going to tell us about her. Trust Mildred to dig up the dirt. The way she's going, we could form a "Anti Mildred" support group. Me 'n

Mattie, and Dorothy, even Bev and Sherri, throw in Kevin and his crowd. The list goes on."

A huge sheet of flame flared up as the fire found a fresh hold. Boris rubbed his hands together. "Wow! What a fire! Wonder if I can get a closer look?" He pressed forward, and I lost him in the crowd.

At this point, the Auxiliary Van arrived and stopped near me. The door flung open, scraping my shoulder. Sherri and Bev stumbled out, both looking with awe at the fire before them.

"Don't stand there gaping!" Mildred's voice cut over the roar of the flames. "Go and find out where they want us to set up."

Both women remained in place, transfixed by the sight.

"Awful, isn't it?" I said to Sherri. "Looks like Kevin will lose the whole place this time."

"What? Oh, I didn't see you, Charles." Sherri turned to me in surprise.

Bev said nothing, and I could see from her face that her thoughts were far away from the fire before her.

"Beverly! Sherri! Get going. We don't have all night!"

I could feel the anger rise within me. I seldom lost my temper, but this time, something that had been lurking beneath the surface ever since the A.C.W. Chowder Luncheon, broke free.

"Tell her to go fly a kite!" I said to the women. "Why do you let her boss you around like that? You don't owe her anything after the way she treated you tonight." I slammed the van door shut.

Sherri started as if I'd smacked her. Bev shook her head in bewilderment.

"You don't need to listen to her. She doesn't have a hold

over you any more. No matter what you do now, she'll still call in your loan, Sherri, and as for you, Bev, well, what more can she do than she's already done to hurt you tonight?" I shocked myself with my forwardness. Eric Spratt never meddled in other people's business, but Charles Trenchant could remain silent no longer.

I heard the door open on the other side of the van and braced myself for the confrontation to come. By the time Mildred reached my side of the van, both Bev and Sherri had disappeared. I presumed they'd taken my advice.

"Where are those girls?" Mildred demanded.

"I don't know," I stammered, my newfound bravado dissipating under Mildred's glare. "I suppose they've gone to find out where to put the van."

Mildred snorted in disgust and returned to her seat behind the wheel. The door slammed. The van lurched off towards the Jollimore driveway.

Through the clouds of smoke, I could see Kevin and Clarence standing on the driveway, gape-mouthed as the flames continued to roar. Their faces glowed, whether with success or from the reflection of the flames, I couldn't tell. I wondered how they'd done it this time. I thought this might be a good opportunity to let Kevin know that Ollie would be removing his possessions from my shed in the morning.

Before I could get to them, The Voice rose above the din around me, calling from somewhere down the driveway. "Kevin! Where the hell are you? She's *here!*"

Kevin and Clarence followed the sound of The Voice and sloped off.

I decided to return to my house and see how things were going. I had only gone a few steps, when the sight of the mystery SUV, parked next to my gate, stopped me in my tracks. Where had it come from? To my horror, the two men who had cased the house and broken into my kitchen stood deep in conversation with Ollie. I debated creeping closer to find out what they were talking about, but my good sense got the better of such a rash decision. I should remain out of sight, I decided. I got down on my hands and knees and crept along the verge, keeping well hidden behind the line of cars between me and the SUV.

"Whatever are you doing, Mr. Trenchant?" I looked up and saw Annie standing over me.

"Um, er…" I racked my brain. "I…er…dropped a contact lens," I explained, groping around me in the weeds. Even I heard the thinness of my excuse.

"Well, you'll never find it tonight," she said. "It's worse than a needle in a haystack. You'll have to wait until morning, and even then, I doubt you'll have much luck."

I glanced over my shoulder. The smoke and the darkness hid me from view. Feeling bold, I stood up next to Annie.

"Have you seen Etta Fay?" she asked me. "She came out here with Ollie 'n me, and I was wondering if she wanted a ride back home. She took off like a scared rabbit the minute we got here, and I ain't seen hide nor hair of her since. I hope she's all right. She was some shook up back at the firehall, I thought."

Before I could answer, the rest of the Jollimore roof gave way with a thundering crash. As if in sympathy, the heavens opened, and the storm broke in torrents of rain. Within seconds, it had soaked everyone and everything. Hissing and sizzling, followed by clouds of steam, replaced the earlier roar of the flames and the billowing smoke.

People ran for their cars and trucks, firemen shouted orders to one another, the rain continued to bucket down, lightning lashed and the thunder rolled, showers of sparks flew upwards from the final burning moments of the Jollimore house. Greasy ash covered everything, including me. The stench choked us all. With the rain acting as a grey curtain across the scene and the fire no longer a spectacular sight, the crowds began to disperse. I looked around for Boris but couldn't see him. I presumed Dorothy had escaped the deluge in his car and thought I might join her, waiting out the SUV and its occupants.

Annie and I stumbled along in the darkness and wet, she looking for Etta Fay and I for Boris's car. As we picked our way along the road, blinded by sheets of rain, I bumped into another person coming from the opposite direction. I grabbed her before she could fall, and to my surprise, realized I had Etta Fay Izzard in my arms.

"Are you all right?" I asked her.

"I've been looking for you. Do you want to go home now?" Annie sounded solicitous.

Rain and soot streaked Etta Fay's face, plastering her hair to her birdlike skull. Her thin frame shivered as if the cold rain had penetrated to her very bones.

"You're soaked through," Annie continued. "Come with me. There's an old blanket in the truck. You're going to catch your death of cold. I'll get you home right away and come back for Ollie later."

Annie took Etta Fay's thin arm, guiding her to her truck. "If you see Ollie, tell him I won't be long," she called back to me.

I continued on to look for Boris's car. When I found it, to my surprise, no one waited inside. I wondered where Dorothy had gone. Maybe she'd decided to track down Father Donald. I hoped she hadn't set out for home on her own. She'd be in for a long walk on a very dark wet night.

I sank down into the anonymity of Boris's back seat, where I resolved to wait out the SUV and the rain.

Minutes after I settled in, the front door opened and Dorothy clambered inside.

"Oh, Charles. Isn't it raining buckets? At least it will put a damper on the fire. Too little, too late, I'm afraid, for the Jollimores." I wondered where she'd been all this time. Below her flushed face, her ample bosom heaved under the flowered dress now plastered to her body by the rain. She brushed at her hair and shoulders, wiping off the rain. "I'm soaked through," she complained.

Her hands stilled, then with frantic pats, she began to explore her bosom. She flicked on the dome light, pulled down the visor mirror and peered into it.

"My brooch!" she said in alarm. She dropped down and fumbled on the floor of the car. "It's gone! I've lost my brooch!" She wriggled forward and ran her hands over the seat, pushing down between the cushions. "I was sitting in the back earlier," she said. "Is it back there, Charles?"

I looked about me and shook my head. Dorothy wrenched open the door, got out, and joined me in the search of the back seat, to no avail. To my horror, Dorothy fell onto the seat beside me and burst into tears, a reaction I thought far more severe than a mere loss of costume jewelry warranted.

"Was it very valuable?" I asked.

"Priceless!" she sobbed. "I bought it on my trip to Graceland. It has never left my person since that moment. I can't think what could have happened to it. I must have lost it somewhere." She looked out the window at the scene of utter confusion around the Jollimore bungalow.

If she'd dropped it among that mess, she might as well

kiss it goodbye, I thought but didn't say aloud.

"You'll have to wait until the morning to search for it," I told her, thinking to give her some shred of hope.

She ignored my words and threw herself back in her seat, tears running unchecked down her face. I gave her knee a couple of tentative pats, hoping to comfort her.

At this juncture, Boris returned. He opened the car door, plopped down in the driver's seat, gave one startled glance at Dorothy, raised an eyebrow and said, "What's up with her?"

"She's lost her brooch," I began.

A pounding on the window prevented me from explaining further. We could see Ollie's face peering in through the curtains of rain that still fell. Boris rolled down the window.

"They've found Mildred!" The words tumbled out of Ollie's mouth. "Behind the van. Deader'n a effin' mackerel!"

Dorothy gasped and exclaimed, "Dead? Mildred Barkhouse's dead?"

"How?" Boris asked. "Can't be a heart attack. She didn't have one."

"What happened? I just saw her a little while ago," I said. "She was fine then."

"Murder," said Ollie with relish. "That's what done her in. Murder. Found her with a goddam great knife a-stickin' up out'n her chest."

Eighteen

I'd stumbled to bed in the early hours, cold and exhausted. It seemed only moments later when the jarring ring of the telephone brought me out of a deep dreamless sleep.

"Charles! Charles! You've got to come right away. Oh my soul! Did I wake you up? Well, of course I did, didn't I? I'm so sorry, but it's a matter of life and death. Well, of death anyway. Not my death. Or Dorothy's. Although I suppose it could be, but then, we don't have the death penalty, do we? Although on the other hand, she couldn't possibly have done it, could she? She was with you, wasn't she? Or at least, you were with her, weren't you? That is, you were both together. There. At the fire. Boris saw you, didn't he?" His voice rose. "Didn't he?"

My fuddled brain tried to make sense of Father Donald's incoherent ravings. "Whaa..?"

"Last night! They're coming for her. Well, not *them*, but Sergeant Bickerton is, at least I think he is, although sometimes he sends Constable Blair, a nice fellow, but not too bright, I've always thought, although I have no real evidence of that, except he does tend to ramble when you try to get some sense from him. When I was talking to him about the stolen communion wine, he was quite useless. Although there isn't much you can do when the bottle is empty, can you? It's gone! He didn't seem to be able to grasp

176

this point, and I was perfectly clear in my explanation to him regarding the matter. Oh, I do hope they don't send Constable Blair. I'm sure he's not going to be a sympathetic ally, especially since Dottie called him an 'incompetent nincompoop'. I told her at the time it wasn't a good idea to alienate the police, and now look what's happened…" He sucked in a noisy breath that ended in a sob.

"What's…happened?" I managed to string the two words together.

"What? Oh my stars! Oh my soul! You don't know? Although, how could you know. No one knows. Except Sergeant Bickerton. Even he doesn't really know. It's just preliminary he says. Whatever that means. Preliminary to what? A lynching? A lynch mob at the rectory? Oh my stars! Surely it won't come to that!"

I could tell that I wasn't going to get any sense out of him. "I'll be right there," I said, hanging up.

Sergeant Bickerton and I arrived at the rectory at the same time. "Are You Lonesome Tonight?" brought Dorothy and Donald to the door. Both looked white and strained. Sergeant Bickerton cast an inquiring glance at me.

"Oh, it's all right, Sergeant. I asked Charles to come over," Father Donald said.

"Is he your lawyer?" asked Sergeant Bickerton.

"No, oh my stars, no! A lawyer! I didn't think of calling a lawyer. Do you know any lawyers, Charles? Someone from the city perhaps. Someone really good. Although not too expensive. I read about the fellow who had to pay thousands of dollars just to convince the lawyer to take the case. Although he did get the client off, so I suppose that makes a difference. Not that money can buy a jury or a judge, at least not here in Canada, although I do know that some judges are more lenient than others. Oh, I do hope we get a good judge for you, Dottie. Someone who is sympathetic to women, especially women with nervous complaints."

At this point, I regretted my precipitous arrival at the rectory. The presence of the police put a different perspective on the situation ("Don't draw attention to yourself. Don't even get a speeding ticket."), and here I sat, smack in the middle of God knows what.

"Charles is our lay reader," said Dorothy in a measured tone. "Donald asked him here for moral support. Thank you so much for coming, Charles. I'm sure we can clear this up very quickly." She ushered us into the front room.

"Would anyone like coffee?" she asked. "Or tea, perhaps?" she said in her hostess voice. Only a slight quiver gave any indication of her distress. Sergeant Bickerton and I both declined.

"No? Then perhaps you'd be good enough to tell us why you've come, Sergeant Bickerton." She fixed him with a cold stare. Her composure amazed me.

"Oh my stars! Oh my soul! You know why he's here, Dottie dear. He thinks you did it! He as much as said so. Well, not in so many words, but when the police roust you out of your bed at dawn and say they want you to help in their inquiries, and then tell you not to leave your home until they've talked to you, and insinuate that they have evidence to convict you, although what evidence he could possibly have on you, Dottie, I can't imagine. It's not as if you're the kind of person who would cold-bloodedly plunge a knife into the breast of even your worst enemy, although I suppose, if you were angry enough you might, but then, you'd have to be off your medication for days to get into a state like that, but then, on the other hand, I do know that missing just one pill can make you quite testy, although whether you'd be testy enough to do something as drastic as murder... Come to think of it, there are lots of people who would want to murder Mildred. Why, I can think of at least half a dozen without even trying, so why they should pick on you, I can't imagine!" Father Donald threw himself down on the couch in a dramatic attitude of despair that turned into a scramble to prevent himself from sliding off the slippery surface onto the floor.

Dorothy turned to me, and I noticed a certain sluggishness in her movements. Far from being disconcerted by Father Donald's rantings, she had an air of detachment. I wondered how many of her nerve pills she'd taken already.

"Donald has it in his head that Sergeant Bickerton suspects me of murdering Mildred," she told me. "Of course, I can't deny that we were far from being close friends, but I certainly wouldn't stoop to violence to settle our differences." She seated herself with care in the armchair next to the Elvis photo. She picked it up, gazed at it, traced the inscription with her finger, smiled, and returned it to the table. In her habitual gesture, she reached to pat the brooch she always wore, but stopped in mid-air as she realized it no longer resided on her bosom.

"Well, Miss Peasgood, if I can just ask you a couple of questions, we can clear this up quickly," Sergeant Bickerton began. "Did you speak to Mrs. Barkhouse at the fire last night?"

Dorothy gazed at him, a thoughtful look crossing her face. "Why do you ask?"

"Just let me ask the questions."

Father Donald sat up as if to interject, but Sergeant Bickerton quelled him with a stern look and a shake of his head.

"Well, let's cut to the chase. Several people saw and heard you having an altercation with the deceased earlier in the evening at the firehall. In fact, I have several witnesses who say you and she were having a bit of a tussle."

"A tussle? Dottie? You must be mistaken!" Father Donald leapt up and began to pace back and forth across the room. Several small ornaments shook with each step. Dorothy picked up the Elvis picture and hugged it to her chest. "A tussle? You make it sound like some kind of brawl, well not a brawl exactly, more of a set-to, and I might add that Dottie was perfectly justified in her actions, what with Mildred flying at her like a banshee, and if anyone was hurt, it was I, and indeed, the bruise is still there, in fact I had trouble putting on my shoe this morning, and I know that Dottie didn't indulge in physical violence of any kind, especially against a member of the congregation. Mind, I must admit, she was pretty handy with her fists as a young girl, but then, most brothers and sisters have their ups and downs, and now that we're adults, of course all that is in the past, and I'm sure that the witnesses must have been exaggerating, not that they weren't honest, but so often people get carried away by the scene and I was reading just the other day that six witnesses will give six entirely different versions of the same event, and I don't know if you have six witnesses, but I'm sure that even if you had thirteen or fourteen witnesses, it would be just the same, or nearly…"

Sergeant Bickerton shook his head as if to clear it. "Please sit down, sir," he said in a firm voice of authority, cutting through Father Donald's tirade. "If you don't keep your comments to yourself, I'll have to ask you to leave the room."

Father Donald sank down onto the sofa like a deflated balloon and began to pick at a strand of loose yarn on the sleeve of his knitted sweater.

"Now, Miss Peasgood. Did you speak to Mrs. Barkhouse at any time during the Jollimore fire?"

Dorothy took a firmer grip on Elvis. "No," she said. "I had no reason to speak with Mrs. Barkhouse. In fact, I chose not to watch the fire at all, but waited in the car for Boris and Charles to return."

I started as I remembered that she hadn't been in the car when I returned to it. I struggled to keep my face neutral and hoped that Sergeant Bickerton hadn't seen my reaction.

"So, you're saying that at no time during the event did you see or speak to Mrs. Barkhouse while she was on duty with the Auxiliary Van?"

Dorothy's mouth tightened. "I've already told you that I didn't talk to the woman."

"Then how do you explain this?" Sergeant Bickerton fished in his pocket and flourished a plastic evidence bag. In it, Dorothy's guitar brooch glittered.

"My brooch! My brooch! Oh, you've found it. Thank heavens! I thought it was lost forever!" Dorothy leapt up and snatched at the bag, but Sergeant Bickerton pulled it back from her grasping fingers.

"I'm afraid you can't have this," he said. "It's evidence."

"Evidence?"

"Yes. It was found under Mildred Barkhouse's dead body."

"Oh my stars! Oh my soul! Dottie, what have you done?" Father Donald leapt up, stuffing strands of yarn back into a gaping hole in the sleeve of his sweater. "There must be a mistake. Tell him, Charles. Tell him that Dottie was in the car. Oh my soul! Dottie, what will the Bishop say *this* time? He'll never believe that this was just a mistake, too. Oh my stars! Oh, Dottie! At least last time nobody got killed. Well, there were some injuries, but certainly you couldn't be blamed for all of them. Well, perhaps the horse, but then, it shouldn't have been there in the first place, and who would have thought that the Mayor would have broken his nose in such a slight fall, although the Silver Cross Mother had something to do with it, at least that's what I think, and if the police hadn't been so zealous but had given you a little leeway, for after all, who was to say that you didn't really see what you thought you saw, and indeed, many people have claimed to see the same thing in many other much less likely places, although I must admit, Dottie dear, that I did doubt that he would choose a Remembrance Day service to visit, but then, people are so unpredictable, aren't they, and I do think that altogether too much was made of the whole incident, and now, look what's happened…" He wound down, his voice trailing off in despair. "I think the Bishop is going to be very upset, Dottie, dear." He pulled out a piece of yarn from the hole and began twisting it around his fingers.

"Oh, Donald!" Dorothy's voice had its old crispness. "Don't hark back to that story again. It's over and done with. I'm sure Sergeant Bickerton has no interest in past history."

"As a matter of fact, I do," said Sergeant Bickerton. "It sounds to me as if you've been in trouble with the law before, Miss Peasgood. Would you care to explain what your brother was talking about."

"Don't say a word, Dottie. We'll get a lawyer. A good one. Not too expensive, though, although I'm sure that the Diocesan Legal Fund might help out, although I think that's more for slander and libel and lawsuits and such, although this could very well be just that kind of thing, not that you've abused anyone, or at least, anyone we know, although murdering Mildred could be a form of abuse, especially since she was a member of the congregation…"

"Donald!"

Father Donald stopped in mid-stream.

"It was nothing, Sergeant. A small misunderstanding. I thought I saw someone I knew beside the cenotaph, and the local constabulary wouldn't let me through. I felt constrained to press my way forward, but unfortunately, several people were in my way." She held out the Elvis photo and gazed at it, a fond smile on her face. "He was a very special friend, but by the time I finally reached the cenotaph, he was gone. I had nothing to do with the mountie falling off his horse, or the mayor tripping over the wreath and breaking his nose, and indeed, the Silver Cross Mother saw me coming and could easily have stepped aside. As for the sea cadet, I have no idea how he came to knock several people down with his flag. No charges were laid and the incident is closed."

I realized the full import of the secret that Mildred had been threatening to tell everyone. Dorothy had "seen" her late idol at the Remembrance Day services, and nothing had stopped her from going to him. I could well picture the melee that must have ensued. No wonder Dorothy wanted to keep this story from the citizens of Cormorant Harbour, but I couldn't believe that her embarrassment would lead her to murder Mildred. After all, as Mildred pointed out, the story was public record in Seal Cove.

"I think you'd better come into the station, Miss Peasgood," said Sergeant Bickerton. "We'll need a statement from you. I suggest you get a lawyer. Although we're not laying charges at this point, there are some discrepancies in your version of the evening's events. We have yet to ascertain how your brooch came to be under the deceased." He turned to Father Donald. "Please don't leave town, sir. We may need you for further questioning."

I admired Sergeant Bickerton's professional detachment. The thought of questioning Father Donald would have made a lesser man quail.

"You might as well come in, too, sir," he said to me. "Miss Peasgood seems to think that you can provide her with some sort of an alibi."

My heart plummeted. The police station! Notoriety. Investigations. Disclosure.

"No, no!" I protested. "I didn't see Miss Peasgood after she left us to go back to the car. In fact, she wasn't in the car when I returned to it later." I stopped dead. I could have bitten off my tongue. In my haste to distance myself from the situation, I was incriminating Dorothy. "She was probably looking for her brooch," I added, then realized that she hadn't missed the brooch until she'd returned to the car. I clamped my mouth shut, determined not to say another word.

"Well, you can tell us all about it at the station." Sergeant Bickerton's implacable tone left no room for protest.

"Oh my stars! Dottie! They're taking you away like a common felon! Oh my soul! I'm coming, too. Don't worry, I won't let you face this trial alone." Father Donald drew himself up and tried to look in control. The trailing strands of wool from the hole in his sweater spoiled the effect.

"No, Donald. You stay here. I'll be fine. Charles and I will simply make a statement. I am innocent, and I have nothing to fear. We'll clear the matter up in no time. In fact, I'm sure we'll be home in time for coffee." She put Elvis back in his usual place with exaggerated care, patted her hair and proceeded to the hallway, where she gathered up her coat and handbag. "Shall we go, Sergeant?" she said.

I had no choice but to go with them. Father Donald's voice followed us to the waiting cruiser. "Don't say a word, Dottie. Not a word. They'll use it against you. Especially don't tell them about Mildred and the A.C.W. or the Casino Night, or all that nastiness over the choir gowns, not that they have anything to do with murder, but you never know, and it's always the small things that add up and in the end cause you grief, although sometimes it's best to get it all off your chest, but then, you never know how they're going to take things, twist your words and make you say things you don't mean, especially when they're giving you the third degree. You've got to be strong, Dottie, dear, and watch out for that good cop/bad cop stuff, and remember, you have rights, too, and they can't keep you without a reason, although I guess finding your brooch under a dead person is a pretty good reason…"

Sergeant Bickerton slammed the car door, mercifully cutting off the flow of Father Donald's final incriminating words.

Nineteen

An hour later, I handed in my signed statement to Constable Blair. Although I didn't actually *lie*, I made sure that *my* involvement was as minimal as possible. Even so, I was forced to admit that Dorothy hadn't been in Boris's car the entire time, and that she'd returned to me there, soaking wet and *sans* brooch.

I had a sinking feeling that even making a simple statement such as this would lead me to just the kind of notoriety that I'd been told to avoid. I could see the headlines in the Cormorant Clarion now. "Damning Evidence From Harbour Newcomer Convicts Rector's Sister."

They were still grilling Dorothy when I left. I wondered if Father Donald had found his sister a criminal lawyer whose abilities were not reflected by his fees. I debated whether or not to return to the rectory and offer him my moral support, but in the end, I turned towards home and contented myself with offering up a prayer on his behalf.

Back at Innisfree, I found Annie scrubbing the kitchen floor. She looked pale and drawn.

"I didn't expect you to come in today," I told her. "I'm so sorry about your sister."

Annie leaned back on the mop and looked at me."Well, what's done is done. Life goes on. I'm sure she wouldn't have wanted me to mope about. Better to get on with things.

Takes my mind off it all, it does. 'Sides which, we can't do anything until the police is finished." Annie wrung out the mop, threw the bucket's contents out the back door, set the mop outside to dry and returned everything else to the broom closet.

"You could have knocked me down with a feather when I came back to pick up Ollie, and he told me what had happened," she continued as she set the kettle on to boil. "To think there'd be a murder in Cormorant Harbour, and in our family, too. Poor Mildred. What a terrible way to go. It's a good thing we don't know the end from the beginning. Life's a mystery. I'd thought Mildred would outlive the bunch of us, die in her bed, she would. Strong as horse, she was, not at all as meek and mild as she looked." Annie paused, groped for a kleenex in her sweatpants pocket and wiped her eyes. "Mind you, we was never close, not even as girls. She always thought herself a cut above the rest of us, but blood is thicker'n water, and I wouldn't have wished such a thing on my own worst enemy, let alone my sister." She sighed and shook her head.

I patted her arm in sympathy.

"To think that I just drove away with Etta Fay, not knowing a thing, and my own flesh and blood, lying there dead on the ground. Just goes to show, you never know when life is going to take a turn for the worst." She blew her nose with a loud snort. "Oh, dear!" She clapped a hand over her mouth. "Etta Fay! What with all of this, I didn't give the poor old thing another thought. I hope she's all right. She was soaked right through, and there's not enough of her to shake a stick at. Ah well, I'm sure Vi or Margaret or one of her other bingo buddies will have popped in by now." She poured the boiling water into the coffee maker.

"You were out early?" she said as she pushed the plunger down.

"Yes, indeed." I told her about Dorothy.

"Well, let's have our coffee, and you can fill me in on all the details." She sounded more like her old self.

I told her everything. I left nothing out, since the whole story had no doubt gone twice around the Harbour by now.

"Well, my dear, who'da thought it," she said, leaning back in her chair. "Well, as I always say, there's no smoke but there's fire. Those two have been mortal enemies since the first moment they clapped eyes on each other." She blew across her coffee cup and stirred in several spoonfuls of sugar. "'Still waters run deep', and 'You certainly can't judge a book by its cover', and her the rector's sister and all. Well, I never." She took a noisy gulp of her coffee.

"I don't suppose you happened to see Sherri at all when you were in the harbour, did you?" Annie asked me. "When I come by this morning, Phyllis Smith was waiting outside for her appointment, and it was after nine, and the door was still locked. I went round the back and banged on the back door, but nobody was home. I don't understand it. Her car was still there. I've called several times since I got here, but I just get her machine. It's not like her to just take off without telling anyone, especially when she has customers. She's very reliable, my Sherri."

She took another sip from her cup, and I could see the lines of worry creasing her placid face.

"I haven't seen her since last night. She was at the fire with Bev." The scene with Mildred replayed in my mind. My compulsion to interfere in affairs that did not concern me might have been the catalyst for Sherri's uncharacteristic behaviour. I thought again how I'd urged them to rebel against Mildred's domination. What had I done? Had my outburst of unsolicited advice sent Bev and Sherri over the edge? I tried to picture the two of them committing the foul deed. Would one hold Mildred while the other plunged the knife into her bosom? I shook my head. No, even my writer's imagination couldn't run to such extremes.

I reined in my thoughts and groped for a more reasonable explanation. "Could she have gone to the city?" I suggested to Annie. "She was pretty upset last night after Mildred's performance at the Fire Hall."

"Could be. I don't have Nathan's number there, or I'd call him. I suppose it's really none of my business. She is after all a woman grown and she's entitled to her own life. But I do worry. She's not had it easy these last years. And then, with Mildred on her back all the time…" Annie sighed again. She poured us each another cup of coffee. I took it as a sign that the conversation hadn't come to an end.

I took advantage of the moment to ask the question that had bothered me ever since I'd heard about Sherri's circumstances. "I hope you won't feel that I'm prying, but I was wondering why Sherri didn't just get a small loan from the bank to start off her business rather than borrowing from Mildred. Even now, her business seems to be thriving, and I'm sure that any bank would be happy to loan her enough to pay off Mildred."

Annie looked troubled. She bit her lip and contemplated the cup in front of her. I feared I had offended her.

"Well," she said, "it's no skin off your nose, so I guess there's no harm in telling you. I'm sure I can trust you to keep it under your hat."

I nodded, trying to look as trustworthy as possible.

"She don't have her beauty license. She was just one exam

away, and then Nathan came along, six weeks early. He had lots of problems, medical things. After that, why she just never had the time to go and make up the exam she missed. In the end, they told her she'd have to go back and do the course all over again. She never had the time nor the money to do that, not and take care of Nathan as well. Mildred loaned her the money to buy out Connie Rutledge. It was Connie's shop before, but then her husband got a job in Calgary, and she was glad to sell it cheap. People around here just assume that Sherri has her license."

I didn't get it. "Does it matter if Sherri doesn't have a license? She's a good hairdresser."

"It's the law, you see. You're not allowed to even wash someone's hair without that piece of paper. Dumb if you ask me, but then most laws are dumb, aren't they?" Annie wiped a tear from the corner of her eye. "Too proud to go on welfare, she is, and now with Nathan heading off for college, every penny she's got will go to him." She brightened up. "But then," she said, "every cloud has a silver lining. I know she was my sister, and you shouldn't speak ill of the dead, but with Mildred gone and all…" She paused to blow her nose. "Well…" she continued, "I doubt Bev will be after Sherri to pay up on the loan."

My blood froze. Maybe my wild imaginings weren't too far from reality. Bev and Sherri both had a lot to gain from Mildred's death. Was it beyond the bounds of imagination to think that they had done the dirty deed then taken themselves away from the scene of the crime to wait until the heat died down? I thought not.

Annie gathered up the coffee cups and rinsed them at the sink. "Well," she said, "I'd better get to the vacuuming, or you'll be giving me the sack."

I took her gentle hint to get out of the kitchen and went through to my little study. Twinkles followed after me and settled next to my computer, a favourite spot due to the warmth generated by the monitor.

With some guilt, I realized that my work had been neglected of late. Even while I blamed the circumstances around me for my lack of writing discipline, I knew that the crux of the matter lay in the fact that I had never been on a river in a craft of any kind in my life. My proposed metaphysical symbolism of life's journey would have to take some other form. "Write about what you know," I'd been told. However, what I knew of journeys encompassed several bus trips to Niagara Falls and the daily commute to the office.

I sat in front of my keyboard and toyed with the Niagara Falls analogy, but since I could see nowhere to take it except over the falls, I had little alternative but to compare life's journey with the tedium of the seven fifteen GO train out of Markham into downtown Toronto.

For a moment, I could see them in my mind, my fellow passengers, faces I'd seen every morning as I'd walked to my accustomed place, fourth car, third row from the back, left hand side, window. In fact, I'd often speculated on them, wondering what their real lives were like, what thoughts raced behind those bland faces.

A glimmer of an idea flickered in the back of my mind. I felt a stirring of excitement. Forget life's journey. Forget rivers and boats. Forget metaphysical analogies, esoteric metaphors and psychological symbolism. I would write about what I knew. Each seat on the train represented a story and the trip linked each one to the other.

"*The Morning Train.*" The words formed in my mind like a marquee on a theatre. It was the perfect title.

The blinking cursor beckoned me. Centrespace, bold, all cap, I typed in the words. *The Morning Train.* With a sigh of pure joy, I took a deep breath, looked up at the sun breaking through the clouds and felt the opening sentence begin to form in my mind. I stretched out my hand and stroked Twinkles soft fur, eliciting loud purrs of contentment.

The black SUV swept past my window, turned around in the Jollimore driveway and parked alongside my gate. The two goons got out.

My hands clenched in sudden fear. Twinkles let out a shriek of protest and hurtled past me into the hallway. I followed hot on her heels. Together we raced down the polished tiles, skittering from side to side. One of my slippers flew off, but I didn't dare stop to retrieve it. I had to hide. They were already knocking on the door.

"Annie!" I croaked. She had her back to me as she vacuumed down the hallway towards my bedroom. "Annie!" I cried again. My fear-dampened voice had little power against the steady drone of the vacuum cleaner. In desperation, I yanked the cord from the wall plug. "Annie!" I bellowed into the silence.

Annie swung around. "Whatever is it, dear?"

"I'm hiding in the wardrobe! Don't tell them I'm here. Don't tell them anything. Tell them I've gone away. Tell them I'm dead. Just get rid of them," I jibbered into her startled face.

"Tell who?"

I realized that she hadn't heard the knock on the door.

They knocked again as I turned to the sanctuary of my bedroom. My foot caught on the thick vacuum hose and I tumbled headfirst into the room. I scrabbled across the floor on my hands and knees. "Get Twinkles," I hissed. "Shut her in the bathroom. Don't let her in here." I wrenched open the wardrobe door and rolled inside, banging my shins on the sharp edge of the shoe rack. I pulled the door closed behind me.

"Mr. Trenchant? What are you doing?" Annie said.

I cracked the door. "Go away," I whispered. "Don't talk to me. I'm not here." I could hear the knocks getting louder on the front door. "Just get rid of them." I pulled the door closed and huddled into a small miserable ball in the camphor scented darkness.

"Anybody home?" The voices of the goons echoed down the hall. They must have broken down the door and pushed their way in! "Annie? You here?"

Oh, God! They knew Annie. She and Ollie were part of the conspiracy. I heard Annie's footsteps retreating back into the hall.

"Well, hello, dear. How nice to see you again."

"Ollie said we'd find you here."

"My dears, come in. I'll put on the kettle."

My kettle! They were here to rub me out, and she offered them tea. My tea! I stood up in indignation, bumping my head on the clothes rail.

"I'll just see if Mr. Trenchant would like a cup of tea, too." I heard her footsteps coming back across the bedroom floor. Did they always give tea to their victims, I wondered?

The wardrobe door opened a crack. "Would you like some tea, Mr. Trenchant? Billy Barnes and his son are here. Remember I was telling you about them? This used to be their family homestead. Hope you don't mind if they come in and have a look about." She spoke in a tone reserved for recovering invalids and frightened children.

"Billy Barnes?" I whispered. The name sounded familiar.

"Yes, him what's grandfather used to have this place.

They's visiting down from Ontario. They was here several times looking to come in. Remember? I told you about them."

A vague memory stirred in my mind. Barnes. The Old Barnes Place. It all made sense. I drew myself up and stepped out of the wardrobe as if this were something I did every day. "Tea would be nice," I said, smoothing my hair. "Maybe with some of your shortbread," I suggested.

I followed her out of the bedroom, picking up my slipper on the way to the kitchen.

We spent a pleasant hour as Billy reminisced about the "old days". After a tour of the house, they drove off, well satisfied with their visit. Annie and I watched the black SUV disappear down Lupin Loop. I returned to my study, she to her kitchen, and neither of us referred to the episode of the wardrobe.

However, I heard her mutter under her breath, "Them writers is crazy" and knew that everyone in her circle of friends would have a much-embellished version of my behaviour before the end of the day.

Twenty

The rest of the morning passed in a creative haze as my fingers flew over the keyboard. "The Morning Train" took shape in my imagination. Nothing stood between me and the muse. The black SUV no longer loomed in my mind, and I could pursue my new inspiration free from its dreadful shadow. Slowly, Eric Spratt, accountant, faded away, and Charles Trenchant, writer, burgeoned beneath my fingers.

By the time I wandered out of my study in search of lunch, the first chapter had almost written itself.

In the kitchen, I found Ollie waiting for me.

"I've come to shift that goddam Jollimore trash," he said. He brandished a formidable tool, its long blue handles topped by a pair of lethal blades. Snapping them together several times, he told me, "I brung my bolt cutters. I'll have that effin' padlock off'n there in no time at all. We shoulda done it earlier, what with them goddam fire inspectors and police from the city across the road, and Mildred dead, and the goddam police tape all around the place and all…"

I followed in his grumbling wake out into the yard. I watched in awe as one swipe of the cutters took off the padlock and most of the hasp as well.

"That's got the effin' thing off. 'Twas me, now, I'd take the whole goddam lot to the dump. Ain't even worth the price of gas. Serve the lazy sonofabitch right if I just put the whole shitload back into his yard. Let him explain that to them goddam fancy-pants inspectors. But then, they'd be wantin' to talk to you, Mr. Trenchant, and no doubt, they'd haul me in, too. I could tell them a thing or two…" His eyes gleamed.

I had a moment of fear as I imagined the reaction of Sergeant Bickerton if he found out about my latest involvement with the Jollimore fire and its deadly ramifications.

"Hell, guess I'll hafta take the whole effin' lot down to Clarence's." Ollie stood in the doorway, surveying the pile of Jollimore treasures. "Goes against the grain to waste my good gas haulin' Kevin's goddam junk all the way down to Lower Cormorant, but that's where Kev and Arleen is stayin'. I'll dump it in the yard, and they can do what they wants with it." He hitched up his pants and spat into the grass.

We'd just begun to move the load, hauling an old television onto the back of Ollie's tailgate, when the Jollimore truck pulled up in front of the house.

"Howdy, neighbour." Kevin, followed by his faithful companion Clarence, shambled over towards us.

"Just comin' for a few things," said Kevin, fumbling in his pocket. He pulled out a key. His mouth dropped as he took in the open shed door and his television set perched on the tailgate of Ollie's truck.

"Hey! What're you guys doin' with my stuff?"

Clarence stepped forward and loomed over me. "Yeah, what're you doin' with Kev's stuff, eh?"

I stepped back.

Ollie shoved Clarence aside and stood toe-to-toe with Kevin, scowling up into his face. "Back up, you goddam moron," he hissed, his bony finger poking into Kevin's doughy mid-section. "I know your little game, my son, and it ain't goin' to work. No sirree, not as long as there's breath in this here goddam body. Yous two just take this effin' pile of goddam junk outer here and don't come whining back. Mr. Trenchant don't need no trouble, and trouble is what you're in, iffen the cops ever get wind of your goddam 'lucky strike.'" Ollie jabbed him a several times more to emphasize the words.

"Now, Uncle Ollie, don't be gettin' mad at me." Kevin backed up until the truck prevented him from going any farther. " I didn't do nothing. Leastways, not *last* night, I didn't. It was a real fire. Legitimate, like. The cops told me. Some guys was driving by and saw the lightning hit, right, Clarence?"

"Yeah, some guys was driving by. They saw it. They called in the fire on their cell phone. It was legit. A real fire. Even the insurance can't say nothin'." Clarence shook his head. "Who'da believed it. A *real* lucky strike! Didja ever hear the like? A *real* lucky strike," he repeated.

Ollie looked doubtful.

"Go on, call the cops if you don't believe me. They'll tell you, Uncle Ollie. Right out. It was legit. A fire. A real fire. From the lightning." Kevin's voice rose in righteous indignation.

"Kevin!" The Voice screeched from the cab of the truck. "What the hell you standing there for? We ain't got all day!"

Kevin turned and hollered over his shoulder. "For God's sake, woman, give it a rest." He turned back to us. "Gotta go. I just come for the photo albums and the old Bible, is all. Don't need the rest of that junk. Gonna get all new stuff."

"What the hell you talkin' about?" Ollie demanded. "You shift this whole goddam lot outter here."

"Don't need it no more," Kevin replied, waving at the television on Ollie's truck. He grinned as he stomped into the shed. "Reckon I guess I'll get myself one of them big-screen tellyvisions. Gonna put it in the family room of the new house. Don't want any of this old junk in here. Arleen's thinking maybe having a hot tub, too, and I allus wanted a wet bar in the rec room, and maybe a pool table, and a coupla dirt bikes for me and the young lad, and an ATV as well, and we was thinkin' about having a snowmobile or two for the winter, that is iffen we don't go to Florida, although I allust likes the snow and all, 'specially at Christmas." Kevin rooted about in the back of the shed and reappeared with the albums and the Bible in his arms

"What the hell are you talkin' about?" Ollie shot out his arm and stopped Kevin in his tracks. "You don't got the effin' money for that kind of stuff."

"Well, we will have. We're just on the way to the lawyer's now. Aunt Mildred's left it all to me, you see. She always said she would. And with her gone, she didn't have time to change her will, did she? And then there's the insurance. Gotta pay up, don't they? House got struck by lightning, didn't it?"

Ollie's arm fell from across Kevin's chest. He stood silent. For once, even Ollie had nothing to say.

"C'mon, Clarence. Let's get out of here." Kevin handed the albums to Clarence and the two of them strutted back to the truck.

"Well, it's about time," The Voice greeted them.

We heard the doors slamming, then Kevin shouted out the truck window. "You can have it all, Uncle Ollie," he said. "The whole lot. Reckon you'll make a few bucks if you take it along to Koff's. They's got an auction on Saturday next. You don't have to pay me nothing. It's all yours." He started the motor. It coughed and died several times before catching. "I'll even throw in my truck. Don't need it no more, neither. Gonna get a new 4-by-4, with the power hitch and all."

Before Ollie could reply, the truck shot off in a cloud of dust.

My stomach grumbled. I needed my lunch, but I felt that I should at least offer to help Ollie load the Jollimore junk into his truck. We struggled back and forth, carting numerous boxes and green plastic garbage bags, as well as a pile of fishing rods, several small appliances and a set of truck tires. Ollie had recovered his power of speech enough to keep up a constant tirade against Kevin.

"I mind to send him a goddam bill for haulin' this effin' junk to the dump. Iffen he's so goddam rich now, he can afford to pay for my time and my gas. What a world when lazy no-good goddam bums get rich on the backs of foolish old women who ought to know better. Effin' sin it is, no one's sorry to see her gone, not that she ever did anything to make them miss her, miserable old cow that she was. And our good money going to them goddam insurance companies who'll pay up for any effin' thing except when an honest man needs them, they goddam don't want to hear about it. Sin it is!" He threw the last bag on the truck and climbed into the cab. "Iffen he thinks I want that effin' old pile of junk he calls a truck, he's got another think comin'. Wouldn't give it goddam shed space. Not even good for goddam parts." He spat out the window and started the motor.

Before he could pull out of the driveway, Boris's little Toyota screeched to a halt at the gate. Boris leapt out and started to speak as he strode towards us, his voice crackling with excitement.

"Hello, Charles. Ollie. Thought I'd pop by. Take another look. Heard there was hot-shots in from the city. Forensics, eh? Just like television. Mattie calls me a rubbernecker." He chuckled. "Actually, calls me a voyeur. Sounds more sexy, eh?" He winked at us.

Ollie snorted.

"Big brouhaha in the harbour. Bev's gone missing."

I felt a stab of alarm. First Sherri, now Bev, both missing, and the last time I'd seen them, they'd been together. Perhaps I'd been too hasty in dismissing my dark suspicions.

"Everyone's looking for her," Boris continued with relish. "Police, morgue and the undertaker, all hot on her trail. Only, there's no trail. Vanished. No one's seen her since last night. Mattie says it looks suspicious. Can't see Bev doing the dirty deed myself, although you never know…" He stopped and inspected the pile on Ollie's truck.

"Moving house, Charles? Making a run for it? Blowing the scene of the crime?" He guffawed at his own wit. "Maybe you and Bev are doing a Bonnie and Clyde, eh?"

I opened my mouth to protest, but Ollie leapt in. "Goddam pile of junk belongs to that shiftless sonofabitch nephew of mine. Thinks he's won the effin' lottery, he does. Braggin' left and right 'bout all the goddam stuff he's gonna buy. Stupid effin' jackass! Thinks I want his effin' truck!" Ollie spat out of the truck window.

Boris's mouth dropped open at Ollie's diatribe. He gaped, first at Ollie and then at me.

I shrugged, giving up on any attempt to explain. I felt light-headed and somewhat nauseous. If I didn't get my lunch soon, I would fade away, right here in the middle of the driveway.

Ollie wasn't finished. "Who's gonna pay for the goddam gas? That's what I want to know. Costs money, it does, to run back and forth to the goddam dump. And my time? That costs, too. Take it to the effin' auction, he says. My arse! Wouldn't get a goddam penny for his pile of shit." He smacked the steering wheel in frustration. Then, with a look of relief, he brightened. "'Course I was forgettin' that I was doin' all this in the first place for Mr. Trenchant. On his payroll, I am. Takin' for him, I was. Was goin' to the goddam dump in the first place

200

before that half-assed idiot showed up and told me I could keep his effin' pile of junk." He tipped his cap at me. "So, I'll just be off then, Mr. Trenchant. I'll get rid of this goddam stuff for you, just like you asked me to. No bother at all. Tell the missus I'll pick her up on my way back." He shoved the truck into gear and pulled out of the driveway.

Boris and I stood and watched the precarious load make its way up Lupin Loop. At the corner, the truck pulled around a small caravan of white vans, each with a satellite dish on top, turning into Lupin Loop. "ATV NEWS" emblazoned on the side of the lead vehicle identified the convoy. Behind it "EASTLINK" and "CBC/RADIO CANADA", rumbled hot on its tail.

"Wow! They're all here," said Boris, an edge of excitement in his voice. "Gotta get over there! Looks like they're doing live reports. Scene of the crime. Maybe I'll get my mug on TV. Wouldn't Mattie like that. Don't want to miss any of the fun." The vans pulled up across the road, and people spilled out of every door. I saw television cameras being set up and hoisted onto brawny shoulders. Various elegant looking men and women in designer suits picked their way through the rubble from the fire. "We're big news!" said Boris. "This'll put Cormorant Harbour on the map." He clapped me on the shoulder and loped across the road to engage one of the technical-looking individuals in conversation. I saw him gesture back at me.

I bolted for the house. They mustn't see me! If my face were to be on television, however briefly or inadvertently, the game was over. I would be, as they say, "toast". I slammed the front door shut behind me, making sure that both bolts were in place.

I ran down the hall and burst into the kitchen, my need for lunch forgotten.

"Don't answer the door!" I yelled at Annie as I locked the back door and drew the curtains over the sink. "No matter how hard they knock, don't let them in, " I added as I dashed into the living room and pulled the curtains tightly across the window. I peeked through a crack and saw a phalanx of media types heading towards the house.

Annie stood in the doorway. "Who?" she asked, her eyes narrowing.

"Who what?" I said.

"Don't let who in?"

"Them! The television people!" I scrabbled into my study and pulled the blinds down. "They're coming to see me!"

"Why?"

"Because I'm here. Because I was there. Because it's big news, and I can't be big news. Not now! Not ever!"

I raced into the bedroom to draw the blinds.

"Are you going back into the wardrobe again?" she asked me, a look of resignation on her face. "Do you want me to take Twinkles?"

"No! No!" I grabbed her by the arms and looked her squarely in the eye. I had to make her realize the gravity of the situation. "I don't want to talk to television people," I said, enunciating each word carefully as if to imprint them on her brain. "Or the newspaper, or the radio, or even Boris. Don't let *anyone* in." I couldn't understand why she couldn't grasp such a simple concept.

The phone rang. Annie turned. I grabbed her again.

"Don't! Don't answer the phone, either!"

Annie shook off my hand, drew herself up and snorted. "Suit yourself," she said in a tight voice. "Lunch is ready if you want it." She turned and stamped back into her kitchen, her back registering her disapproval.

I followed her into the kitchen just as the pounding started on the front door.

Twenty-One

Although the media vans gave up within the hour, the phone continued to ring off and on throughout the day. I didn't dare answer it. I wandered through the house, unable to write, feeling a growing sense of disquiet as I pondered the events of the night before.

As far as I knew, Dorothy Peasgood was still the prime suspect. In my own mind, the likelihood of Dorothy perpetrating such a heinous crime, regardless of her anger at Mildred, seemed almost laughable. But then there was her brooch, a damning piece of evidence if ever there was one. On the other hand, the woman I had comforted over the loss of said brooch did not act like a woman who had just committed murder.

I shivered with apprehension. I hoped that this wouldn't be like the numerous cases that I'd been reading about over the past few years. I hated to think of Dorothy Peasgood, shrivelled and old, being exonerated twenty years later due to the tireless efforts of her faithful brother, who had never doubted her innocence, while all the while the true culprit remained at large.

There must be other suspects that the police were investigating. Bev and Sherri, for instance. The police must be wondering at their sudden disappearance, especially after the scene at the Fire Hall, with Mildred threatening both of them. The more I thought about it, the more I began to realize that their disappearance was out of character. Where could they have gone? And why?

Come to that, what about the Jollimores? I had no doubt that Arleen could resort to violence. Her assault on Mildred earlier in the evening proved that. By now, even the police must know of the Jollimores' financial hopes. What better reason to knock off Mildred?

Boris? I dismissed the idea even as I thought of it. Boris's bark was worse than his bite. His antipathy towards Mildred wouldn't go as far as murder.

Mildred had upset a lot of people last night. From Sherri to Etta Fay, even Annie and Ollie, few had escaped her vicious tongue.

The murderer could have been anyone in the crowd at the Jollimore fire. Hadn't I heard as much all that time ago on my first visit to Sherri's? Although I couldn't recall who'd said it, I remembered the venom in the woman's voice, "Why, leave a loaded gun on the table, and someone's gonna pick it up and shoot Mildred Barkhouse for sure." Loaded gun or butcher knife? What difference did it make? The weapon was at hand, and someone had seized the opportunity.

By eight o'clock, I was exhausted. I fell into my bed and slept deeply until the shrilling of the phone woke me. Twinkles leapt off the bed with a meow of protest. Befuddled by sleep, I answered the phone without thinking. It took me a moment to realize what the caller was trying to say.

"Oh, Charles! Thank God you're in. I've been calling all day, well not all day, but most of the day, when I could, that is, when I wasn't with Dottie and the lawyer and the police. It's been hell, simply hell, not that I know what hell is like, but if hell is anything like the day I've just put in, then, I'm very glad I'm not going there, at least, I certainly hope I'm not going there, not that one knows, of course, but one can presume some assurance, being of course a Christian…"

"Father Donald?" I cut in.

"Well, yes, who else would it be? Were you expecting another call? It is quite late. Oh my stars! Oh my soul! I had no idea it was *this* late. Oh shoot! Did I wake you? Well, I must have, mustn't I? It's nearly eleven o'clock. Far past my bedtime, 'early to bed', Dottie always says, but who could sleep after the day we've had, or at least, Dottie's had, not that I haven't had a bad day, too, but she's the one who…"

"How *is* Dorothy?" I interrupted again, moving into my Father Donald mode.

"Dorothy? Oh, yes, Dottie. That's why I called you. She's out. Sprung. Free. Well, not entirely free. She can't leave Cormorant Harbour, but at least she's not in jail, not that she was actually *in* jail, but the possibility was always there, even though the police didn't say they were charging her, but it was quite clear, at least to me, that her hours of freedom were numbered, although in the spiritual sense, I guess one could say that all of our hours of freedom are numbered, in fact, it might make a good sermon subject, very topical under the circumstances, although I doubt Dottie would let me…"

"What happened?" I sat up on the edge of my bed, now wide awake. "Have they found someone else?"

"Oh my stars! It was a miracle! An answer to prayer. Of course, the lawyer helped, too, a very good man, came all the way in from the city, well recommended by the Bishop, who by the way, is being very supportive, most unexpected, given the circumstances, but then, he is our Shepherd after all, and when one of the sheep is in trouble, it's his duty to come to their aid, not *my* aid, but Dottie's, and technically, she isn't exactly one of his sheep, but in the broadest sense…"

"What did the lawyer say?" I felt a small headache beginning behind my eyes.

"The man was absolutely brilliant, and not too expensive, either. It's the legal mind that cuts to the heart of the matter. Oh, dear! Maybe I should rephrase that, considering the method of Mildred's sad demise. Anyway, he was the epitome of logical reasoning. His arguments certainly put the police in their place. They were like puppydogs with their tails between their legs when he finished with them. Not a shred of evidence, he said, barring the brooch, of course, which could have fallen on the ground at any time during the fire. And Dottie's clothes were the clincher."

"Dorothy's clothes?" I asked, still struggling with the various metaphors that Father Donald had thrown at me.

"Yes. Clean as a whistle, which is kind of a funny phrase, isn't it, Charles? Why is a whistle clean as opposed to what? A trumpet? A drum."

The headache moved into a more serious phase. "So Dorothy's clothes were clean?"

"Yes. Not covered with blood."

In a flash, I realized that Donald was right. Dorothy had been soaked with water, not blood, when I saw her. Whoever killed Mildred would bear the evidence of the bloody carnage on his or her person. Even the rain wouldn't have washed away all the evidence that easily.

"Of course," continued Father Donald, "the fact that they had a witness who'd seen Dottie's small disagreement with Mildred and watched her walk way, and in fact, had collected a cup of coffee from Mildred's own hands soon after the event, may have had something to do with Dottie's release. The lawyer immediately realized the significance of this additional piece of information. He pounced on it like a cat on a mouse. He was magnificent, worth every penny of his fee. Dottie was out in no time, well, it took an hour to do the paperwork, but no time at all in terms of the life imprisonment that faced her."

"That's wonderful!" I was much relieved that my statement wouldn't lead to Dorothy's incarceration. Perhaps now, the police would lose interest in me as a witness. With any luck, my name and face would remain anonymous.

"Now, we can all get back to normal," Father Donald continued. "At least normal for us, not that we're not as normal as others, but…"

"Well, goodnight then," I hinted. "Thanks for calling me with the news. Please tell Dorothy how happy I am that everything went well."

"Oh! Oh! Shoot! Before I forget! Sunday!"

My heart sank. Now what?

"I know Sunday will be your first day back since your unfortunate accident, and I just wanted to remind you that it's Nursing Home Sunday."

My heart sank even lower. I'd forgotten. Nursing Home Sunday meant an afternoon visit, complete with Boris and his accordion, plus assorted members of the choir, for a service at the seniors' facility attached to the hospital, culminating in weak tea, stale fruit bread, and a dear little lady who thought I was her nephew, uncle, father or brother, asking me impossible questions such as, "Whatever happened to Auntie Phyllis?"

"Is there anyone in the hospital who needs communion?" I asked, knowing that Father Donald liked to combine the two events.

"Yes, one or two, but it shouldn't take us long, well, not as long as if there were six or seven, not that there has ever been that many, what with so many Catholics in the area, and I must say, they do seem to be a weaker crowd than our own, although the Baptists are seldom in the hospital, and I've often wondered…"

"Fine." I cut him off. "I won't forget. See you on Sunday. Goodbye. " I hung up before he could think of anything else he needed to tell me.

I think I was asleep within seconds.

The next morning, although it was a Saturday, I noticed that the police were still poking around the Jollimore property. The media vans were nowhere in sight. I supposed that some other tragedy had claimed their attention.

Twinkles and I settled ourselves down in the study. In minutes, I was deep in *The Morning Train*, my thoughts leaping ahead of my typing fingers. The words and phrases formed themselves with no effort, and I was thrilled to see the pages filling up, not at all like the weeks of struggle with my old manuscript. I found myself smiling. To think that I had doubted my ability as a writer.

It was Ollie's shout in the kitchen that tore me from my muse.

"Mr. Trenchant? You here?"

I was almost glad of the interruption. My neck hurt. My fingers were stiff. I stood up and stretched. "I'm in the study," I called out.

Ollie clumped in, brandishing a piece of paper. "I brung you the bill," he said.

"Bill?"

"For the dump. They charges, you know. Not like the old days. Time was a man could just leave his goddam stuff and be done with it. But not now. No, gotta put it in the right effin' place. Gotta pay for the privilege of doing their goddam work." He hitched up his trousers and sat in the chair I had vacated. "Been workin', eh?" he said, peering at the screen.

I reached past him, hit the save icon and closed down the file. I felt protective of my work, not willing to let it be seen by any eyes other than my own.

"Yes," I said. "It's only in the rough stages, right now. You can read it when I'm done."

"Oh, no need for that. Ain't much of a one for readin'," Ollie assured me. "Annie neither. But our Sherri, well, that's another thing altogether. Allus has her head in a goddam book, she does. Loves to read."

"Did you find Sherri? Annie was worried about her yesterday?"

"Oh, she 'n Bev was in the city. Seems like they took it into their heads to leave Mildred with the goddam van. Don't know where they got that idea from. Not like them at all." He tipped back his cap and scratched his head.

I knew where they'd got the idea. I felt a twinge of guilt. Perhaps if Sherri and Bev hadn't taken my unsolicited advice, Mildred might be still in the land of the living.

"Got a ride back to the Harbour and took Bev's car. Stayed at Nathan's. Sherri said Bev was pretty goddam upset. Over Clarence and all the rest of that stuff Mildred was dishin' out at the Fire Hall and thought she needed to get away from Mildred for a bit." He looked up at me from under his shaggy brows. "Mind, she's away from her for a effin' good bit now, and that ain't bad news for Bev, iffen you ask me. Mildred might have been her goddam mother, but she run that poor girl ragged."

"Did the girls talk to the police?" I asked, still wondering whether there was more to the story than Ollie knew.

"Yes, they did. Had a good long chinwag with that Bickerton. He was waitin' for them. Lot of goddam questions, he had. I was of a mind to get a lawyer from the way that goddam Bickerton was carryin' on, but he changed his tune onct' he got the clothes they was wearin' on the night.

"The same thing happened with Dorothy Peasgood," I said. "Once they got a look at her clothes and didn't find any blood on them, they had to let her go."

"Right enough. There'd be effin' blood aplenty. Why, Mildred was covered in the stuff. Great effin' gobs of it all over the place. All over the goddam van and the sandwiches, and all. Who'da thought such a little dried-up scrap of a woman woulda had so much goddam blood in her. Anyone close enough to stick that effin' knife in her woulda got hisself covered with it." He rubbed his hands together in relish.

I felt rather queasy.

"In fact, they was tellin' me that the police are getting' the clothes from all of us what was still there after the rain began. They figured out that's when Mildred got it. Some fellow picked up a cup of coffee offen her just afore the downpour. He's the last one what saw her alive. 'Cept for the one what killed her, course, and he ain't talkin'. Young Blair was by to look at our goddam clothes this morning—Annie's and mine. Don't doubt but he'll be comin' to see you, too."

The front door bell rang. Ollie peered out the window.

"See, what did I tell ya? It's the cops. Or at least that Blair fellow. He's a bit of a sissy to my mind, not like good ol' Freddie Cooks what was here afore. You could talk to Freddie, man to man like, but not Blair. Goddam fancy-pants from the Valley. Likes himself he does, 'specially in that goddam uniform. You'd better let him in. He ain't goin' away, believe me." He glanced out the window again and settled back into the chair with the air of someone preparing to enjoy the show.

I sighed in resignation and went to let Constable Blair in. He towered over me, and I was forced to back up. Ollie crowded into the study doorway, unabashedly eavesdropping.

Constable Blair was all politeness, inquiring after my health. He took off his cap and laid it on the hall table, then asked if I had any more details to add to my statement.

"Oh," I said, feeling my heart plummet. "I thought you wouldn't need my statement, what with Ms Peasgood being exonerated and all."

"Just a formality, sir," he assured me as he smoothed his blonde hair in front of the hall mirror. "We like to gather as much information as we can. Try to get a complete picture, so to speak." He gave his tie a tweak.

"Well, no, I think I pretty well covered it yesterday. Is that all?" I said, my hope rising.

"Actually, I wonder if we might have a word in private, Mr. Trenchant?" Constable Blair looked at Ollie as he said this.

"No need for secrecy," Ollie said, slipping his hands in his pockets and leaning back against the door jamb. "I already told Mr. Trenchant here all about the goddam clothes. You wantin' to see them and all." He shot Constable Blair a triumphant look.

"Well, yes, um…" Constable Blair looked uneasy. "I suppose it'll be all right, that is, if Mr. Trenchant doesn't mind."

I did mind, but I couldn't say so without hurting Ollie's feelings.

"It's fine, Constable. I understand you want the clothes I

was wearing at the fire. Annie does washing on Mondays, so they'll still be in the hamper. I'll get them for you." I left Constable Blair and Ollie glaring at each other and hurried down the hall to my bedroom.

The clothes were bundled up in a heap, still damp and smelling smokey. I grabbed the pile and brought them back to Constable Blair.

"Here you are," I said. "These are the ones."

Constable Blair put on a pair of plastic gloves before he took each article from me, shaking it out and examining it with great care. I'd dressed up that evening for my visit with Father Donald in what I thought was Cormorant Harbour semi-formal. My Dockers pants were very much the worse for wear, and I doubted that just a washing was going to restore them. My socks were grimy and dirty. When I saw the rumpled mess that was my Calvin Klein shirt, I regretted having chosen it for the occasion. Constable Blair discarded each piece onto the hall chair.

As I handed him my good navy Arnold Palmer knit pullover, I could see it would never be the same.

Constable Blair took one look at it, frowned, and walked over to the window. Ollie followed him. Blair's height frustrated his attempts to see what Blair was looking at on my pullover.

"I'm going to have to take this into evidence, sir, for forensics to have a closer look." Constable Blair turned back to me. "There seems to be some sort of suspicious staining on the front. Do you have any idea what it might be?"

I was nonplussed. "Staining?" I squeaked, sounding all the world like a guilty party. "I don't know what you're talking about." My voice trembled.

"Let me have a gander," said Ollie, pulling the sweater

from Blair's hands. "Sure looks all the world like effin' blood to me."

"Blood!" I felt myself grow faint and groped for the hall chair. I pushed the clothes off and fell down on it. "Blood?" I faltered.

"Give that back!" Blair commanded, reaching out for the pullover. "You're tampering with evidence, and that can land you in jail."

Ollie dropped the garment like a hot potato.

Constable Blair pulled out a plastic evidence bag from one pocket, picked up the sweater and bundled it into the bag. He scribbled out a receipt and handed it to me.

"I'm afraid I'm going to have to ask you not to leave the area without informing us of your whereabouts. This is a serious matter. and until we have resolved it, consider yourself a material witness." With that, he put on his hat, checked it out in the mirror, and left.

"Material witness, eh? Sounds goddam serious. Whew!" Ollie grinned. "They thinks you done it! Got her good and proper!" He started to chuckle. "Told you he was an effin' idiot. Don't know his arse from his elbow. Don't you go worryin' none, Mr. Trenchant. Bickerton'll put him straight. Though I gotta admit, that sure did look like goddam blood to me, and I'se seen plenty of it in my time, what with huntin' and all."

I sat in the chair, surrounded by my discarded clothing, unable to think of a single thing to say. I was a material witness! How could this have happened to me? I wondered what my agent would think when she heard about this.

"Well, no time to stand here jawin'. I gotta go and get the missus. She's over at Etta Fay's. I dropped her off on the way. She wanted to see how the old girl was doin'." He slapped me on the shoulder. "Buck up, my son. It can't be all that bad. Iffen it was, he woulda arrested you right here and now." He laughed again. "Wait'll I tell Annie she's working for a goddam material witness. Won't she be surprised." He was still laughing as he slammed the door behind him.

I don't know how long I sat in the hall, racking my brains, trying to think where I might have got the stains on my pullover. I didn't remember spilling any food, and apart from crawling around on my hands and knees in the ditch, there were no other times when I could have gotten dirty.

Lurid visions filled my head. I saw myself in the dock, judged guilty by a jury of my peers, sent away to prison for life for a crime I didn't commit. I began to understand how the Bacciaglias must have felt. No wonder they hated me so much. How ironic it would be if I were incarcerated in the same soulless prison as they were. I doubted I'd see the light of a second day if that were to happen. I sobbed in despair.

It was Twinkles who roused me from my state of collapse. She rummaged through the pile of clothes on the floor, twined herself around my legs and jumped up into my lap. She pushed her face against my beard and kneaded my chest with her paws. I took comfort from her loud purrs of contentment. Who would love Twinkles as I did if I were sent to jail?

"Poor thing," I whispered to her. "You'll be an orphan again."

I must be strong for Twinkles, I told myself. I am all that stands between her and a return to the animal shelter. I decided to ask Father Donald for the name of Dorothy's lawyer. I knew I was innocent. It would be madness for me to take the fall without fighting for my freedom.

Feeling much heartened, I took Twinkles into the kitchen and opened us a can of tuna for our supper.

Twenty-Two

After a sleepless night, I dragged myself to St. Grimbald's, where I hoped that the ageless liturgy of the church might take my mind away from the cycle of worry and fear that had consumed me since the moment when Constable Blair had confiscated my sweater.

Father Donald conducted the service with an air of unrestrained ebullience. His enthusiasm over Dorothy's release spilled over into his homily, where he waxed eloquent on the vagaries of time. I doubted anyone in the congregation had the slightest idea of his meaning. I tried to concentrate on his words, if only to stop myself from falling back into the grip of despair.

The Coffee Hour, scheduled by the A.C.W. in memory of their late President, caught me by surprise. Instead of whisking off to the Seafarer's Memorial Hospital and the Ebb Tide Nursing Home as we usually did, Father Donald, Boris and I found ourselves in the basement of St. Grimbald's, immersed in a sea of gossip and speculation.

Mildred's sad demise formed the hot topic of conversation ("Died in the line of duty, she did, what with being at the fire and all…", "Better'n being strangled, I suppose; no closed coffin, and I always say that Farris's does a wonderful job of the laying out…", "We'll need to have another election for President soon…").

Dorothy's brief incarceration caused quite a stir as well, ("Well, I still say that where there's smoke there's fire...", "Whatever Mildred knew about Dorothy will go to the grave with her, more's the pity...", "I doubt Dorothy will feel she can run for president now, what with the circumstances being what they are...").

Since Dorothy hadn't been in church, she had no opportunity to rebut any of these remarks.

The surprising news that Etta Fay had been taken to the hospital the day before added spice to the conversational pot. Annie had found her and now held court in the centre of the basement.

"Could have knocked me over with a feather," she said to her rapt audience, "seeing her lying there like that, so pitiful. Poor soul, musta fell and knocked her head in the bathroom. Probably trying to wash off some of the soot, it being on everything and all. Took myself nearly an hour to get it out of my hair after the fire, specially with it being rainy and all. Looks like she just crawled into bed, still half-dressed. Terrible mess everywhere. She only had a little cut on her forehead, but them little head wounds bleed something awful. I knew she was in a bad way when I dropped her off, soaked to the bone and all. I should have gone in with her, but I thought she'd be able to take care of herself. Looked like she hadn't moved from the moment she crawled into her bed, poor soul. Gave me a nasty turn, it did, seeing her like that. For a moment, I thought she was a goner. The ambulance was there in no time, but they told me she wouldn't have lasted much longer like that. Pneumonia," she finished up with relish. "It's what gets them every time."

Much to my horror, the story of my visit from Constable Blair had also made its rounds of Cormorant Harbour. Unlike the openness with which they discussed every other topic, this one elicited sideways glances and sudden silences as I drew near. I caught a phrase here and there, none of them encouraging, ("Well, we have no idea who he really is, do we...?", "Where's there's smoke there's fire, I always say...", "You never can tell with these come-from-aways; they seem nice on the outside, but..."). From what I could gather, they all would have preferred to have had a stranger like myself commit the murder, rather than one of their own.

Father Donald wandered from group to group, carrying a large plate of sandwiches with him.

"Eat up," he urged me every time our paths crossed. "We won't be getting lunch today, and it's a long time until the Nursing Home serves tea."

We didn't break away until after one o'clock. That left Father Donald and I little time for the hospital visits before the Nursing Home service at two. We couldn't dislodge Boris from his conversation with Annie, so we agreed to go ahead and meet him in the Ebb Tide Nursing Home lounge.

As we drove to the hospital, I told him the full story of Constable Blair's visit.

"Could I have the name of the lawyer you got for Dorothy?" I asked him. "He sounded like an able man. It seems that I might need some legal help before this is all over."

"Oh my soul! Oh my stars! Charles! Material witness! Surely they don't suspect you? Why, you're a pillar of this community, well, maybe not a pillar, having been here for such a short time, although it does seem much longer, now that we have become so close, but, I would at least consider you to be a stalwart supporter of the parish, if not a pillar, since generally speaking, pillars are those people who have been with us for many generations and whose history is an open book to us all, and I must say, we know so little about you, not that there's things we should know, dark secrets and skeletons in your closet and all that kind of thing, although I'm sure that some of the pillars have skeletons in their closets if we were to look closely…"

"Thank you for your confidence in me," I cut in, "but I'm afraid these days the police aren't impressed by pillars or even supports of the church."

We got out of the car and between us loaded up with the paraphernalia of a full-blown hospital visit.

"The lawyer's Richard Mervinski. I'll call you with his number later," Father Donald said as he juggled the prayer books and communion case. "I'm sure he'll take you on. He seems rather eager for high-profile cases."

I cringed at the thought of once again being a player in a high-profile court case, since it seemed that this time my role would be that of the star, but I had little choice. I followed Father Donald's bulk into the hospital.

"There's only two we have to see," he told me. "Poor old Amos Beaver, on his last legs, they say, although why they say 'legs' when he's been bedridden for ten years, I'll never know. Anyway, I think it's time to administer Last Rites, not that we call them Last Rites, not wanting to upset anyone, but you know what I mean. I tried to persuade the family to wait until tomorrow, what with the Nursing Home service due to begin at two, but they were anxious that I get it over with as soon as possible, it being the weekend, and everyone here…"

We tiptoed into Amos's room. I saw a small, wizened figure, hardly discernible beneath the bed covers. The tip of his nose showed over the edge of the sheet, and wisps of grey hair fell across his waxen forehead. Only the slight movement of the counterpane indicated that we weren't too late. It surprised me that no members of the family hovered around his bed.

"Oh shoot! They must have gone for lunch." Father Donald glanced at his watch. "We don't have time to go and look for them. Just to be on the safe side, I'll do the Prayers for the Dying now and come back later, if there is a later, for the rest of it." Father Donald draped his stole around his shoulders and launched into the liturgy. I strove to keep up with the responses as he sped through the service.

In record time, we hit the last prayers.

"Depart, O Christian soul, out of this world," Father's Donald intoned in his best ecclesiastical voice.

The figure in the bed sat up. Father Donald gasped and stopped.

The three of us gaped at each other.

"For the love of God! They told me I was going home tomorrow, but I didn't think they meant that kind of home!" The astonished recipient of Father Donald's ministrations groped for his teeth on the bedstand and shoved them into his mouth. He smoothed back his hair and sat up straight, looking from one to the other of us.

"Amos! You're not Amos! Oh my stars! Oh my soul! Don't tell me I'm in the wrong room!"

"You lookin' for Amos Beaver? He was moved into palliative care last night." The patient waved at the empty bed next to him. "That was his bed there."

Father Donald checked his watch again. "Oh shoot! We're getting later by the minute. Let's just pop in and see Etta Fay. We'll come back for Amos right after the Nursing Home Service."

"Have we got time for Etta Fay?" I asked.

"Oh my soul, yes. Just a few prayers to keep her going. I doubt she's awake, but you never know." Father Donald lumbered off down the hallway.

At Etta Fay's door, we met Boris, who'd come to look for us.

"Natives are restless," he said. "Don't like waiting. Got 'em all in the lounge. Can't keep 'em much longer. Mobile ones keep wandering off. Ones in the wheelchairs keeping nodding off. Come on, let's get this show on the road."

"We won't be a minute," I told him. "Father Donald wants to pop in and see Etta Fay."

"I'll come with you," said Boris. "Not going back to face that crowd. Not on my own, I'm not. Can't handle those old birds alone."

The three of us wheeled into Etta Fay's room, a small single unit at the end of the hall, already filled by a bed that took up most of the space. A narrow metal clothes locker hung on the wall on the far side of the bed, as well as a night table at the head of the bed. The corner across from the door held the single visitor's chair.

Mattie blocked the bedside nearest the door as he adjusted the flow of an intravenous line. Father Donald and I crowded in. Father Donald moved to the far side of the bed, positioning himself in front of the locker. With little room for his bulk between the locker and the bedside, I stood in the corner near the chair. Boris lingered in the doorway. I felt a tinge of claustrophobia.

Etta Fay lay in the bed, her eyes wandering around the room as she took in our faces. Father Donald plunked his belongings down on the wheeled table positioned across the bed.

"Is that you, Father?" she asked in a thin voice.

"Yes, yes! It's me! How are you today?" Father Donald's cheerful bedside voice boomed in the quiet room.

"Have you got a nice rabbit?"

Father Donald looked nonplussed. "Um, er…" he began.

"Momma said we would have rabbit stew today for supper when you came home."

Father Donald looked around the room as if to find a rabbit lurking in the corner.

"I think we've reverted to our childhood. Fever sometimes does that," Mattie whispered. "Just play along with her. She'll probably snap out of it in a few minutes."

"Oh, yes! Well, um, Etta Fay…dear…" Father Donald tried to get into the spirit of the moment. "Rabbit. Yes. Delicious, I'm sure. Um…"

"Perhaps we should come back later," I whispered to Boris. "I don't think this is going to work."

"Rabbit!" Father Donald began again. "I have two. Two rabbits, Etta Fay…dear. Enough for a big pot of stew. We'll ask…um…Momma to cook it for us. Yum. Yum."

"Father Donald! Whatever are you talking about?" Etta Fay's eyes snapped open. She regarded Father Donald as if he had two heads.

"I think we're back," Mattie whispered.

Out of the corner of my eye, I could see Boris in the doorway, his face red with suppressed laughter, his shoulders shaking.

"Oh my soul! Oh my stars! Etta Fay! Are you feeling better now?" Father Donald leaned over her and took one of her thin hands. "We've all come to say a little prayer for your recovery."

"Prayers aren't going to do me any good," she muttered, pulling her hand away.

"Now, now, I know you're feeling low, and of course, everything is all upset at the moment, but I'm sure that you'll be up and bouncing around in no time, what with the miracle of modern drugs, and you're still relatively young, such a lot to look forward to, and it's important that you keep a positive attitude…"

Etta Fay shook her head. Two tears trickled down her pale cheeks.

"Now, now," said Mattie. "No need for us to get upset. We'll all feel better later, if we just have a little nap." He turned to Father Donald. "Perhaps you should come back later, Father Donald, when she's feeling up to it."

Father Donald checked his watch. "Yes, we should be going. I'll see you later, Etta Fay," he said, reaching for the communion kit and books on the table. Too late, I lunged forward to catch the glass of juice behind them.

"Oh shoot! Now look what I've done!" Father Donald said in dismay as a dark cranberry juice stain spread across the white bedcovers. He whipped out his handkerchief and bent forward to lay it over the stain. As he did so, his ample backside hit the locker behind him with a resounding clang.

"Oh my soul!" He rebounded off the door and caromed into the side of the bed, which rolled towards Mattie, who grabbed for the intravenous bag.

Father Donald staggered sideways and collapsed onto the night table, knocking a k-basin and a stack of towels onto the floor.

The locker door, released by his bulk, sprang open in front of him. A large plastic bag fell out.

I stood, transfixed by the scene. Boris's laughter, far beyond containment, filled the room.

"Stop it!" commanded Mattie. "Out! All of you!" He pointed dramatically towards the doorway.

Constable Blair walked in. "Mr. Trenchant! They told me I'd find you here." He elbowed his way past Boris. "I'm afraid I'm going to have to ask you to come with me for further questioning," he said as he tucked his cap under his arm.

My mouth went dry and I could feel the blood draining from my face. "What! Why?" I croaked.

"If you'd just step outside, sir," Constable Blair began.

"Don't say a word until you've called the lawyer!" Father Donald's muffled voice came from behind the locker door.

"You don't have to go," said Boris. "Not without a warrant. Can't make you. Gotta have a pretty good reason to drag you in."

Constable Blair wheeled on Boris. "I must ask you not to interfere in the process of the law, sir." Unlike Ollie, Boris remained unimpressed by Blair's officious manner.

"Stand your ground, Charles. We're with you," he said, his beard bristling in indignation.

I took heart from Boris' words. "May I ask why you wish to speak with me?" I said, trying to sound calm and controlled.

"It's your sweater, sir. Those stains are blood. Human blood. Same type as the deceased." Constable Blair enjoyed the sudden silence that met these ominous words. "We don't need a warrant to ask you to come along and help us with our inquiries."

"Blood!" I squeaked. "Impossible! How would I get Mildred Barkhouse's blood on my sweater?" I sank back into the visitor's chair, my head whirling, my stomach churning. All of my worst nightmares had come true. I'd become the chief suspect in a murder one case. It would be the chair for me. Oh no, not the chair. Not in Canada. Worse, life imprisonment with big goons like the Bacciaglias, who would think I was a killer of little old ladies, and no doubt would find me cute to boot. All of my efforts to remain anonymous, to lead a quiet, unassuming life, to disappear in this Nova Scotia backwater, would be for naught. Oh God! My case worker would be furious! And what would become of Twinkles? And *The Morning Train?*

"We need to find that out," said Constable Blair, laying a hand on my shoulder. "That's why I must ask you to come with me now."

I cringed from his touch.

"Don't be ridiculous!" Father Donald pushed the locker door away from him, knocking over the plastic bag which blocked it. The contents spilled out around my feet. They were Etta Fay's clothes, bundled into the bag by the hospital staff.

I kicked aside the clothes and stood up. "I didn't go near Mildred," I told Blair, my voice rising in desperation. "Lots of people can tell you where I was. On the road. All the time. Ask Ollie. He was at my gate with one of the other constables. Ask Dorothy. She saw me in the car. Ask Sherri and Bev. They saw me on the road. And so did Annie. She met me there when she was looking for Etta Fay. Etta Fay!" I waved towards the figure in the bed. "Ask her now. Etta Fay? Don't you remember? I bumped into you. When it was raining. You fell into my arms On the road. I was with Annie. She was looking for you to take you home. Remember?"

A long silence greeted my outburst. We all looked at Etta Fay. She didn't meet our eyes, but instead, looked down at the stain seeping through Father Donald's handkerchief.

"Blood. Blood. Everywhere. Father, must you kill the little rabbit here?" She touched the stain.

I felt the skin prickle on the back of my neck. Boris and Constable Blair took a step away from the bed.

"An eye for an eye, isn't that right? She killed my grandbaby." Her eyes skewed around to Father Donald. "Don't give me any rabbit stew, Father. I've been very bad." She slumped back onto her pillow, her gaze fixed on the ceiling.

Father Donald sidled out from the corner. He closed the locker door, and stooped to put the clothing back into the bag, all the while, keeping an eye on Etta Fay.

As Father Donald picked up Etta Fay's dress, I knew what had happened. "You'd better leave those there," I told him. "I think Constable Blair is going to want to look at Etta Fay's clothes."

Father Donald looked at the dress in his hands. "Blood! Oh my soul!" His eyes rolled up and his face paled. He sagged like a deflated balloon, sliding down the wall, his legs disappearing under Etta Fay's bed.

Mattie sighed. "It's always the big ones who can't stand the sight of blood."

Twenty-Three

Father Donald held Etta Fay's funeral a week after Mildred's. Everyone felt it was a mercy that she succumbed to the pneumonia and hadn't had to stand trial for Mildred's murder. The tests on her clothes coupled with her cryptic confession at the hospital proved beyond any doubt that she had wielded the knife. Of course, as I suspected, they soon found out that the residual blood on my clothes had come from my collision with Etta Fay on the night of the fire.

The horrible crime and Etta Fay's obvious descent into insanity hadn't prevented the entire community from turning out for her funeral. The general consensus was that Etta Fay had been provoked beyond any human endurance.

Her son, Randy, came home from Alberta to attend the funeral. Much to everyone's delight, he and Bev picked up where they'd left off twenty years earlier. Father Donald predicted a Christmas wedding.

Mildred Barkhouse's will turned out to be the surprise sleeper of the summer. She died virtually penniless, having put all her money into high tech mutual funds. With the crash of the dotcom bubble, Mildred lost everything. Kevin ended up with a little under five thousand dollars after the funeral expenses. Bev, on the other hand, who'd only been left Mildred's house, stood to make a nice profit on the sale of the Victorian monstrosity to Boris and Mattie.

"Gettin' out of the teachin' game," said Boris with a smug smile. "Sick of the little buggers. Mattie's always wanted a B&B. Once he's done it up, all House and Garden, you won't recognize the place. Four star. Tourist attraction. Put Cormorant Harbour on the map."

As for myself, I soon slipped back into my daily routine. I maintained a wary posture, knowing that my enemies might still surface at any moment. After the close call of Kevin's fire, I realized that I lay at the mercy of circumstance. Nevertheless, I remained stoic in the face of the vagaries of fate.

The Morning Train continued to evolve and grow under my fingers. Page after page slipped off the screen, and I revelled in the joy of creative expression. I began to think that I might, after all, have a life in Cormorant Harbour, complete with my duties in the church and my friendships in the community.

By the end of September, I'd reached the final chapters of the book. The characters were bringing themselves to conclusion. I only needed to listen to their voices in order to have them reach their final destinations.

As I sat in my study one morning, looking out across the road to the blackened bulldozed area once occupied by the Jollimore shack, a strange car pulled up at my gate. For a moment, my old terrors overwhelmed me. Then, I recognized the person coming up the walk. My heart sank.

My case worker from the Witness Protection Department strode up the walk with a confident air, her tall figure in a grey suit, pressed and pristine as always, her short-cropped black hair hardly ruffled by the wind off the ocean. She carried a large briefcase. I could only think that her arrival didn't bode well for me. Why would she be here unless someone had blown my cover?

As I sat transfixed in front of the window, stroking Twinkles, who had insinuated herself onto my lap, a sense of impending loss overwhelmed me. Having at last come to terms with my new life and persona, indeed, having embraced them, it seemed that they were both to be snatched away from me by the cruel hand of bureaucracy.

It took all my willpower to go to the door and let her in.

"Mr. Trenchant!" she said, remembering to avoid the use of my old name.

"Ms Smith," I replied, using the pseudonym that facilitated our communication. "Please come in."

She followed me into the living room and seated herself in one of the over-stuffed chairs. Without a moment's hesitation, Twinkles jumped up onto her lap.

"Get down!" she said, brushing the cat off with a less than gentle hand. "I hate cats," she told me with a grimace of distaste.

Twinkles stalked off across the room, tail in the air. I didn't think it would be the end of her feline assault.

"Why are you here? Has my cover been blown?" I didn't have time for the niceties. Better to have the bad news stated and over with. Then I could deal with it.

"No…not really." For the first time, Ms Smith looked uneasy. She bent down and opened her briefcase, pulling out a sheaf of papers. She seemed reluctant to continue. Twinkles jumped back up onto her lap.

This time, Ms Smith grabbed Twinkles around her ample middle and dumped her onto the floor. "Go away," she said.

I hid a small smile. It had been Ms Smith's idea that I should have a pet. I wondered why she'd chosen a cat for me. Twinkles circled her chair.

"Derek Street is dead," she said. "Killed by a hit-and-run driver early yesterday morning."

"Derek Street?" Could he be the person who had blown my cover?

"Yes. You might remember him from the trial. He was the Bacciaglia's accountant." She shuffled her papers and cleared her throat several times.

"I must confess I really didn't notice many people at the trial." The memory of Lucia Bacciaglia flashed through my mind, the only face I remembered seeing in the courtroom. Lucia, who I thought might be related to Zerena? Was this the weak link in the armour of my new identity?

"Derek Street was the one who blew the whistle on the Bacciaglia's operation. He turned crown witness in exchange for protection and gave us all we needed to bring down the whole group." A flush of embarrassment crossed her normally impassive face.

"Doesn't look like he got much protection," I said, wondering if she had come to tell me of a similar danger to my own life. Could the gang be closing in on all of us?

"Well, um…you see…that's the problem." Twinkles leapt from a nearby table and landed squarely in Ms Smith's lap. She shrieked, stood up, and helped Twinkles out of the room with the toe of her boot. "Can't you lock that thing up?" she said.

To save Twinkles from further assaults, I picked the indignant cat up and closed her in my study, whispering a few words to comfort her.

When I got back to the living room, Ms Smith had regained her composure.

"Now, as I was saying… There was a slight problem with Mr. Street's protection."

"*Slight* problem!" The man was dead, and she was talking about a slight problem. What kind of people was I involved with? How safe was I after all?

"You know, we handle hundreds of protection cases every year, and sometimes, problems arise, especially when names and professions are similar. However, in the very unlikely situation, such as yours and Mr. Street's, when the descriptions and personal details are also similar, mistakes can occur." She slumped back into her chair as if delivering this piece of information had exhausted her.

"Similar? Mistakes?" I didn't understand the implication of her words.

"Yes. Eric Spratt and Derek Street. Accountants. Fifty-five years old. Slight build. Bachelors. No family. You can see how it could happen, can't you?" She looked at me with pleading eyes.

I couldn't. "What could happen?"

"I'm afraid you got Derek Street's witness protection, and he got nothing."

"You mean, I should have got *nothing?* After I put my life on the line to be a key witness in this case? Nothing!"

She leaned forward and her voice softened. I detected a note of pity. "Actually…Eric…to be perfectly frank, we would have prosecuted even without your testimony about finding the briefcase. We did appreciate your coming forward with it, but in the overall big picture, it had very little to do with the final outcome. It was Derek Street's testimony that brought down the Bacciaglia gang, not yours."

My head reeled. "You mean this was all a mistake?" I whispered, waving my arm around the room. "Cormorant Harbour, Charles Trenchant, Twinkles…everything?"

She nodded.

For a moment, we sat in silence. Then Ms Smith pulled out several sheets of paper from the pile.

"We realize that you might have some recourse against

the Crown. In any case, the embarrassment from the bad publicity would be damaging to the Witness Protection Department. To that end, we are prepared to reinstate you in your old life if you should so choose, and of course, offer a small monetary compensation for your mental stress brought on by this mistake."

I tried to imagine returning to Eric Spratt.

"However…" Ms Smith paused. "There is an alternative."

"An alternative?"

"Yes. We are prepared to leave you here as Charles Trenchant with the identity papers and background which we provided, remaining intact. The house and its contents will be yours, and of course, a small monetary compensation to show our good will. This is by far, in our opinion, the best course to follow to maintain the integrity of the Witness Protection Department." She paused and looked at me. "Eric, I know this is an awful alternative, but if you could see it in your heart to let sleeping dogs lie, to stay here as Charles Trenchant, your government, and I, will be most grateful."

"Let me get this straight. There are no goons after me. I am not in any danger of being rubbed out by the mob. This was all a mistake. I can go back to being Eric Spratt in Markham with perfect safety?"

"Yes."

"Or, I can stay here, and you'll keep my new identity intact?"

"That's right. Personally, I think it's an appalling alternative, asking you to remain here in this godforsaken backwater, but my superiors have asked me to present it to you. From my point of view, to remain here would be an act of selfless patriotism, far beyond what most Canadians would be willing to do for their country."

I could almost hear "O Canada" playing as she spoke.

An hour later, when Ms Smith left clutching her briefcase full of signed disclaimers and releases, I was officially Charles Trenchant, writer, a free man. She would never know that my decision had nothing whatsoever to do with patriotism. I thought it good to have someone in high places in the government who now "owed me one".

I let Twinkles out of the study, and we sat back together in my armchair as I revelled in my newfound sense of freedom. No more anxiety. No more fear. No more need to hide.

I could take up my duties at St. Grimbald's. I could pursue my friendships. I could become part of the community with no fear of sudden disclosure. Strangers would no longer fill me with apprehension. I wouldn't look for an enemy behind every tree. I wouldn't suspect innocent bystanders like Ollie and Annie. I could put to rest any suspicions I might have held about people like Zerena.

Zerena. I smiled as I contemplated the fact that she had no involvement with the Bacciaglias. That left the way clear for me to pursue the interest I felt in her. Perhaps a little dinner, or afternoon tea, I thought. I hadn't really thanked her for her kindness to me when I'd hurt my ankle. Now I could do so with complete confidence.

I looked down at my runner-shod foot. That was another thing. The jeans, the shoes, the flannel shirts—they could all go. I'd bundle them up today and give them to Annie for the next rummage sale. I didn't need to blend in any more. I could be *me.*

I decided to change and go into the Harbour to celebrate. I thought a cup of Rudy's excellent coffee and a slice of his strudel would do justice to my elation.

With great pleasure, I donned my grey flannel pants, my favourite shirt and tie and slipped on my navy blue blazer.

Surveying myself in the mirror, I decided that my beard, now grown into its full splendour, called for something a little more dashing. I pulled off the tie and slipped an ascot around my neck. Tucking it into the open shirt collar, I almost wished that I smoked so that I could sport a pipe to complete the image before me. I felt ready to face the world.

With a sense of reckless abandon, I left the door unlocked.

As I came to the road, I saw the Jollimore truck barrelling down towards me. It screeched to a halt. Kevin jumped out.

"Howdy, neighbour."

Even the sight of Kevin, as dishevelled and dirty as ever, couldn't spoil my current mood.

"I was wonderin'," he began, looking hopeful, "whether there was anything left of mine in the shed."

"Left?" I said. "No. Ollie took it all to the dump on the day after the fire. Don't you remember? You told him to get rid of it all. In fact, I think you said he could have your truck, too."

Kevin stepped back and laid a proprietary hand on the hood of his truck. He looked around as if expecting Ollie to appear and claim ownership.

"Well, that was then, and this is now," he said. "Too bad about the stuff, though. I coulda used it. Things didn't work out the way I expected."

I thought that was the understatement of the century. "I'm sure Arleen must be very disappointed."

Kevin's face clouded, and he licked his lips. "Yah, well. Let's just say I'm not getting much these days. Has her tits in a twist, she has. What with Aunt Mildred's money not being what we thought it was, and the insurance and all, she's not fit to live with."

"How did you make out with your insurance?" I asked. "I suppose you'll be starting to build soon."

Kevin shuffled from foot to foot. "Goddam insurance companies. Can't trust nobody. Says they'll pay, and then they don't. And it was legitimate. A *real* fire. Anybody knows that. But they calls it an 'act of God'. What the hell is that supposed to mean? Everything's an act of God, ain't it?"

"Well, weren't you fully insured?" I asked him, beginning to get a sense of impending disaster.

"Nope. I guess not. You see, I was only thinkin' of a regular fire. You know, the usual kind. Wiring, paint rags, candles, wood stove, you know, regular fires. Not some goddam bolt of lightning from the sky. Whoever would have expected something like that? Woulda cost me a bundle to insure for something like that." Kevin looked up at the sky and scratched his chest. "Act of God? he repeated. "Well, I hope He's satisfied."

"It always pays to read the fine print," I told him.

Kevin snorted.

"Did they give you anything?"

"Yah, I got a coupla thousand for the contents of the house. Just as well it burned to the ground, else they'da found out the good stuff was in your shed. But, I can't complain," he said brightening. "Found a real nice deal. Even Arleen's okay about it. In fact, here it comes now." He pointed.

A huge flatbed trailer filled the road. On it, a decrepit house trailer, paint peeling, rust showing through in great orange streaks, tarped roof held in place with a half dozen old tires, dingy windows and sagging door, sat in solitary splendour. Clarence sat behind the wheel.

"Used to belong to Amos Beaver," Kevin told me. "Poor old bugger. Had it out back of his son's place. Got a good deal. Furnished and all. Only have to hook 'er up to the well and the power pole, and we can move in tonight." His eyes glowed. "She's a beauty, in't she? Bigger'n our last place, too. Kid'll have his own room and all. Better'n sleeping on the couch. Better for me and Arleen, too." He treated me to a lascivious wink.

"Kevin! Get your ass over here!" The Voice reverberated from the passenger's side of the flatbed cab.

"Oops! Gotta go! Iffen I play my cards right, I might get lucky tonight!" He grinned and punched me on the shoulder. "Iffen you get my drift. After all, Charlie, old son, a man's gotta take his luck where he finds it."

Kris Wood (left) and Pat Wilson (right) have been friends for over thirty years and have collaborated on a multitude of projects all through mail, email, fax, telephone and the occasional brief visit.

Pat and Kris have co-authored several short stories for mystery collections by the Ladies Killing Circle and two full-length books on Maritime subjects.

Both are current residents of Nova Scotia.